Bolan needed one of them alive

Scanning the pier, he spied one pirate shouting orders at the others, directing them to first one speedboat, then another. Bolan took a chance and slammed a bullet through his shoulder, dropping the man in a shuddering heap on the pier.

That done, he swept the dock and speedboats, picking off the pirates one by one or in small groups where they huddled together, accepting the illusion of safety in numbers. A couple of them sighted Bolan's muzzle flashes and tried to return fire, but their efforts were halfhearted and clumsy.

The wounded pirate on the dock was going nowhere, as Bolan turned his weapon and attention toward the camp that had become a bloody killing ground.

MACK BOLAN ®
The Executioner

The Executioner®
Don Pendleton's®

SEA OF
TERROR

A GOLD EAGLE BOOK FROM
WORLDWIDE®

TORONTO • NEW YORK • LONDON
AMSTERDAM • PARIS • SYDNEY • HAMBURG
STOCKHOLM • ATHENS • TOKYO • MILAN
MADRID • WARSAW • BUDAPEST • AUCKLAND

First edition February 2004
ISBN 0-373-64303-9

Special thanks and acknowledgment to
Mike Newton for his contribution to this work.

SEA OF TERROR

Printed in U.S.A.

The sea speaks a language polite people never repeat. It is a colossal scavenger slang that has no respect.
>   —Carl Sandberg, "Two Nocturnes"

Water, gentlemen, is the one substance from which the earth can conceal nothing. It sucks out its innermost secrets and brings them to our lips.
>   —Jean Giraudoux, *The Madwoman of Chaillot*

It's time for the sea to give up one of its secrets. And this time, all the water in the world won't quench the cleansing flame.
>   —Mack Bolan

For the 113 persons killed, wounded or kidnapped
by pirates worldwide between
January 1 and March 31, 2001.

Prologue

South China Sea

"Tell me again how you know where we are."

Kim wasn't whining exactly, but her voice had an edge to it, grating on Jeffrey Ryan's nerves. He forced a smile as he answered his bride of three weeks, eyes hidden behind mirrored Ray•Ban sunglasses. "It's the GPS, Sugar. I told you before."

"I don't remember," she said, almost pouting.

"The global positioning satellite gear," he explained. "Space-age stuff. It's like sonar from outer space. You send a signal out, it bounces back and bingo! It plots your location anywhere on Earth, with a three-foot margin of error."

"Three feet?" Kim sounded skeptical.

Ryan turned his head slightly, admiring her sleek, oiled body in the electric-blue thong bikini. The view made up for her tone—so far, at least. "Three feet," he assured her.

"So where are we, again?"

Good God.

"We're three hundred miles southwest of Manila," he told her, concentrating on the ripe swell of her breasts to keep from snapping. "Palawan Island lies a hundred miles to port. The Spratly Islands are a hundred miles ahead of us."

"Who picked that silly name?"

"I wouldn't know, Sugar."

"I thought you were the answer man," she said, teasing.

"I got the answers right last night, as I recall."

Kim shushed him, coming up on one elbow and glancing back toward the wheelhouse, where Albert had the helm. The move deepened her impressive cleavage before she slowly settled back onto the sun pad at Ryan's side. "Don't talk like that," she said, dropping her voice. "He listens."

"Kim—"

"He *does*. I always hear him sneaking past the stateroom."

"Babe, we're on a boat. This is our honeymoon. He knows we're not playing canasta in bed."

"Never mind that. Just keep your voice down."

"You didn't keep *yours* down this morning."

"Jeff, I'm serious!"

"Yeah, yeah. All right."

He closed his eyes and concentrated on the tropical sunshine baking into him. It felt good, lying on the *Valiant*'s forward deck without a care in the world, enjoying the sun and the sea and the beautiful woman beside him. Granted, he'd enjoy Kim more sometimes if she kept her mouth shut, but that was too much to hope for.

The yacht was a wedding gift from Ryan's parents, a Regal Commodore 4160 with all the bells and whistles. It measured a hair over forty-four feet, stem to stern and tipped the scales at 20,375 pounds with its twin 7.4-liter engines and three hundred gallons of fuel. The forward stateroom featured an oversized berth, a cedar-lined hanging locker and a built-in TV-VCR with satellite reception. Two smaller staterooms—one unoccupied this trip—had their own private heads and hardwood doors for maximum privacy. The main salon featured a nine-foot leather sofa, overhead cabinets and an oval pearwood dining table that converted to a coffee table in seconds. The spacious galley included a side-by-side refrigerator-freezer, a microwave, a hidden two-burner stove and yet another TV-VCR.

Jeffrey Ryan didn't know exactly what the yacht had cost.

He'd grown up in a family that didn't need to ask such questions, and he loved it. As far as Ryan was concerned, the claim that money won't buy happiness was just another baseless rumor circulated by the poor.

Screw 'em, he thought, and cut another sidelong glance toward Kim. He wished she'd lose the blue bikini top, at least, but Albert made her nervous. Not that he'd ever done or said anything to merit such a reaction—far from it, in fact. He'd served the Ryan family for thirty years or more, starting before Jeff was born, and like any good retainer he knew how to keep his mouth shut.

Never mind. Another ten minutes or so in the sun and he'd say he needed a shower, ask Kim to join him below and help scrub his back. When she was finished, Ryan could scrub her front and see where it went from there. Albert could handle the *Valiant* alone while the newlyweds got some exercise.

Ryan felt a familiar stirring in his trunks. He stretched, arms above his head, and stared off across the flat, lifeless sea. He was surprised to see another boat sitting becalmed, perhaps three-quarters of a mile away to starboard.

"Where'd that come from?" he muttered.

Kim peered down at the front of his bathing suit, smirking. "Same place it always comes from, babe. Shall I guess where you want it to go?"

"I mean *that*," he said, pointing across the sun-bright water. "What?"

Instead of answering, he rose and moved back toward the wheelhouse. "We've got company," he told Albert.

"Yes, sir. I see," Albert Hatcher answered.

"Just sitting there."

"So it would seem."

"Think they're in trouble, Albert?"

"Doubtful, sir. The sails are furled."

"Give me the glasses, will you?"

"Certainly."

Ryan took the binoculars forward and sat on the sun pad,

removing his sunglasses and raising the binoculars to his eyes. It took a moment for him to find the boat, fine-tuning the focus for maximum definition. Naked masts, empty decks.

"It looks like a junk," he said, passing the glasses to Kim.

She spent a moment focusing, then replied, "You can say that again. I'm surprised it can float."

He took the glasses back and frowned. "A junk's a kind of Chinese boat," he said.

"I *know* that, Mr. Wisdom. Where's your famous sense of humor?"

"Sorry." He was suddenly nervous and didn't know why. "You think they need help?"

"Do you see a distress flag?"

"No," he admitted.

"Any flares? Someone hopping around on deck with a semaphore flag?"

"Maybe they're sick belowdecks," he suggested.

"Maybe it's their honeymoon."

"Maybe." There was an unwritten rule about helping out with maritime emergencies. "We should check, anyway."

"Excuse me?"

"Just in case."

"And do what?" Kim demanded. "We don't even speak the language."

"What language is that, babe?"

"Chinese. You just said—"

"That the boat is a junk. We don't know who's on board."

"And I like it that way." She was sitting up beside him now, arms crossed beneath her ample breasts. "It's weird, Jeff. Let it go."

"Suppose there's nobody aboard?"

"This isn't the Bermuda Triangle."

"We could claim salvage rights."

"And take their chopsticks? Maybe grab an old, used wok? Terrific."

"I think we should— Hey! What's this?"

A speedboat had appeared from nowhere, circling into

view from where the junk had hidden it, trailing a white wake as it powered toward the *Valiant*.

"FASTER!" Nguyen Tre Minh commanded. He stood close to the pilot in the Chaparral 200 speedboat's open cockpit, one hand clutching the windscreen's polished frame while the other clutched a Chinese Type 56-1 assault rifle against his hip.

The pilot seemed to cringe as he answered. "Thirty-five knots, sir. It won't go any faster!"

"Try harder!" Nguyen snapped, raising his voice above the throaty snarl of the speedboat's 4.3-liter Mercruiser engine.

In fact, they were making good speed, the Chaparral's bow lifting slightly as if it were straining to fly. It was a privilege of command to call for impossible feats and keep the flunkies hopping. His crewmen expected no less.

Nguyen glanced back at the other four seated behind him, each armed with an assault rifle or submachine gun. He'd left two men aboard the junk to man the tiller and the radio. If need be they could double-team to operate the Type 80 machine gun concealed by a tarp on the deck.

They were gaining on the yacht, but none too rapidly for Nguyen's taste. The larger boat was cruising at a steady speed of ten or fifteen knots with no attempt to flee so far, but that could change at any moment. Nguyen's crew had the advantage of surprise, but he assumed the targets had to have seen them. They'd be wondering about the speedboat, possibly preparing to defend themselves.

Nguyen released his grip on the windscreen, leaning into the Chaparral's instrument panel for support as he lifted the binoculars he carried on a leather strap around his neck. They were some rich man's glasses, stolen the previous month. Their lenses made the yacht seem close enough to touch.

Nguyen was startled for a moment when he found a naked white man staring back at him through glasses not unlike his own. A closer look corrected his erroneous first impression, picking out the man's skimpy swimsuit. Beside the sunbather

sat a blond woman, wearing little more than her companion.
They were talking now, excitedly, but Nguyen couldn't read
their lips. Instead he scanned aft to the yacht's wheelhouse
and saw an older man dressed all in white, handling the wheel
and speaking urgently into a microphone.

"Faster!" Nguyen repeated, punching his pilot's shoulder
for emphasis. "They've seen us and they're sending a distress
call."

"Sir—"

"Faster!"

And for a moment he imagined that the speedboat surged
ahead at his command, adding another knot or two to its
shuddering pace. Through his glasses Nguyen saw the nearly
naked man and woman rise and move back toward the wheelhouse, huddling briefly with their gray-haired pilot before
they went belowdecks.

Fat-cat tourists, Nguyen thought. The young people were
lean but not hard, and their pilot was going soft with age.
None of them looked like fighters, but if they were armed the
boarding could be hazardous. Nguyen's late ancestors would
be humiliated if he let a lazy white man take his life. He'd
never hear the end of it for all eternity.

The pride leader turned to the members of his boarding
party and found them watching him. The speedboat hit a swell
just then, causing him to stagger through an awkward little
dance step on the deck. One of the crewmen—a Korean
named Kim Sung—started to laugh, but Nguyen's scowl silenced him as effectively as a slap across the face. These men
knew their captain's temper and would hesitate to draw his
wrath.

"They've seen us now and run belowdecks," Nguyen said.
"They may resist."

"How many?" Kim asked. He added "sir" before Nguyen
could call him on the oversight.

"At least three," he said. "A woman and two men. There
may be more below."

His crewmen smiled at mention of the woman. One of the

Chinese, Sun Yau, raised his assault rifle and answered, "Let them fight. They won't last long."

"I want the younger pair alive, if possible," Nguyen replied.

"If possible," Sun echoed, smiling.

"Rich whites, perhaps Americans." Nguyen had their attention now. "They may be worth more than the boat."

"Ransom?" The question came from Julio Marcos, a Filipino.

"There's no telling if they're dead," Nguyen reminded all of them. "Corpses are fish food, hostages are gold."

The crewmen took a moment to think that over, then bobbed their heads in collective agreement. Nguyen didn't expect them to hold their fire if the yacht's crew started shooting, but at least the thought of a fat ransom payoff might make them a little less trigger-happy. If nothing else, perhaps he'd have a chance to claim the blond-haired woman for himself.

A captain's privilege.

They'd closed half the distance to the yacht, their pilot correcting his course to intercept the larger craft in motion. Boarding was the tricky part, but they had grappling hooks and rope ladders aboard. It would be best if they could force the yacht's pilot to turn off his engines, but Nguyen couldn't count on it.

One way or another, he was claiming the yacht as his prize.

Nguyen raised his binoculars again and felt a moment's dizziness as the yacht zoomed into focus. The old man at the helm was no longer speaking into his radio microphone. He watched the speedboat drawing closer with a grim expression on his face, handling the wheel and throttle with obvious experience. He had a cool head, Nguyen thought, but he wasn't good enough to outwit Nguyen Tre Minh.

"Faster!" the pirate captain cried from force of habit, leaning forward into the wind.

ALBERT HATCHER HADN'T killed a man since 1968, but he still remembered how it felt to pull a trigger, send a bullet on its way and watch his target fall. He'd been nineteen years old the last time, a U.S. Army corporal trying his best to survive in the Mekong Delta, and he'd raised his share of hell during a twelve-month tour of duty. He hadn't counted corpses then—after the first few, anyway—and didn't like to think about it now, but anyone who doubted his credentials as a killer could go talk to Mr. Charley.

The Army had been Hatcher's first steady job out of high school. His next—and last—had been with the Ryan family, hired on as a young bodyguard two months after discharge, guaranteed lifetime employment after he'd foiled a half-assed kidnapping attempt on Howard Ryan back in 1972. The family had damn near adopted him after that—or at least they'd let him get as close as any hired help ever would. They trusted him enough to have him tag along with Mr. Jeffrey and his new bride on their honeymoon, much to Kimberly's displeasure, and now it looked like it was time for him to earn his keep again.

He set the Commodore on automatic pilot long enough to duck below and fetch his hardware from the lounge. He'd stowed an Ithaca Model 87 12-gauge shotgun aboard when nobody was looking; the twenty-inch model with an 8-shot magazine was loaded with alternating buckshot rounds and rifled slugs. He'd reckoned fifty rounds of ammo ought to be enough for once around the Orient, then packed a hundred, just in case.

Whoever these men in the speedboat were, Hatcher didn't plan to let them come aboard. Not while he still had strength enough to aim and fire.

Hatcher hoped the Ryans would stay below until the worst of it was over. She'd been in a panic when she passed him, bouncing in her blue bikini, but he couldn't always tell about Ryan. The nervous look he had could be excitement in disguise. Ryan got anxious sometimes and couldn't keep from jumping, even if he put himself at risk. Hatcher was hoping married life would calm him down, make him more level-headed, but they hadn't counted on pirates.

Pirates? Hatcher thought. What else could it be, out in the middle of nowhere?

They'd been warned in the States, quoted facts and figures about the growing incidence of armed robbery at sea. Five hundred incidents in the past year alone, most of them in the Far East, but there'd been no dissuading the newlyweds from their exotic honeymoon. "Asia or bust," Ryan had said, flashing his boyish smile.

Now here they were, and Hatcher feared they were about to get busted.

He had the Commodore at top speed, and still the speedboat gained on him, its lighter weight and superior maneuverability making the difference. Hatcher reckoned he could outdistance the smaller craft, all things being equal, even with nearly one-third of their fuel burned since leaving Manila, but something told him the speedboat's crew didn't plan on a protracted chase. He knew a bit about the way these pirates operated, hit-and-run with few survivors left to tell the tale. He might not be outmuscled where the engines were concerned, but he was almost certainly outgunned.

There were two ways to play it, Hatcher realized. He could hold the throttle open and hope for the best, make it hard for the strangers to board without risking their lives, but if he took a bullet in the meantime, the Ryans would be alone. Kim would be worthless in a fight, and while he guessed that Ryan had nerve enough to defend himself and his bride in a pinch, there was a world of difference between sparring with drunken frat brothers on Saturday night and fighting for his life with no holds barred.

His other option was to ease back on the speed or stop the *Valiant* dead in the water, and devote his full attention to the inevitable fight. His adversaries had a better shot at boarding that way, but they could only come up on one side, and Hatcher would have something to say about that before they cleared the rail. The Ithaca 12-gauge would have something to say about it, too.

He made his choice and hauled back on the throttle, scowling as the *Valiant* responded on cue, wallowing to a dead stop. Grim-faced with anticipation, Hatcher switched off the twin engines and picked up his shotgun, pumping a round into the chamber. He was feeding another cartridge into the gun's magazine when Ryan called up from belowdecks, "What's going on?"

"Stay where you are," Hatcher commanded, discarding his servant's role for the first time in decades. It was close to ass-kicking time, and the newlyweds were simply a distraction now.

"Hey, wait a sec—"

He slammed the hatch between them, cutting off Ryan's protest. Focusing on the starboard side, Hatcher watched the speedboat approaching, her pilot backing off the throttle as he closed the gap. Hatcher didn't need binoculars to count heads, or to see that the strangers were armed. He made it six to one against him, with the other side sporting automatic weapons.

Never mind, he thought. They still have to come over the rail. And unless they were wearing body armor he couldn't see, they'd find that a hazardous task.

Hatcher sat in the pilot's chair and braced his shotgun on the nearby rail, waiting for a target to reveal itself.

"All aboard," he whispered.

NGUYEN TRE MINH was suspicious when the yacht began losing speed, before stopping altogether. The captain had dropped out of sight, no one visible on deck, and he took that as another bad sign. He didn't trust the rich white tourists to surrender peacefully—and he didn't intend to be the first man over the rail.

Nguyen clutched his rifle tightly as the Chaparral drew even with the yacht. His pilot throttled back and brought the speedboat kissing-close to the larger vessel, cutting the wheel so their port side was against the *Valiant*'s starboard flank. The captain knew enough to leave the engine grumbling, ready for a high-speed getaway in case they were surprised by unusual resistance and found themselves unable to board.

In that case, Nguyen reflected, he would use the thermite

grenades stacked neatly in a footlocker beside the captain's seat and leave the *Valiant* burning as they sped away. It would be his yacht or no one's.

But first, someone had to go aboard.

The choice was automatic, made almost without thinking. "Kim Sung!" Nguyen snapped. "Lead the way!"

The Korean blinked at him, hesitating long enough to see Nguyen shifting his rifle around to a firing position, then Kim scrambled from his seat toward the port rail. He scooped up a grappling hook with nylon line attached and tossed it overhand, catching the brightly polished rail on the first attempt. Submachine gun dangling from a shoulder strap, Kim scrambled up the line like a nimble monkey. He had one leg over the railing when a gunshot rang out and the Korean vaulted backward, somersaulting over the speedboat to splash down on the other side.

"Pull back!" Nguyen shouted. "Retreat!"

The pilot instantly obeyed, gunning the Chaparral away from the yacht and swinging it northward, circling back toward the junk. They left the grappling hook attached to the *Valiant*'s rail, line trailing in the water.

"Far enough!" Nguyen said, when they'd put a hundred feet or so between themselves and the yacht. He'd recognized the shotgun's sound and knew they were in no immediate danger of taking lethal fire.

There was no sign of Kim Sung, but Nguyen wouldn't miss him. Raising the binoculars, he focused on the yacht and saw its captain crouched in the wheelhouse, peering over the side to observe them. Without the glasses, he was a dark silhouette.

Good enough.

Nguyen shouldered his rifle and sighted on the white man's head and fired a burst of 7.62 mm rounds across the water, enjoying the rifle's noise, its kick against his shoulder and the impact of his bullets on the target. Nguyen wasn't sure about the man, but he was tearing hell out of the *Valiant*'s wheelhouse. Lee Sun would be angry at the damage, but his boss always said targets should never be permitted to resist.

Besides, there might still be some money in the operation if he took the other whites alive and found someone willing to ransom them. If not, at least they could provide some sport before they died.

Nguyen fired off half his 30-round magazine before he lowered the rifle and gave the yacht another look through the binoculars. There was no sign of the *Valiant*'s captain, but the wheelhouse was pocked and scarred with bullet holes where his rounds had torn through wood and plastic.

"We try again," he said to no one in particular. His pilot glanced at him, frowning, but Nguyen glowered back at him and snapped, "Proceed!"

Reluctantly, his wheelman nosed the speedboat forward, closing the gap once more between them and the *Valiant*. Nguyen kept his eyes locked on the bridge, waiting for the yacht's captain to show himself again, but nothing moved on board the great white boat.

When they were back in place against the *Valiant*'s starboard side, Nguyen spit out rapid-fire orders to the remaining members of his crew. Sun Yau moved to seize the dangling line already attached to the yacht, while Julio Marcos crawled over the Chaparral's deck with a second line in hand, tossing it up to snag a different section of railing. Nguyen reasoned that the *Valiant*'s captain—if he lived—could only kill one man before the other cut him down. If he was wrong, or if the other whites on board also had guns and joined the fight, it would be time for the grenades.

"Go on!" Nguyen barked at his hesitant crewmen. They swarmed up the ropes in seconds, slipping over the rail within a heartbeat of one another.

Almost immediately, the shotgun roared again. Sun returned fire with his Vietnamese K-50M submachine gun, hosing the deck with 7.62 mm Soviet rounds. Marcos quickly joined in with his AK-47, hammering short bursts at the enemy.

Nguyen was torn between fear and anger, seasoned with a measure of embarrassment. The last two members of his crew were watching him, waiting for him to take action.

He had to either lead the final charge or call his crewmen back to safety and retreat. Climbing the rope meant releasing his weapon, if only for a moment. He'd be completely vulnerable at the rail until he swung across and reached the deck.

Now or never.

"Come on!" he told Min Szo, the final member of his boarding party. Nguyen grabbed the nearest rope and started climbing, feeling more than seeing Min scramble across the Chaparral's deck to seize the other line. He'd know within another moment if he was a hero or a fool.

The *Valiant*'s wheelman got off one more shot as Nguyen swung across the rail. He didn't know what kind of load the white man's weapon carried, but he saw Sun lurch backward, blood exploding from an exit wound between his shoulder blades. The Chinese pirate went down firing, blasting divots in the yacht's long deck before his SMG ran out of bullets.

Nguyen saw the white man swing around, pumping another round into his shotgun, but the pirate captain was faster, triggering a burst from his assault rifle, watching the rounds strike home with a spray of crimson. Marcos and Min fired at the same time, making the dead man dance before he dropped out of sight in the wheelhouse.

Nguyen approached the *Valiant*'s bridge as if a nest of cobras waited for him there. He knew he should reload, but didn't dare release the rifle's trigger now. The yacht's captain was far beyond resisting, but that still left at least two persons below. A burst of automatic fire had sprung the door that sheltered them below.

Nguyen crouched in the wheelhouse, his surviving crewmen at his back, and called to the survivors in broken English. "Come out, hands up!" he shouted through the door, down the companionway. "Maybe we don't kill you."

KIMBERLY RYAN HAD SLIPPED one of her husband's shirts over her blue string bikini. It wasn't much, but she'd been in a hurry when they rushed belowdecks, anxious to cover herself, babbling questions about the speedboat and what was happening above. Her husband had ignored her at first, pulling on jeans and a T-shirt, finally snapping at her to shut the hell up and let him think.

She sat on the berth in the master stateroom, arms crossed, folded in on herself, fighting the storm of conflicting emotions that threatened to make her start screaming. She was frightened, angry and hurt, all at once. It was a toss-up which emotion would win out—until she felt the speedboat bump the *Valiant*'s starboard flank.

"Jeff, what—"

"Quiet!" he whispered, stepping into the galley and coming back a moment later, a long carving knife in his hand.

"What's that for?" she demanded.

Ryan turned on her, livid. "Can you please just shut your mouth until I know what's going on? Is that too fucking much to ask?"

Tears stung her eyes, but Kim felt the adrenaline that came with fury kicking in. He never talked to her like that, even when he'd been drinking with his college friends. It told her he was frightened—and before she knew it, fear replaced the anger burning in her chest.

She kept her mouth shut, waiting out the scuffling sound from starboard. Was someone coming aboard from the speedboat? Why would Albert let them—

Blam!

The gunshot made Kim yelp, sending her scooting back on the berth into a corner, stopping only when her skull and shoulders met the bulkhead with a solid thump. She heard the speedboat's engine revving, then receding. Hopeful, she remembered to breathe, willing herself to relax.

A sudden storm of gunfire sent her squealing to the deck, while Ryan crouched beside the doorway to their stateroom. Kim would've gladly crawled under the bed, but there was no space there, thanks to the storage drawers that saved on cabin space. She cringed between the berth and bulkhead, sobbing, while the gunfire seemed to last forever—though in fact, she guessed, it raged for no more than a minute.

Trembling where she lay, Kim heard the speedboat coming back. Its engine noise was muffled, but it came through all the same. Ryan edged into the galley, calling up to Albert, but the older man didn't reply. Kim had a mental picture of him lying dead on deck, blood everywhere. She still had no idea who'd started shooting or why. Was it the strangers in the speedboat? If so, why had they retreated after the first shot was fired? Had Albert brought a gun aboard? Would he know how to use one if the need arose?

Kim Ryan had never fired a gun in her life, but she wished for one now. Her husband enjoyed quail hunting and made fun of her when she refused to eat the birds he'd shot. How different could it be, shooting a man in self-defense?

Of course, Jeff had no gun now, when he needed it.

And quail didn't shoot back.

She heard more scuffling sounds to starboard, then another gunshot echoed from the wheelhouse, instantly followed by the rattling sound of what she took for machine guns. Someone was screaming in the cabin, and it took a moment for Kim to realize the high-pitched voice was hers.

"Shut up!" Ryan raged at her. "Shut up before they hear you, damn it!"

Kim shut up, biting her tongue and swallowing the screams that tried to escape against her will. It was the hardest thing she'd ever tried to do, just keeping silent while the battle raged above them on the *Valiant*'s deck. She tasted blood, grimacing, uncertain how much longer she could stay quiet—when, suddenly, it was over.

The shooting stopped, replaced by a cautious shuffling sound of footsteps overhead. A twangy voice called down to them from the wheelhouse, "Come out, hands up! Maybe we don't kill you!"

Oh, God.

Without saying the words, that voice told her Albert was dead, their last hope gone. She feared for Jeff, but even more so for herself. Who could predict what these strangers would do? Death was one thing, but Kim had heard stories...

"Now!" the strange voice shouted, sounding closer. "You come out quick or we start shooting! Maybe sink boat, too!"

"Jeffrey?" Kim heard the pleading in her tone and hated it.

"We haven't got much choice," he whispered back. Raising the knife, he added, "I can't fight their guns with this."

"Albert?"

"If he was still alive, we'd hear him," Ryan replied.

"Oh, God."

Ryan looked at her and frowned. "Put on some jeans, will you? Don't give these bastards any bright ideas."

Kim shuddered, scrambling for the drawer where she'd stowed her pants. Taking out a pair of blue jeans, she began to slip them on, struggling. It would be easier if she stood, but Kim was frightened of a bullet coming through the bulkhead any second.

"Hurry!" the stranger called to them. "Last goddamn chance!"

"We're coming," Ryan replied, tossing his knife away. "Don't shoot, for God's sake. We're unarmed."

Kim zipped her jeans, stood and suddenly remembered she was barefoot. She was moving toward the stateroom's closet when her husband grabbed her arm and pulled her toward the door.

"I need—"

"Come on!" he hissed.

"My feet!"

"You're walking on them, aren't you? You can't do that if you're dead."

Kim pulled away from him, quickly grabbed her shoes and said, "You first."

"I'm sorry, Kim."

She didn't tell him to forget about it, didn't say it was all right. Why should she lie?

"Go on," she said, and followed him across the galley, toward daylight.

Arlington National Cemetery

Mack Bolan walked the hallowed ground and listened for voices, wondering if the fallen warriors had anything to tell him. He could sense their presence—not in any melodramatic, chain-rattling sense—but in the hush that enveloped the place. The air of sanctity was almost palpable. Drivers passing by on Jefferson Davis Highway laid off their horns. Even birds sang more quietly there.

It was ironic, Bolan thought, that the highway skirting Arlington National Cemetery should be named for the Confederate leader whose rebellion had put so many soldiers there in the first place. Ironic, but not unprecedented. The last time Bolan had walked this ground, he'd been visiting the grave of a traitor who'd spent his last moments on Earth atoning for, as well as restoring some vestige of respect to the military uniform he had dishonored. Bolan had watched the man die and avenged him. Leaving the graveside, one emotion that he *hadn't* felt was satisfaction.

The visit was strictly business, with no time for nostalgic distractions. Still, he kept his mind open, alert for any messages or suggestions his fellow warriors might want to share. And as always when he visited this place, Bolan reflected on his own mortality. He'd already been buried once—a ruse to get the Mafia off his back—but his marker wasn't here. It would've been a curiosity to stand before it, reading his own name in marble, but it wouldn't happen this day.

"Maybe next time," he told the breeze. But even as he spoke the thought aloud, Bolan knew it was wrong. Next time he was planted—assuming enough was recovered to justify a funeral—it wouldn't be his name that went on the stone. For all intents and purposes, Mack Samuel Bolan was gone, officially erased.

Only the Executioner remained.

And he had work to do.

He didn't know what the job was, wouldn't know until he kept his morning rendezvous with Hal Brognola from Justice, but he knew it had to be serious. The director of the Sensitive Operations Group didn't call unless it was a case of pressing need. He wouldn't use a sledgehammer to kill an ant.

A viper, possibly, but not an ant.

Bolan was in the viper-stomping business, figuratively speaking, but his targets were two-legged predators who came disguised as human beings. Unlike reptiles, which only kill when hungry or cornered, Bolan's adversaries went out of their way to spread misery far and wide—for profit, for revenge, for politics or religion, even for the sheer hell of it. He tracked them down, eliminated them, or fought them to a draw because he could.

Because someone had to.

Bolan scanned for the big Fed and checked his track from force of habit. There was nothing to suggest that he'd been followed, no reason anyone should look for him in Arlington, but caution was a part of Bolan's life. Without it he would have no life, in fact. It was the first thing he had learned in combat at a tender age, when high-school friends were on their way to college or their first real jobs. His job, Bolan discovered in his eighteenth summer, was eliminating human predators.

And he'd been at it ever since.

How many had he killed since then? Enough to fill a cemetery of his own, but not this one. Of course, he wasn't finished yet.

He didn't stop to look for names he'd recognize, though some of them were here. More could be found across the river, inscribed on black marble. There wouldn't be time for him to revisit the Vietnam Memorial on this trip, but he didn't need to see it anyway. The names of comrades lost were branded on his heart. Bolan would take them with him to his own true death, whether that came this day or thirty years from now.

He made another scan for Brognola and picked out the stocky figure this time, a hundred yards or so ahead. Brognola had staked out a point due north of the JFK Memorial and its eternal flame. He would've dodged the crowd that way, if there'd been one. As it was, they almost had the eastern quadrant of the cemetery to themselves. Groundskeepers were mowing the grass around Arlington House, but there were no mourners or tourists in evidence so far.

No one to eavesdrop on their talk except the dead.

Brognola saw him approaching and lifted a hand, then stuck it back in his pocket. He wore a trench coat like the old-time Fed he was, having come up the hard way when merit and results counted for more than connections and lip service to politically correct ideas. The head Fed had endured in an ever-changing world, more or less intact, because he got the job done and that ability still had value in Washington, even when his nominal superiors pretended the job didn't exist.

They'd privately referred to the nation's capital as Wonderland, once upon a time, because it seemed that damn near anything could happen there. These days, it sometimes felt as if there were no surprises left, that Bolan had truly seen and done it all, fighting his way to a place where duty consisted of nailing down the same short-term victories again and again. Sometimes he felt as if there were nothing new under the sun.

But in his heart he knew better.

As long as human beings had free will, some of them would find new ways to victimize their neighbors, either individually or en masse. The techniques were fluid, constantly evolving with each new scientific or technological discovery. The world of crime changed every day. Only the motives were frozen in time.

They were as old as history. As old as man himself.

And Bolan's visceral response was still the same.

"Always punctual," Brognola said in greeting. His handshake was the same as always: firm, dry, brief. He carried too much power to engage in knuckle-crushing schoolyard games.

"It sounded urgent," Bolan said.

"What else is new? Let's take a walk."

Bolan fell into step beside his oldest friend. He didn't focus on the markers that appeared to go on forever, as far as the eye could see. Brognola would get down to business in his own good time.

As if on cue, Brognola asked him, "Striker, what do you know about pirates?"

Bolan shrugged. "Peg legs and parrots. Rum and eye patches. Fifteen men on a dead man's chest."

"I never understood what that one meant," the SOG director said.

"Me, either."

"Anyway, forget about Blackbeard and Long John Silver. We're going after modern pirates again, with speedboats and machine guns. Hit-and-run on the high seas."

"Take down one outfit, more pop up," Bolan replied.

"More all the time. An outfit called the International Maritime Organization has been keeping track of piracy since 1991. They've recorded close to twenty-five hundred incidents since then, with nearly one-fifth of those logged last year. So far this year, we're on track to set another record."

"The press doesn't seem to find this newsworthy," Bolan stated.

"Just the occasional feature," the big Fed said. "One problem is that two-thirds or more of the cases occur in the Far East, from the South China Sea, through Indonesia and on to the Bay of Bengal. Most of the pirates *and* their victims are

Asian, so it doesn't hold much interest for your average businessman in the States. Also, there aren't many arrests, so various governments and police agencies try to downplay their own failures—if they're not locked in for a cut of the take."

"Are they hitting your basic pleasure craft?"

"No, anything that floats," Brognola said, "from cabin cruisers to freighters and oil tankers. You name it. The smaller boats get a paint job, names and registration numbers changed before they're sold or put to work for the pirates. Bigger scores go to the highest bidder. If an oil company won't pay to get its cargo back, the pirates can always lay it off somewhere between Manila and Sri Lanka. No one knows exactly what they're grabbing, but a conservative estimate for last year pegged the take around sixteen billion dollars."

"Billion?"

"You heard me right. And that's conservative. For all we know, throw in black-market cargoes that the shippers can't report, they could be pulling twice that in a record year."

Twice sixteen billion made it roughly ten times the yearly American take from illegal gambling, double or triple the various estimates of narcotics sales in the U.S.

"Big business," Bolan said.

"Big and bloody," Brognola replied. "Pirates are killing an average of fifty people a year in the Far East, wounding or kidnapping three times as many."

"Kidnapping?" Bolan didn't like the sound of that.

"Most times," the head Fed said, "they'll grab some kind of cargo ship and make the crew sail it to a neutral anchorage. Once in a while there's a ransom demand—more likely when they take a pleasure craft and figure out the skipper's family has deep pockets."

"If they don't?"

It was Brognola's turn to shrug. "That depends on the hostages. Men are basically worthless, without ransom. Women and children, on the other hand..."

"The slave trade," Bolan finished for him.

"It's going strong, as you're no doubt aware. More stories

in the magazines and newspapers, but precious little action in the courts. Between child labor and the global prostitution market, it's basically a bottomless pit."

Filled with misery and death, Bolan thought.

The soldier had mopped up slaving operations in the past and wouldn't mind tangling with another one, but he still wasn't sure where his friend was going. "What's the angle?" he asked.

"A kidnapping," Brognola said. "Eight days ago, a pair of newlyweds were snatched by pirates in the South China Sea, sailing from Manila to Kuala Lumpur. A mail plane out of Puerto Princessa heard part of the distress call but couldn't get a fix. Two days later, a Vietnamese fishing trawler found their yacht adrift, north of the Spratly Islands. It was shot up pretty good and had a body in the wheelhouse, subsequently identified as one Albert Hatcher, employed by the groom's family."

"The groom being...?"

"Jeffrey Ryan," Brognola answered, "of the oil and pharmaceutical Ryans. His blushing bride Kimberly is the only child of Milton Stroud."

"That wouldn't be Ambassador Milton Stroud, by any chance?"

"The very same," the big Fed said. "Newspapers like to call him the 'first friend,' because he's so close to the White House. Stroud made his millions the old-fashioned way—he inherited the family steel mills and railroads."

"I'll play the long shot and say there's been a ransom demand?"

"Try thirteen, at last count," Brognola replied. "So far, they've heard from rebels in the Philippines, the Japanese Red Army, South Moluccan separatists and a Palestinian outfit calling itself Allah's Righteous Fist. The other demands apparently came from apolitical groups or individuals chasing a payday. Three were e-mailed—in order of arrival, from Jakarta, Quezon City and Singapore. Four others were mailed to newspapers or corporate offices scattered from Mindanao to Calcutta. One was handwritten, stuffed in a bottle and tossed through the window of a police station in Darwin."

"Australia?"

"None other," Brognola said. "The kooks are out in force on this one."

"That's twelve," Bolan remarked. "You left one out."

"Saving the best for last," Brognola said. "The one that counts was left at a church in Kota Baharu, Malaysia. Along with the ransom note, they left an earring. Family members swear it's Kimberly Ryan's, a custom job."

"How much are they asking?"

"Ten million."

"Chicken feed to that crowd."

"Except that Mr. Stroud has a problem."

"What's that?" Bolan asked.

"He's on record from day one of his public career as opposing any ransom payments or negotiation with terrorists. His friend in the Oval Office agrees with him. They can't do a one-eighty now, just because it's Stroud's daughter in jeopardy."

That wasn't strictly true, of course. The rich and famous could do damn near anything they wanted to, but some would sacrifice their own flesh and blood to avoid embarrassment.

"So, let the Ryans pay," Bolan suggested. "They're not diplomats or politicians."

"Pressure has been brought to bear opposing that idea," Brognola said. "I understand the in-laws aren't exactly chums right now, but they're presenting a united front in public."

"And in private?"

"Ryan's folks would cough up ten million in a New York minute."

"There's your answer, then."

"Not mine," Brognola said. "Not ours."

"Go on and drop the other shoe."

"The Man wants us to take it on. Specifically, he wants the bride and groom returned, alive and more or less intact, if possible."

"And what about the pirates?" Bolan asked.

"He wasn't so particular."

"Nobody plans to prosecute, I take it?"

"We're fresh out of volunteers," Brognola said. "Some of the countries where these pirates operate don't recognize the problem. We suspect they're getting paid to look the other way, but maybe it's simple embarrassment. If you can't control the pirates, make believe they don't exist."

"So what about the others?" Bolan asked.

"They do their best with what they've got. In most cases, that means a navy smaller than the U.S. Coast Guard, using gear that dates back to the 1970s. They log arrests from time to time, convict a few pirates. For every one who goes away, you've got a hundred waiting for their shot at easy money."

"We can't fix all that," Bolan reminded him. "We couldn't the last time."

"Agreed. Nobody's asked us to. The White House wants two hostages retrieved, if possible. Whatever happens to the kidnappers, they brought it on themselves."

"The FBI does work like this."

"The FBI," Brognola sadly replied, "has shot itself in the foot so many times, it's hopping around like a one-legged man in an ass-kicking contest. You heard about the guy last week?"

"Briefcase?" Bolan asked.

"That's the one."

"I heard."

A high-ranking FBI agent, well respected by his peers and supervisors, had recently lost a briefcase filled with sensitive documents pertaining to national security. The incident, though relatively minor in itself, climaxed a string of scandals running back to Ruby Ridge and Waco, a decade or more of nonstop bad publicity for the G-men who'd once been America's knights in shining armor. Brognola himself had been an FBI agent when he met Bolan. Now he was upstairs commanding various operations, including the ultracovert Stony Man Farm. It obviously pained him to see the Bureau taking hits, but he was professional enough to recognize a self-inflicted wound.

"What about the CIA?" Bolan asked.

"Even worse. You know their reputation in the Far East. They can work in the Philippines without too much hassle, but Indonesia's tough. Malaysia and Sri Lanka don't want them at all."

"They don't want us? Since when?"

"Since Ryan Petroleum started threatening to shut down operations in the area for security reasons. Since Ryan Pharmaceuticals decided it wasn't safe to ship medicine in from the States."

"Terrific."

It was bad enough hunting Asian nationals on their home turf, where Bolan didn't speak the language and was instantly recognizable as an outsider; now he'd have the extra handicap of working with locals who resented and despised him. Cooperation induced by a gun to the head was never wholehearted and seldom effective.

"It's not as bad as it sounds," Brognola said.

"You mean it gets worse?"

"You'll be starting in Malaysia, where they found the earring. There's a cop out there who's anxious to cooperate, show you around, interpret—whatever you need."

It just kept getting better. Bolan knew what "anxious to cooperate" meant, when the orders came down from on high. For all he knew, he might find himself saddled with a guide who despised him and wanted him back on the next flight to the States. At best, it would mean wasted time and effort; at worst, he could be dealing with a cop who'd sold out to the very predators they were stalking. In that case, Bolan would become the hunted and the body count would blow sky-high.

"Any other good news?" Bolan asked.

"Odds and ends," Brognola replied. He reached into the left-hand pocket of his trench coat and withdrew a CD in a flat plastic case. "I put some stuff together on the hostages, the region, recent incidents of piracy. Look through it when you get the chance."

"No more surprises? These guys haven't got a neutron bomb set to go off at midnight?"

The head Fed grinned. "I think they would've mentioned it."

"Okay. I'll check it out."

"You'll be met in Kuala Lumpur," Brognola said. "The cop's name is David Yun. They talk him up like some kind of hero, but who knows? If you believe advertising, the Whopper's six inches thick."

Bolan knew all about false advertising and the tendency of most police departments to paint a flattering picture of themselves. The worst cop on the force could be billed as a hero if it suited the needs of his superiors—and the men behind the scenes who paid their unofficial salaries. Then again, some heroes were exactly that.

Bolan decided he'd follow his usual course of action, expecting the worst and hoping for the best. If reality fell somewhere in between the two extremes, he'd still be points ahead. And if his expectations were fulfilled, he'd be ready to kick ass.

Which brought him to his next question. "What about equipment?"

"Hard to carry it on a commercial flight," Brognola answered, stating the obvious. "I thought about using the Air Force, but thought you'd prefer anonymity going in."

"You thought right."

"Your contact should have lines on anything you need, within reason."

"Who decides what's reasonable?" Bolan asked him, dead serious.

"That would be you," Brognola said. "If something stinks, you walk. We don't take suicide missions."

Right. Except that each new assignment had the potential to become exactly that: a one-way ticket to the boneyard.

"When do I fly?" he asked.

"Whenever you're ready," Brognola replied. "We're holding seats for you on the next three flights out of Reagan. Here's a list of times."

Bolan pocketed the slip of paper without looking at it. They were down to small talk now, but he had one thing left to say before he split. "You know they may be dead already. They're probably dead."

"It's a gamble," the big Fed acknowledged. "The Man's willing to risk it."

Bolan had to smile at that. The Man would risk nothing. Win or lose, he wouldn't even break a sweat on Pennsylvania Avenue. He damn sure wouldn't spill a drop of presidential blood.

"I'm packed already," Bolan said. "I'll take a look at the CD and try to catch the next flight out."

"Okay." Brognola shook his hand again. "Striker, I meant it, about scrubbing the job if it doesn't smell right."

"Understood." It was a game they played between themselves, both knowing that he'd never backed down from a mission in his life once the battle had been joined. "I'll see you."

"Soon," Brognola said, and turned away. He moved off at an angle, moving back toward the Potomac through the rows of grave markers. Bolan watched him for a moment, then turned back toward his waiting rental car.

There was a laptop on the passenger seat, charged and ready. He loaded the CD Brognola had given him and opened the only file displayed on the monitor. It had no title, but he knew roughly what to expect.

Photos first. The yacht, before and after, then two young people smiling on the deck, waving to the anonymous photographer, while an older man busied himself in the wheelhouse behind them. There were no captions, but Bolan didn't need them. It was a bon voyage party, the send-off for Jeff and Kimberly Ryan at the start of their ill-fated honeymoon.

A few more shots depicted preparations for sailing, one framing the *Valiant*'s stern with its name boldly painted in black on a stark white background. The newlyweds were happy enough to be models posing for a bridal catalog. They obviously didn't know a wicked ogre would be waiting for them at the climax of their fairy tale. The older man hung back, made himself scarce, appearing in some of the photos as if by accident, wholly absent from others. Bolan assumed he was the late Albert Hatcher, lost while defending the *Valiant* and its masters.

"Bad luck, Albert," he told the man's unsmiling image.

The last dozen photos were forensic shots, more or less. They'd been converted from Polaroids or some equivalent, taken after the yacht was found adrift in the South China Sea. Brognola was right about the damage. Someone had poured concentrated gunfire into the vessel's wheelhouse, killing Hatcher in the process. Two shots of his body revealed that he'd taken multiple hits, any one of them potentially lethal. The rest of the yacht was undamaged, though, and Bolan wondered why the pirates had left it behind. Were the controls impaired? Or did they calculate their hostages were worth enough to make the raid a success, all by themselves?

Ten million dollars. It was petty cash to Milton Stroud or Howard Ryan, sitting on top of their family fortunes, but Stroud and the White House had drawn a line on principle. The pirates might not be aware of that position, since there'd been no public statement on the kidnapping so far, and common criminals in Southeast Asia weren't necessarily tuned in to the fine points of American diplomatic policy. True, there'd been a "no compromise" policy in effect since 1979, but its enforcement was erratic at best. The Iran-Contra scandal proved that, Bolan thought, and corporate ransom payments were routine in the Third World, from Central America to the Middle East and Indonesia.

So the pirates had made their demand—and they were about to get more than they'd bargained for.

The main question in Bolan's mind right now was whether he had any chance of finding the newlyweds alive. If so, he had a rescue mission on his hands. If not, it would be payback, plain and simple.

But he had to find out first if Jeff and Kim Ryan were still alive. And for that, he'd need cooperation from the detective who awaited him in Kuala Lumpur.

The rest of the CD file was divided into personal data—

the bare-bones scoop on Jeffrey Ryan and his bride, enough to help him recognize the pair—and official documents from the International Maritime Organization's Safety Committee. Brognola had included half a dozen quarterly reports on modern piracy, spanning the past eighteen months. Maps and graphs summarized the problem, while detailed chronologies described the individual attacks.

He scrolled down the depressing list. Ships looted while docked at Chittagong anchorage, Bangladesh. Hijackings in Manila harbor with exchange of gunfire. Pirates armed with machetes boarding vessels in the Malacca Strait. Firebombs hurled from ship to ship at Labuan anchorage, Malaysia. One incident after another in the South China Sea, with captains and crewmen wounded or killed, sometimes set adrift in lifeboats. The targets ranged from humble junks and fishing boats to tramp steamers and huge cargo ships. A distressing number of the cases ended with the grim notation No official action taken.

Part of the problem, he assumed, was bad logistics. How could the Malaysian coast guard, for example, hope to pursue and capture pirates in Philippine or Indonesian waters? Even if jurisdictional disputes could be resolved, where would they start the search?

Where would Bolan start his?

Seventy percent of the earth's surface was covered in water, much of that the great oceans and seas. Ninety percent of all cargo transported around the globe—be it machinery, petroleum, food, medicine, clothing, whatever—was carried on ships. The lure was irresistible, and more predators were rising to the bait every year. Bolan could no more eradicate that plague than he could cure the common cold.

But he could give this mission his best, try his damnedest to retrieve the missing bride and groom. Failing that, he could treat their killers to a taste of justice that the international courts were unable or unwilling to dispense.

His face would be the last some of them ever saw.

Packing was easy. Bolan traveled light, and he'd be lighter

still without the side arm he habitually carried. Brognola was right about the risk of smuggling guns abroad, but there would be more danger of exposure if he hopped a U.S. military flight from the States to Kuala Lumpur. If it felt wrong at the other end, or if his contact couldn't set him up with the equipment he needed, Bolan could always turn around and come back.

Yeah, right.

He wondered how much the Malaysian detective would know about his mission and the way Bolan worked. They could have trouble if his guide turned out to be a straitlaced devotee of law by the book. In fact, if David Yun couldn't adjust to Bolan's style of warfare, they had no future at all.

First things first.

He put his Beretta 93-R and its shoulder harness in a plastic shopping bag and stashed it in a long-term locker at Dulles International Airport. The locker's key went into an envelope, addressed to Hal Brognola at the Department of Justice. Also inside the envelope was a metered ticket from the airport's overnight parking lot and the key to his rental car. The person Brognola dispatched to make the pickup would need cash on hand, but that was his problem.

That done, Bolan consulted his list of flight times and presented himself to the appropriate airline's ticket counter. A stoic clerk examined his passport, confirmed that no strangers had handled Bolan's bags or given him anything to carry on board the plane, then sent him on his way to the departures terminal. He had ninety minutes to kill before boarding and spent part of it in a concourse bookshop, then retired with his paperback purchase to a nearby restaurant where coffee and a doughnut cost as much as a steak dinner in the real world outside the airport.

It was highway robbery—make that *runway* robbery—but he didn't have time to argue. Besides, Bolan's traveling fund came courtesy of his enemies. The wad of bills he carried now, undeclared to customs or the IRS, had been lifted two days earlier from a Mafia numbers bank in New Jersey.

If he ran short on the trip, Bolan was confident he'd find another source of ready cash somewhere along the way.

One of the first things that he'd learned in Special Forces training at Fort Benning, Georgia, had been tricks for living off the land. His instructors in those days had never mentioned robbing pimps, pushers and loan sharks, but in Bolan's mind it all came down to the same thing. Whenever possible he let his adversaries pay the tab for their own destruction, recycling some of their ill-gotten gains. And if a thug in Jersey had the wherewithal to help him bust some pirates in Malaysia, why, so much the better.

What goes around, comes around—and sometimes it lands on the bad guys, right where it belongs.

Bolan was apprehensive about his new mission, not because he anticipated failure, but because he questioned whether Jeff and Kim Ryan were still alive. They had value to their captors, as long as they were breathing, but he couldn't count on the pirates to realize that or to care. Some predators killed because it was convenient, others killed simply because they could.

Either way, if the newlyweds were history, his job description changed. In that case, he could swap the kid gloves for brass knuckles and punish the bastards responsible without restraint. If there was no one left to save, he didn't have to pull his punches.

If.

And finding out the answer to that question would be Bolan's first order of business. He had to know if the Ryans were alive, before he calculated his response to their abductors. One way or another, it had the makings of another trip to Hell on Earth.

2

Kuala Lumpur, Malaysia

Bolan's flight from Washington to Kuala Lumpur didn't literally take forever; it just felt that way. His first stopover was Chicago, followed by a longer flight to San Francisco. Changing planes again, he then embarked on the marathon transpacific leg of his journey, with further stops at Honolulu and Manila before final touchdown in Malaysia. Bolan had finished his novel before they took off from Frisco, watched a Jackie Chan comedy between California and Hawaii, then slept through a Tom Cruise action flick en route to the Philippines. He remembered to drink lots of water while flying, and ate the food they put in front of him as if it were digestible.

The first thing that impressed new arrivals to Southeast Asia was the weather. Steam heat enveloped them as they stepped from their air-conditioned planes, threatening to smother them while it squeezed sweat from every pore. The short hike from runaway to terminal felt like a marathon's last mile. First-timers had been known to collapse on the tarmac—and some old-timers, too. For those who came in search of trouble or adventure—often one and the same thing—the weather was a warning: Watch your step.

Bolan had grown up in the tropics, not from infancy, but in the years when he was learning how to be a man. The sudden rush of heat affected him like anybody else, but he could

live with it. He *had* lived with it, or in spite of it, while those
around him failed to make the cut, or else got blown away on
either side. He could feel the jungle waiting for him, even
though he couldn't see it yet.

The Executioner was home.

The international date line had cost him a day, on top of
the twenty-odd hours he'd spent aboard planes and in airports
since talking to Brognola back in Arlington. It was pushing
two p.m. when he entered the arrivals terminal and found the
air-conditioning was either on a break or broken down completely. The place was wall-to-wall with bodies, most of them
in motion, all of them perspiring heavily. Someone had
propped the doors open to help, and mosquitoes had found
their way to the feast. It reminded Bolan of Danang, except
that nobody was shooting at him.

Yet.

He followed multilingual signs, moving through the crush
toward a row of sluggish baggage carousels. He half expected
to discover that his bag had gone to Singapore or Tokyo, but
there it was, rocking along on the conveyor belt with only
three or four new scars. Bolan retrieved it, got in line to let a
skinny cop check out his baggage and was advancing slowly
when a man stepped up beside him.

"Mike Belasko?"

Hearing his alias, Bolan turned to face the stranger. He was
Asian, probably late thirties, clean shaven, with short dark
hair. He wore plain clothes but palmed a badge and what appeared to be police ID.

"David Yun, I presume?" Bolan said.

"The same. Shall we move on?"

Yun badged the skinny uniform and Bolan followed him,
jumping the line. Some of the waiting travelers were plainly
curious, others sullen and resentful. They didn't know where
he was going, but they envied him regardless. After so much
time in transit, Bolan guessed that some of them would rather
go to jail than spend more time standing in line.

The heat hadn't improved since Bolan disembarked from

his flight. Yun led him to a brown no-frills sedan parked just outside, standing defiantly alone against a red-painted curb, three feet from what Bolan assumed was a no-parking sign. Yun left Bolan to stow his own luggage, climbing into the driver's seat and removing a dog-eared cardboard sign from the windshield on his side. Bolan couldn't read the sign, either, but he knew it had to identify Yun's four-door as a police car, thereby immune to parking tickets or towing.

"You had a good flight?" Yun asked, as they pulled into sunshine and traffic.

"I had a *long* flight," Bolan answered.

"So true. You've come a far distance for two young people."

"That's how it works."

"Americans," Yun said, shaking his head. But he was smiling, and he didn't seem to disapprove. Not quite.

"You wouldn't follow up?" Bolan asked.

"We live in different worlds, Mr. Belasko. May I call you Mike?" His English was precise, textbook.

"Suits me."

"Americans—most Westerners, in fact—are often startled or outraged by things the so-called Third World takes for granted. People die, they disappear. It happens every day. We punish crime whenever possible of course, and often more severely than your courts in the United States. By the same token, I don't believe my government would send a man halfway around the world to supervise the search for two young people kidnapped on a pleasure cruise."

"I wasn't sent to second-guess your people," Bolan said. He didn't need a pissing contest with the local cops to slow him. If Yun was looking for an argument, Bolan hoped he could head it off and save them both some time.

"Please understand me," his escort replied. "I'm glad you've come. These pirates need a lesson, but I fear the hostages you seek may already be dead."

"In that case," Bolan said, "I'll want to meet their killers."

"Vengeance." David Yun was smiling. "This, I understand."

"It's just a job," Bolan replied.

Yun cast a sidelong glance at him and lost the smile. He said, "It's more than that, I think."

Bolan ignored the observation, leaving Yun to think whatever pleased him. They'd known each other less than half an hour, and he wasn't in the mood for being psychoanalyzed. "They told me in the States that you could set me up with some equipment, yes?"

"Firearms? Assuredly." Yun didn't seem to take offense at the rebuff. "I took the liberty of filling out the necessary paperwork on your behalf." Yun reached inside his jacket and removed a laminated card. It bore the name of Mike Belasko and some numbers that appeared to be the present date, but Bolan couldn't read the rest of it.

"A carry permit?"

"Yes. I thought it best, in case we should be separated at some point. It authorizes you to travel armed throughout Malaysia for a period of thirty days. I trust your business will be done by then?"

"Believe it," Bolan told him. One way or another.

"I assume you don't wish to borrow an official side arm?"

"Better not."

"In that case," Yun replied, "we need to speak with Mr. Chang."

Bolan sat back and let his escort chart their course through teeming streets. He felt the quickening of pulse that always came at the beginning of a hunt, a tingling of his nerves. It wasn't show time yet, but they were getting close.

And when the curtain rose, there would be hell to pay.

THE ARMS DEALER operated from a pawnshop on the edge of a slum district on Kuala Lumpur's east side. His continuance in business was a personal embarrassment to David Yun, but the American appeared to understand and didn't seem to judge him for the fact that Chang was obviously bribing someone in authority. It was the same in the United States, Yun understood, but possibly without such flagrant violation of the law.

There was always a market for weapons in Malaysia. It dated from British colonial times and the first insurrection, fueled in later years by rebels and drug lords alike. Pirates were included in the black market now, both as customers and vendors. Arms shipments were highly prized as targets, since the thieves could pick and choose the best weapons for themselves before selling the rest to other criminals. Yun knew brother officers who'd been killed by some of those guns, but high-ranking authorities still protected the traffic, to their everlasting shame.

Yun found a curbside parking space and returned the cardboard sign to his dashboard. He didn't fear a parking ticket, but rather hoped the placard might induce young thieves and vandals to leave his car alone. A question now occurred to him, as he was opening his door. "You do have cash, I trust?" he asked.

Bolan smiled and said, "Assuming Mr. Chang takes U.S. dollars."

"I believe you'll find him most accommodating on that subject."

It was dark and cramped inside the shop, a little bit of everything on display, from arcane musical instruments and stuffed animals—the rearing cobra was a standout—to jewelry and an improbable selection of fur coats. Chang was alone in the shop, as always. In all the years he'd known the dealer and observed his operation from a distance, Yun had never seen Chang miss a day of work or share the load with anyone. He had to have help of some kind, the detective reasoned, but if so his aides remained invisible.

"Detective Yun!" The old man came around his counter, smiling, as if they were bosom friends. "You've brought a guest to visit my humble establishment. How kind of you."

Any intended irony was swallowed by Chang's ear-to-ear grin and subservient attitude. The old man had learned early on how to deal with police. He kept a civil tongue in his head and paid his bribes on time, without being asked twice.

Yun swallowed his discomfort, telling Chang, "My friend

needs equipment for a hunting expedition. I've informed him that you may be able to supply his needs."

Chang raised an eyebrow—not missing the irony now, with Yun cast as a customer for the first time in their long association—and turned to Bolan, addressing him in near-perfect English. "Of course! Anything for our friend, the American sportsman. What is it you require, sir?"

Bolan was calm. "I'd like to see your inventory," he replied.

"Most certainly!" Chang shuffled past them, locked the front door to his shop and turned the plastic sign around to indicate the place was closed. "This way, my friends. This way."

They followed him around the counter, past the register and through a beaded curtain to a combination storage room and office in the back. A flight of stairs led steeply downward into darkness, suddenly illuminated as Chang found a switch on the wall. He climbed downstairs, jingling keys in his hand, to unlock and open a steel door below. Another light came on as Yun and Bolan followed Chang into his bunker.

The place was an arsenal, packed wall to wall with weapons, ammunition and some unlabeled crates that made Yun especially nervous. Roughly three hundred square feet in area, the basement contained more lethal hardware than the armory at Kuala Lumpur police headquarters—and it was all on sale, freely available to the highest bidder. Some of Chang's weapons had no doubt killed policemen and soldiers; many more had killed unarmed civilians, but Yun was forbidden to touch him.

He swallowed his anger and disgust, watching his new partner browse along a rack of automatic rifles. The American picked out a folding-stock AKMS assault rifle, the Russian model chambered in 7.62 9mm, and asked Chang, "Do you have spare magazines and ammunition for this one?"

"Of course, my friend. Whatever you require."

The American fieldstripped the weapon in seconds flat, checking the firing pin and other critical components before he reassembled it with equal speed. "I'll need a dozen loaded magazines," he said, "and boxed cartridges for reloading. Call it seven hundred rounds?"

"No problem," Chang assured him.

Bolan moved on to the handguns, displayed in boxes and hanging on wall hooks. He chose a new Beretta 92-F and asked the same questions of Chang, settling for 150 rounds of 9 mm Parabellum ammunition in 15-round box magazines and a black leather shoulder holster.

Hand grenades were the last item on the American's shopping list, Chang beaming as he showed off an assortment of American, British and Russian antipersonnel devices. Yun's new partner chose ten of the Dutch NR-330 fragmentation grenades, Chang adding two canvas satchels to contain his selections. The arms dealer looked surprised when there was no haggling over price. He asked for fifteen thousand ringgits or four thousand U.S. dollars, whereupon the American produced a fat roll of currency and peeled off forty hundred-dollar bills, counting them into the pawnbroker's hand.

Chang was clearly impressed, and he found it difficult to tear his eyes away from the man's remaining bankroll. "Always happy to do business with Americans." He beamed, smiling wide enough to show off gold-capped molars. "Come back often, please! Anything you need, if it's not here, I can get it!"

"I believe you," the American replied, slipping his jacket off long enough to don the shoulder rig and settle the Beretta in its place below his left armpit. Pouches on the right held two spare magazines; the rest joined his other acquisitions in the olive-drab satchels. "You need anything?" he asked Yun.

The detective shook his head, frowning. Chang kept up a cheerful patter as he led them back upstairs, unlocking the door to the street. He wished Bolan well on his "hunting trip" and repeated his offer to find whatever special items might be needed later on. "More ammunition, not a problem," Chang declared. "Maybe a bigger gun for larger game?"

"Let's see how I do with this batch," Bolan said, leaving Yun to disengage as he left the pawnshop. At the car Yun watched him stow his purchases out of sight, on the floor behind the passenger's seat.

"You think all this is necessary?" Yun asked.

The American responded with a shrug. "We're hunting pirates," he said. "No word on how many or what they'll be packing. I'd rather have it and not need it than the other way around."

"Of course," Yun said, disguising his uneasiness as best he could. "I hope our next stop may provide more information on the men you seek."

"The men *we* seek," Bolan said, correcting him.

"Of course," Yun answered, wishing he were anyplace but in the tall man's company. "That's what I meant to say."

"I never doubted it," Bolan answered.

"WE ARE GOING to see a man who deals in stolen property," Yun said. He drove skillfully, avoiding cyclists and erratic pedestrians on the crowded street without using the old sedan's brakes. "I think you call such men fences?"

"That's right."

"This fence is named Mahmoud Safi. He's been named in our investigations as a friend of certain pirates operating from Kuala Terennganu and Kota Baharu."

"Where the ransom note was found," Bolan stated.

"Correct. Unfortunately, evidence is lacking to connect him positively with the gang in question. We only have rumors, what you call hearsay?"

"That's what we call it," Bolan replied.

"I've questioned him myself on two occasions, but without some evidence..."

"Maybe he'll talk to me," the Executioner suggested.

"It's a possibility."

Bolan watched the streets as Yun drove, memorizing landmarks in case he was left to his own devices in Kuala Lumpur at some point in the future. He sensed the detective's reluctance without having to study Yun's face. He had Yun figured as a cop who played things by the book whenever possible, chafing at the corruption that surrounded him. Yun didn't like the system as it was, but so far he'd stopped short of openly rebelling—and he might find it impossible to go along with Bolan when the game got rough.

"You need to understand something," Bolan said.

"Rest assured, your mission was explained to me."

"Let's hit the abridged version, anyway. I've got two jobs. The first, hostage retrieval, may turn out to be impossible. I won't know that until I poke around and turn up the heat. My second job is to locate the men responsible and put them out of business."

"You mean kill them," Yun replied.

"Your people haven't had much luck so far with the conventional approach."

"I've read that in your country some policemen look the other way while crimes occur. They're paid to break their oath of office. Others who work with them may be honest, but they keep the secret out of loyalty to their comrades. This is true?"

"I'd guess it happens every day," Bolan acknowledged.

"Then you understand my problem. In Malaysia," Yun went on, "the punishment for drug offenses is extremely harsh—at least by Western standards—but narcotics still remain available. Some traffickers remain untouched. An officer of my acquaintance who arrested one such man was reprimanded and reduced in rank. Later, investigators searched his locker at headquarters and discovered heroin. He sits in prison now. I always thought that rather curious."

The message came through loud and clear. Bolan could offer little in the way of reassurance, other than to say, "I understood cooperation on this job had been cleared at the highest levels."

"So I understand, as well, but situations change, sometimes."

"If you feel a change coming," Bolan remarked, "I'd like to have some warning, if it doesn't put you in too much danger."

"Agreed." This time, Yun managed an approximation of a smile, more irony than mirth in his expression.

"Meanwhile, how much farther is it to this fence we're going to see?"

"Not far. Perhaps one more kilometer."

That meant another fifteen minutes, dodging foot traffic and rickshaws, bicycles and motor scooters, as the streets filled up with evening traffic. Night fell swiftly in the tropics, but Kuala Lumpur's neon did a fair job of keeping the darkness at bay—at least until Yun left the main drags behind and started winding through a warren of smaller side streets where outdoor lighting was sparse to nonexistent. Noise and pale light spilled from the doorways of occasional taverns, gambling clubs, brothels, perhaps the occasional opium den thrown in for variety. Local residents kept the blinds drawn over windows in their tiny apartments, while an equal number slept rough on the streets and in dark alleys.

Bolan recognized the neighborhood, although he'd never passed this way before. He'd seen its mirror image in a hundred other cities, from Asia to Europe and Latin America, and he knew that any tourists who found their way here after nightfall were gambling with their lives. This was rock bottom, where the people lived hand-to-mouth and some didn't make it at all. Police would visit in groups or stay away entirely, perhaps ignoring the lesser emergency calls and trusting urban nature to follow its own brutal course.

"Almost there," Yun announced, killing his headlights as he made a left-hand turn into another dark and narrow street. He parked near the intersection and switched off the sedan's engine. A half-dozen shops were still open, by the look of things, but there was no foot traffic on the street to encourage their proprietors.

Across the street and three doors down, a nondescript business with blacked-out front windows emitted the throbbing bass line of recorded music played at ear-damaging levels. Bolan took it for some kind of nightclub, his judgment confirmed when Yun pointed to the source of the noise and said, "Mahmoud Safi owns the Leung Chung Club."

"Leung Chung?"

"The Happy Dragon," Yun translated. "This dragon isn't happy when police drop in to visit unexpectedly."

"No problem," Bolan said. "I'm not police."

"It's all the same to him."

"His problem, then, if he gets rowdy. How's he fixed for reinforcements?"

"On a normal night, two bouncers, maybe three. If he expects trouble, there may be more."

"What do they carry?"

Yun frowned in the darkness. "There are strict laws in Malaysia governing the ownership of firearms."

"We've already seen how well they work," Bolan replied. "Same question."

"Normally," Yun said, "the bouncers carry saps and knuckle-dusters, sometimes knives. Mahmoud would probably keep the guns in his office."

"That narrows it down. Are we ready?"

Bolan had his fingers wrapped around the inside handle of his door when Yun replied, "One moment." Headlights speared the street downrange and Bolan saw a black Proton Juara van approaching from the east. It stopped outside the Happy Dragon Club, the driver remaining in his seat while doors came open on both sides behind him. Three long-haired hardmen in dark suits emerged, the last one on his feet manhandling a slender woman out of the back seat.

Before the headlights died, Bolan could make out few details of the woman's appearance. He got his best shot when her three escorts jostled her into the club: Asian, with long black hair, wearing a sleek kimono-style dress that flattered her athletic figure. Age-wise, she could've been eighteen or thirty-five; the dark and distance ruined any shot he had at pinning down more details from across the street.

"Is that how Mahmoud gets his dates?" Bolan asked Yun.

"She's not a date," Yun answered, opening his door. Bolan was thankful that the dome light didn't work. "Unless I'm very much mistaken, we've just witnessed an abduction."

SACHIKO HIRAWA was frightened. She'd tried to tell herself otherwise, from the moment Safi's thugs had snatched her off the street until they'd reached the Leung Chung Club, but the bravado wasn't working. She was definitely frightened.

Make that terrified.

She was also embarrassed and angry with herself. It was humiliating to be taken by surprise, when she should've known better. Two weeks in Kuala Lumpur, nearly a month overall since she'd left home on her private quest, and she *did* know better than to let herself be caught napping. There'd been a moment on the street when she could've fought back, perhaps eluded her captors, but one of them had shown her a gun and she'd panicked, forgetting the moves she'd practiced since childhood.

Now Hirawa feared that moment of weakness might cost her life. There was a chance, she thought, that Safi would simply threaten her again—present her with a final warning—but she doubted it. He'd been quite emphatic in their last conversation, commanding her to leave Malaysia and go home to Sapporo, forget about her loss and realize that there was nothing she could do to make it right.

That warning hadn't fazed her, naturally, any more than the advice from local police had changed her mind. The police had been less threatening, more patronizing in their attitude, though one of them had been quite courteous. It made no difference in the end. Hirawa knew her duty, her obligation to her family. If she had to do the dirty job herself, so be it.

Now, though, it appeared that she would never have the chance. Because she had been weak and slow to act.

It wasn't in her nature to concede defeat, but Hirawa admitted to herself that things looked bad. She'd let herself be taken without a fight, and now she'd been delivered to Mahmoud Safi's lair. The Leung Chung Club was little more than an underworld hangout disguised as a nightclub, somewhere the bandits and assassins could relax when they weren't robbing innocents of their life savings or killing them for sport.

She wasn't finished yet, though. Even in the serpent's nest, Hirawa still knew a trick or two that might surprise them—all the more since she'd surrendered so meekly on the street earlier.

Give me Mahmoud, she thought grimly. That much, at least, before I die.

In truth, death wasn't the fear that troubled Hirawa the most just now. She was afraid what else her captors might decide to try for fun before they let her die.

Fear sharpened her resolve to repay pain in kind at the first opportunity. She followed the two escorts in front of her as they crossed the loud, smoky barroom, keeping track of the third man behind her all the way. Her captors were relaxed now, comfortable on familiar ground. It was their turn to be careless, convinced that a mere women posed no threat to them.

So far, indeed, she hadn't. But Hirawa planned to change that very soon. All she required to set the stage was one clear shot at Safi.

Her escorts brought her to a door marked Private in four languages, including Japanese and English. She waited while the tallest of her captors knocked and a voice from within bade them enter, barely audible above the music throbbing from the club's jukebox. It wasn't just tobacco smoke she smelled now, and Sachiko had begun to feel a bit light-headed from the hashish in the Happy Dragon's thick, polluted atmosphere.

Safi's office was an architect's afterthought, more impressive for its clutter than its size. Hirawa hadn't seen the man's cramped inner sanctum before. Their last meeting had taken place in the club's main room, before it opened for business. Standing in the office now, adjectives like cramped and claustrophobic came to mind, but she supposed the little room could work in her favor. If she had to fight—which seemed more likely by the moment—her opponents would have trou-

ble striking back without hitting one another. She, on the
other hand, could lash out in any direction at will, making
each kick or punch connect with flesh and bone.

Not yet.

The room's one piece of halfway decent furniture, a heavy
desk, stood between herself and Safi. Two of his men flanked
Hirawa, standing close on either side, while the third was still
behind her. She could feel the eyes moving over her body like
rude, groping hands, but she focused on the man who had
frustrated her so far, blocking her search for those she sought.

Safi addressed her in English, since he spoke no Japanese.
"You should've gone home when I told you to the first time,
little girl," he said. "You're in some trouble now, asking rude
questions in the street."

"What would you do in my place?" she inquired.

His shrug was lazy. "I understand your feelings, truly, but
you must see when there's nothing more that can be done."

"I haven't reached that point," she said defiantly.

"You disappoint me, Sachiko." He smiled. "You don't
mind if I call you Sachiko, I take it?"

"You may call me Miss Hirawa."

"Sachiko," he said, ignoring her, "you've placed me in a
difficult position."

"How unfortunate."

"It is—for you. The men I work with, those you're looking for so urgently, trust me to keep their names a secret."

"I don't know their names," she told him. "Yet."

"I can appreciate your feelings," he repeated, "but—"

"I doubt that very much."

"Insults don't help your case with me."

"What would?"

Safi considered it, frowning. The effort brought his thick
eyebrows together in a long, unbroken line across the middle
of his face. It made him look more simian than ever. Under different circumstances, Hirawa might easily have laughed at him.

She wasn't laughing now.

"You ask an interesting question," Safi said at length. "Already, you've ignored my efforts to protect you and annoyed me in the process. Disrespect is something that a man in my position cannot tolerate."

"I would respect you if you helped me find the men I seek," she said.

A sudden flare of anger turned his frown into a snarl. "You don't tell me what I must do!" he raged. "This is my city. *I* tell *you*, and you ignore me at your peril."

Hirawa thought it couldn't hurt to try another tack. "If that's the case, if it's your city, why are you afraid?"

An angry flush suffused his sallow face. Safi lurched to his feet, braced on his knuckles as he leaned across the desk.

A few more inches and he would be close enough.

"You speak of fear?" he said, taunting. "I'll teach you what it means!"

"From personal experience, no doubt."

"You say that I'm afraid of you?" He forced a yelp of laughter through his crooked teeth.

"Of what I may discover," Hirawa replied. If she couldn't escape, she needed to provoke Safi and draw him closer. Close enough to reach his flabby throat.

"You've wasted two weeks and discovered nothing," he replied, sneering. "You'll *never* find the men you seek."

"If you believed that, I'd be back at my hotel and you'd be busy pimping little girls, instead of sweating through that shiny suit."

Mahmoud Safi trembled in his rage. He poised as if to hurl himself across the desk, frozen with one leg raised when someone started pounding on the office door.

"What is it?" he shouted, forgetting to switch back from English.

"Trouble!" a man's voice replied in the same language.

As if to prove it, a gunshot rang out from the main room of the Happy Dragon Club. Safi was blinking, startled, when Hirawa launched a roundhouse kick into his sweaty face.

David Yun was first through the door, badge in hand as two bouncers moved up to intercept him. Bolan, close behind him, saw the muscle separate as if to let Yun pass, but they were shooting glances back and forth, noting that Yun still hadn't shown his gun. The bouncer on the left said something Bolan couldn't understand. It sounded like a challenge, and Yun replied in angry tones. The bouncer flashed a smile with no sincerity behind it, shrugged and launched a roundhouse swing at the detective's head.

Bolan was ready as the second bouncer came for him. He had six inches on the Asian, but the man was solid, snarling with a face crosshatched by scars. That face said, "You can hit me hard, and it still won't take me down."

We'll see, Bolan thought.

The wiry bouncer's first move was a looping kick with his right leg. It could've fractured Bolan's cheekbone, but he blocked it with an arm and answered with a forward snap kick of his own. The bouncer danced away from glancing impact on his chest and came back swiftly with another kick. Left leg, this time, with everything he had behind it.

Bolan saw his opportunity and seized it—literally. Pivoting inside the kick, he grabbed his adversary's left ankle and gave the upraised leg a twist. At the same moment, still turning, he kicked back with his right leg, heel impacting on the bouncer's right kneecap. A squeal covered the softer crunching sound, but Bolan felt the knee buckle and let his enemy collapse into a squirming heap.

He turned in time to see Yun drop his dazed opponent with an elbow to the face. Two down, and while he'd hoped for that to be the end of it, Bolan saw two more bouncers moving in, these men armed with sticks resembling sawed-off pool cues. Yun called out to them again, barking a single word that Bolan took to mean police, but the advancing thugs were unimpressed. Behind them, gathering like storm clouds cast in human form, approximately two-thirds of the Happy Dragon's customers had formed into a growling mob, while the remainder slipped out through an exit at the rear.

To hell with this, Bolan thought. He was not about to brawl bare-handed with a gang of thugs, at odds of ten or twelve to one. Assuming he and Yun survived the fight—unlikely, any way he sliced it—they'd still blow their best shot at helping the woman and cornering Mahmoud Safi.

Bolan drew and fired his Beretta in one fluid motion. The closer of the two club-wielding bouncers saw it coming but had no time to protect himself. The Parabellum round drilled his left shoulder, spun him on his heels and dropped him face-down in the path of those who pressed forward behind him.

Bolan turned toward the second armed bouncer and found him retreating, dropping his club as he backed away. Three or four of the bars' scowling customers had drawn knives, but they seemed in no hurry to use them, surging backward like a single organism in the face of Bolan's gun. The wounded bouncer made no effort, content to curl up on the floor and mutter in his misery.

Yun looked as surprised by the shooting as anyone else in the bar, and nearly as unhappy. He'd drawn his gun in reflex, on hearing the shot, but he didn't seem sure where to point it. Angling its muzzle toward the floor, somewhere between himself and the crowd of surly nightclub patrons, barking orders at them in a language sounding vaguely like Chinese.

Movement behind the Happy Dragon's bar distracted Bolan from his coverage of the mumbling crowd. He turned to find the bartender rising from a crouch, holding a submachine gun clutched against his chest. The gunman had his finger on the weapon's trigger but he wasn't aiming yet, and Bolan didn't plan to let him get that far.

Sighting quickly, he released a quick 9 mm double tap into the barman's upper chest and slammed him back against the shelves of bottles. Some of them toppled, shattering, before the dying shooter's trigger finger clenched and brought his SMG to life. Numb hands couldn't control the weapon, and it kicked free after firing roughly half a magazine, but not before it sprayed the ceiling and the long north wall above the heads of their collective audience.

That was enough to break the crowd and send its members racing for the exit. Yun called after them, as if to bring them back, but short of firing for effect into their backs there was no stopping them.

Bolan considered it a lucky break and let them go. He looked for other doors and came up with the entrance to a narrow passageway beyond the north end of the bar. Yun was beside him as he moved in that direction, following his pistol through another beaded curtain, not unlike the one they'd seen at Chang's pawnshop.

"We could've done this without shooting," Yun remarked, as they were entering the dimly lit hallway.

"I didn't feel like leaving in a body bag," Bolan replied. And then, "Look out!"

In front of them, the first of three doors suddenly burst open to disgorge a slender Asian man dressed in a lime-green leisure suit. He wore a hat to match, and mirrored sunglasses despite the hour, but the most important thing about him was the nickel-plated pistol in his hand, seeking a target as it wavered back and forth.

Bolan fired once before the human string bean could decide, sending the man sliding down the wall, leaving a gaudy streak of crimson in his wake. The gunner managed one shot, but he did no better than the bartender, his bullet plunking through the ceiling to unleash a rain of plaster dust.

The Executioner was moving past him, checking out the room he'd left for any further threats and finding none, when crashing sounds of combat echoed from the far end of the hall. A muffled gunshot sounded from behind another door, this one shut tight and marked with multilingual signs demanding privacy. The shot aside, it sounded as if someone in the closed room had decided to redecorate with a sledgehammer. A woman's squeal cut through the scraping, banging sounds.

Bolan was on the move in that direction, gaining speed, when Yun cried out a warning from behind him and a storm of gunfire swept along the corridor.

FOR DAVID YUN, a split second made the difference between life and death. That, and a nervous shooter who was too high-strung to keep his mouth shut when it mattered. If the stranger had been able to assert more self-control...

There was no time to analyze it during the event, of course. Yun was staring at a dead man in a green suit as he slithered down the wall, smearing the faded paint with blood. Dust filtered down in front of him, from where the gunman's bullet had drilled through the ceiling overhead. It could've been Yun's blood staining the wall and carpet, but the American had been quicker than their enemy. His partner was moving on toward other targets, following the sounds of struggle from a closed room at the far end of the corridor.

Mahmoud Safi had his office there, Yun knew from prior experience. The woman had to be there, as well. It sounded as if she were being beaten, then a gunshot echoed from behind the door and Yun feared they were already too late.

Bolan rushed the office, and in that way missed the sound of gunmen coming up behind them. Yun would almost certainly have missed it, too, but one of those arriving late was obviously startled by the sight of the green-suited corpse and gave a little yelp of anger or surprise. Thus warned, Yun turned to face them, crouching, and called out a warning to Bolan as the shooters opened fire.

He counted three of them as he slumped sideways, slipping down the wall in an unconscious parody of the dead man behind him. Yun had no idea where they had come from, but assumed there were other rooms he'd missed extending from the barroom. Two of the new arrivals carried Japanese SCK submachine guns, while the third was armed with two snub-nosed revolvers.

All three opened fire in unison, raking the hallway, but they seemed to value racket over accuracy. Hunched against the wall, Yun heard the first rounds strike a yard above his head and aimed his 9 mm Daewoo DP-51 pistol at the nearest of the men who sought to kill him. It had been five years since Yun last fired a shot in anger at another human being, and he'd missed his target then, but now he fired as if his life depended on it, four quick rounds aimed at the shooter's torso, aiming for center mass.

The gunman staggered, scarlet splashed across the front of his beige linen shirt. His short legs buckled and he dropped to his knees with a jolt, gasping in startled pain. He tried to hold the submachine gun steady, bringing it to bear on Yun before his life ran out through leaking holes between his ribs, but Yun squeezed off another shot that drilled the thug's forehead and slammed him over backward in a twitching sprawl.

That still left two, and both of them were leveling their guns at Yun now, furious and frightened after he had dropped their friend. With eight rounds left and precious little time, Yun wasn't sure if he could stop them both, but he was bound to go down fighting.

Before Yun had the chance to fire again, Bolan shot the other submachine gunner, a clean shot through his neck that spouted blood from wall to wall across the corridor. Choking, the gunman grabbed his throat with one hand but continued firing with the other, emptying his magazine before another Parabellum round tore through his chest and took him down.

The gunman with the two revolvers—a Korean, Yun saw now—found himself the last man standing and was none too happy with the situation, if his twisted features were a gauge of how he felt. Bleating a wordless squeal of anger or alarm, he started running backward, firing both revolvers wildly as he went.

Yun guessed he meant to fire one piece at each of his opponents, but the jerky effort came up short in both directions and he used his last half-dozen rounds without scoring a hit. The hammers fell on empty chambers almost simultaneously and the shooter turned to flee, but he had stalled too long. Yun and Bolan fired simultaneously, five rounds altogether, the impact of their bullets propelling the target toward a head-on collision with the nearest wall.

Yun had lost track of how many times he'd fired, but the slide on his Daewoo hadn't locked open, so he knew there was at least one live round still remaining in the pistol. Scrambling to his feet before anything else could happen, he faced Bolan and found the American moving once more toward Mahmoud Safi's office. Sounds of struggle continued from behind the closed door, but they seemed less urgent now, as if the fight were nearly over.

Yun followed Bolan, breathing in the reek of cordite that reminded him of mornings on the practice firing range—except that there was another smell beneath it: the metallic tang of fresh blood.

Five dead, the dazed detective thought. *And we aren't finished yet.*

HIRAWA'S FIRST KICK found its mark on Mahmoud Safi's cheek, pitching him backward and away from her, against a nearby filing cabinet. The impact of his body jarred a stack of papers loose from their precarious position on the cabinet and sent them all cascading around Safi as he collapsed.

Her three escorts were stunned, torn between responding to the gunfire from the nightclub and protecting their boss. By the time they decided, Hirawa had picked her next target, spinning to her left for another high kick at the face nearest to her.

This time the target anticipated her move and was quick enough to protect himself, raising an arm to block the kick. The impact still rocked him, but he wasn't disabled or even stunned. In fact he struck back with a fist that caught the woman high on the inside of her thigh, making her grunt with pain. Her leg was tingling when she drew back, forcing her to hop a little as she braced herself for the next move. Her adversary took advantage of the moment, rushing forward to strike again, but Hirawa raised her trembling leg as if to launch another kick and he retreated out of range.

Not that it helped, a second later, when one of the others struck her from behind. He didn't aim at the back of her head or neck for some reason, and it proved to be a critical mistake. Propelled into the nearest wall, Hirawa raised an arm to save her face, ignoring the bruises she got in return. Rebounding from the wall, she spun to meet the sucker puncher as he aimed another clenched fist at her face, perhaps trying to make up for his first-time oversight.

Hirawa rolled away from the punch at the penultimate moment, pleased with the sound of knuckles striking brick. Still moving, she spun beneath the blow and drove her right elbow into her enemy's ribs, putting her full weight and momentum behind it. Something cracked and he bellowed a cry of pain, stumbling backward with a bruised hand clutching his side.

"Finish it!" Safi rasped from behind the desk, speaking through blood. Two of Hirawa's escorts immediately reached inside their jackets for weapons, warning her that she had to do something now or miss her last chance.

Trusting her right leg more than she wanted to at the moment, Hirawa hopped forward, found her mark and threw a side kick into the nearest thug's body. Her foot caught his forearm with the hand inside his jacket, cracking the long bones against his sternum. A gunshot thundered in the confines of the tiny office, as his finger clenched around the trigger of a hidden pistol. Hirawa recoiled from the sound, amazed to see flames licking from the left side of the shooter's polyester sport coat. Her adversary noticed it an instant later and abandoned his attempt to kill her, focused instead on the effort to save himself from a critical burn.

The woman might've kicked him unconscious and left him to smolder, but she had other enemies to deal with at the moment. With Safi shouting, "Kill her! Kill her!" at the top of his lungs, Hirawa's two uninjured escorts scrambled for their pistols. There was one on either side of her in the cramped office, and she got no satisfaction from the knowledge that a cross fire might've killed them both, along with her. The object of her mission was revenge, but she could only reach that goal if she survived the night.

The gunmen had her flanked. So near and yet so far. Ignoring either one of them could give him time to draw and fire, a killing hit at this range virtually guaranteed. To save herself, Hirawa had to stop—or stall—them both at the same time.

Nothing to lose, she thought, and made her move. To an observer, it may have resembled something from a grim ballet. Half turned in profile to her would-be killers, all her weight supported on one leg, Hirawa kicked out to the left and simultaneously bent her torso to the far right, both arms shooting out together, fingers hooked like claws.

She nearly missed the kick, heel barely grazing her first target's chin, but it was still enough to stagger him and spoil his aim with the shiny automatic pistol he carried. Her aim was better with the hands, fingernails biting deep into her second adversary's forehead and ripping bloody furrows down his screaming face.

She spun out of the long kick for another, going low this time and to the left. The gunman she had staggered with the face kick was recovering—at least, until she cut his legs from under him and dropped him on his backside, grunting as he hit the concrete floor. A third and final kick connected with his temple, hammering his head against Mahmoud Safi's desk, and he slumped over backward. Dazed or dying, Hirawa didn't know and didn't care.

The bleeding shooter, fumbling a pistol clear of his jacket, fired before he was ready. She felt the hot wind of a bullet's passage on her cheek, already lashing out with her right foot to crack his knuckles, and sent the pistol spinning uselessly to a neutral corner of the room.

The gunman had to rush her. It was in his blood, and much of that was smeared across his pale silk shirt by now. He had no style and no apparent training, arms flailing as he came at her. Even in the confined office space she was able to side-step his clumsy charge, whipping a heel into the back of his head and dropping him like an oversized marionette with the strings cut.

Easy.

Well, not quite.

Before Hirawa could congratulate herself, she heard the sharp click of a pistol hammer being cocked behind her. Thick with malice, spiced with pain, Mahmoud Safi's voice told her, "It's time for you to die."

MAHMOUD SAFI FELT as if he'd awakened from the worst binge of his life, hung over terribly, to find a stranger slapping him across the face. His head throbbed viciously behind the eyes, and there was something wrong with his jaw where the woman had kicked him. Clenching his teeth against the pain, he found they didn't fit together properly, and when he spoke his tongue felt thick and heavy, like an alien appendage inside his mouth.

Safi had reached for his pistol while the woman finished with his men. If they survived the night, he meant to fire all three. If they were competent, his ears wouldn't be ringing now. What kind of soldiers let a woman pummel and disarm them after she kicked their employer in the face?

The dead kind, Safi thought. Maybe it wouldn't be enough to simply fire them after all.

"It's time for you to die," he told the woman, but Safi still didn't squeeze the trigger of his Star 30-M pistol. It was trembling in his fist, the sights fixed on the woman's face, but now he hesitated, wondering if he might need the woman as a hostage.

What in hell had happened to the club? One moment his men returned from their errand with the woman he'd sent them to find and retrieve, the next, shouting and gunfire were competing with the jukebox, while Hirawa proceeded to mop up the office with Safi and his men.

The fence didn't like surprises, least of all when they were painful, dangerous, or cost him money. His worst-case scenario in life was a surprise that fit all three descriptions—and Mahmoud Safi had a sinking feeling that he had such a surprise in store for him right now.

"Who followed you?" he asked the woman, taking full advantage of a lull in firing from outside.

"I wouldn't know," she said, sneering at him. "Your thugs refused me when I asked to drive the car."

"You may regret that attitude of yours," he hissed. "Who's working with you?"

"No one." This time, from her tone and the expression on her face, Safi almost suspected that she'd told the truth.

Another burst of gunfire rocked the Happy Dragon Club. This one was closer, from the corridor outside his office. As if to prove the point, a bullet pierced the wall beside his door and smacked into the filing cabinet across the room. He ducked instinctively, hating the way his pistol wavered, but he kept it pointed at Hirawa all the same.

"You still say no one followed you?"

"A man like you makes enemies," she said. She stressed the word "man" as if it were a curse or possibly a joke.

Fuming, Safi knew she was right—he had no end of enemies, around the country and beyond—but it struck him as too coincidental for belief. His troops brought in Hirawa for a grilling, while some unrelated foe chose that very instant to attack the club? It was incredible, nearly beyond belief.

"I'll ask you one more time," he said, thrusting the pistol forward as if two or three less inches made its threat more imminent.

"Once or a hundred times," she said, "it makes no difference. My answer is the same. I work alone. If someone followed your men here, I don't know who they are." A sudden smile lit up her face. "I hope to watch them kill you, though."

"You bitch!" Safi circled around the desk, careful not to close within reach of the woman's quick feet. "What have I ever done to you?"

"You mean besides ignoring my requests for information, lying to my face and having me kidnapped?" The sneer was back. "Nothing at all."

"You poke your nose in where it isn't wanted," Safi said, "and now you have to pay the price."

More shooting from the hallway distracted both of them, bullets pecking at the heavy door this time. One of them struck the doorknob and dislodged it, leaving twisted metal and a fan of wooden splinters in its place. Another moment, and Safi knew someone would come bursting through the doorway to destroy him, weapons blazing.

Furious and frightened, energized by both emotions, Safi threw himself at Hirawa, swinging his pistol as a bludgeon. He aimed for her temple, but she either felt or saw him coming, maybe both, and turned to take the blow across one cheek as she recoiled. Safi bored in, clutching at one of her wrists, drawing back the pistol for another swing.

The door burst open on his left, but Safi had no time to deal with the intruders just now. He jerked Hirawa toward him by her arm and swung the Star 30-M pistol at her face.

BOLAN HAD NO WAY of knowing if the office door was locked, so he took the knob off with a point-blank pistol shot and followed with a kick, lunging into Mahmoud Safi's private office. Yun was behind him somewhere, staying close.

Bolan hadn't known what to expect, but the scene in the office was startling. The three goons from the Proton Juara van lay scattered about the office floor, one of them beating feebly at the smoking ruins of his coat with blistered hands, the other two apparently unconscious. In the middle of the room, the young woman he'd come to save was grappling with a man he'd never seen before—presumably the fence who ran the Happy Dragon Club.

Before Bolan could intervene, Mahmoud Safi tried to club the woman with a pistol. She blocked the swing with her free hand, then slammed a heel down on his instep, grinding while he wailed. Safi released her other arm and she immediately hit him with a one-two combination punch that rocked him backward, fresh blood splaying from his broken nose.

Lurching, Safi retreated several awkward steps beyond the woman's reach and tripped on an immobile figure slumped beside his desk. The fence went down, arms flailing, but he kept a tight grip on his gun. The woman tried to follow up her first advantage, closing on him, but Safi already had her in his sights. It seemed impossible for her to bridge the gap before a bullet found her, slammed her back and down.

Bolan wanted Safi alive for questioning, but there was no time for trick shooting in the half second or so before the fence's index finger tightened on the trigger. It was a head shot or nothing, and Bolan made it two rounds from ten feet out, spilling the best part of Mahmoud Safi's brain across the cheap green carpet that was decorated with a dragon.

The woman gaped at Safi for a moment, then rounded on Bolan in apparent fury. She spoke first in rapid-fire Japanese, then caught herself and switched to English in midsentence. "That was brilliant! Stunning! Now he'll never tell me what I need to know!"

"From where I stood," Bolan replied, "he was about to say goodbye."

"It was under control!"

Bolan scanned the office battleground, three bodies on the floor, one struggling to get up. "I see that now," he said, leaning across to slug the smoky hardman with his pistol, putting him away.

The woman rolled her eyes in disbelief. "And now I won't get anything from him!" she said.

"The only thing you need is to get out of here," said Bolan. "The sooner, the better."

"I've been working toward this moment for the past two weeks!"

"We can discuss your choice of suicide techniques another time. Right now, we need to move."

The woman took a long step backward, putting space between them. "And you think I'd leave with you?"

Yun tried playing peacemaker. "If I may say—"

"You may *not* say," the woman cut him off. "I don't know either one of you, and I don't *want* to know you. You've barged in and ruined everything, destroyed whatever chance I had...."

She broke off, choking on the words and on a sudden rush of tears. The overflow from almond eyes did nothing to diminish her exotic beauty or disguise the rage that seethed inside her. Bolan didn't have a clue what she was doing there, but he would bet the farm that one or more of those who'd fled the Happy Dragon earlier were spreading news of trouble even now, maybe returning to the club with reinforcements for a little housecleaning. And while he understood some of his fellow countrymen staged reenactments of old battles as a pastime, Bolan didn't plan to make the Leung Chung Club his private Alamo.

"Okay," he told the woman. "I don't know what you had going here, and frankly I don't care. You want to come with us and get out while the getting's good, you're welcome. If you'd rather stick around and roughhouse with Mahmoud's boys, be my guest. We're leaving either way."

Yun started to protest, raising a hand as if he were directing traffic. "We cannot—"

"Force her to do the smart thing?" Bolan interrupted him. "You're right, we can't. She wants to stay and fight an army, that's her call." He turned back to the woman then, and said, "Good luck asking your questions from beyond the grave."

She blinked at that, shifting her mental gears. "You'd leave me here?" Like that, the thought seemed to amaze her.

"We're not kidnappers," Bolan replied. "We tried to help you out and evidently screwed that up. Good luck. You're on your own."

"No, wait!" The lady flushed with anger or embarrassment, maybe a bit of both. "I haven't got a car."

"You want a ride, now? After all that other—"

"Please!" She nearly whispered it, her voice taut with urgency.

Bolan pretended to consider it for all of fifteen seconds. Finally he said, "All right, let's go."

Before they reached the main room of the Happy Dragon, he knew they'd stalled too long. A swell of voices sounded from the barroom, some angry, none of them pleased. He didn't know how many men or weapons they'd be facing when they cleared the beaded curtain, but he didn't like the feel of it.

"That doesn't sound much like the welcoming committee," Bolan said. "We need a little icebreaker."

Reaching under his jacket, Bolan palmed the Dutch frag grenade he'd held out from his purchase at Chang's pawnshop, unclipping the cool metal orb from his belt. At 465 grams it weighed slightly more than the standard U.S. hand grenade, 156 grams of that weight the egg's payload of RDX plastique.

"How many ways can you two say 'Grenade'?" he asked.

They didn't hesitate, the woman calling out in Japanese, while Yun voiced the alarm in Malay, Cantonese and English. Bolan waited for the exit rush to start, then pulled the grenade's safety pin and tossed the bomb sidearm into the barroom without looking first to count heads. It blew five seconds later, rattling fixtures and shattering glass.

"We might consider going out the back door," Bolan told his two companions.

4

Kuala Lumpur

Nguyen Tre Minh saw the police lights flashing ahead and pulled his Perodua Kenarii miniwagon to the curb when he was still two blocks east of the Leung Chung Club. There was trouble ahead, and he wouldn't blunder into it like a fool.

That was someone else's job.

Nguyen turned to his companion, a Laotian named Mansay Boanam, and said, "Go see what's happening."

The pirate blinked at him, red and blue flashing lights giving his face a sickly hue. "Why me?" he asked.

"Because I said so." Nguyen didn't have to strive for menace in his tone.

"All right, I'm going."

"And be careful. Don't attract attention to yourself."

"You don't want me to ask what's happening?"

Stupid, Nguyen thought. "Don't ask the pigs. Use common sense, if that's not too much strain."

He watched Mansay move along the sidewalk, shoulders hunched, hands in his pockets. The Laotian was unremarkable, a perfect fit for the seedy neighborhood. There was nothing about him to make police single him out as suspicious. If Mansay kept his wits about him, talking quietly and only to civilian bystanders, he should be fine.

But just in case...

Nguyen reached beneath the driver's seat he occupied and found the Hungarian KGP-9 machine pistol he kept there for emergencies. He hoped not to need it, but they already had trouble—or, rather, Safi did—and if Mansay was careless, the fourteen-inch SMG could cover Nguyen's retreat with a barrage of 9 mm Parabellum rounds rattled off at a cyclic rate of 900 rounds per minute.

Nguyen sat with the gun in his lap and watched Mansay merge with the crowd milling about outside Mahmoud Safi's nightclub. Guessing the cause of the trouble was pointless. Knowing Safi and the Happy Dragon, it could be anything from a drug raid to a bloody drunken brawl between his customers. There was no reason to suppose it involved his business with Safi, but it was a damned annoyance all the same.

Nguyen rolled down his window, preparing to light a cigarette, and his nostrils picked up something on the breeze. It was a familiar scent—but what? Something like gunpowder, but not exactly.

Squinting against the strobelights, Nguyen thought he could see a thin haze of smoke in the street outside the club. He wondered briefly if the place could be on fire, but an absence of fire trucks and hoses negated that option. An ambulance was parked near the club, beyond the idling squad cars, but its attendants were standing by with their arms crossed, in no hurry to service the sick or injured.

That told Nguyen one of two things had transpired. Either someone in the club had minor injuries and the police were grilling them before the medics were allowed to do their work, or else the wounded were beyond all earthly help. It wouldn't be the first time someone had been killed at the Happy Dragon—nor even the first time this year. Safi paid dearly for his license and the forbearance of police who ignored his shady dealings for a price. This disturbance could be anything.

In which case, why did Nguyen suddenly feel nervous?

He was troubled by the kidnapping, admittedly. It had been his idea and Lee Sun had approved it after consultation, but Nguyen was having second thoughts. He had begun to fear there would be trouble if they pressed their ransom demand for the two Americans. It would be safer, he believed now, to dispose of them and write off the matter as a bit of unfortunate business. Lee had overruled him, insisting that the money had to be paid.

Ten million U.S. dollars.

Cash like that was always welcome, and two hostages were easier to maintain, safer to exchange, than an oil tanker filled to the brim with black gold. Nguyen could hide the prisoners in a car trunk, if need be—and he could leave them there to die if anything went wrong at the delivery.

Simple.

Except it had been anything but simple to the present time. There were delays, procrastination by the families and the U.S. government. The woman's father was some kind of diplomat, apparently, who'd pledged that he would never sit down to negotiate with terrorists. Nguyen himself saw no conflict, since terrorists were zealots by definition, while he and Lee were entirely apolitical—virtual poster children for the new free enterprise.

Still the one family—Stroud, their name was—refused to give in and retrieve their child. The Ryan clan seemed more amenable, but they were influenced by the Strouds and by official U.S. policy on ransom negotiations. Overall Nguyen believed it would be best to kill the male hostage and sell his wife for whatever the market would bear in Penang, Bangkok, or perhaps even Algiers. Young, white flesh still demanded a premium price in some quarters, from collectors who had no fear of personal exposure or reprisal.

If he could just convince Lee Sun...

Nguyen saw Mansay returning from the nightclub, moving with the same studied nonchalance. This time he watched the crowd with narrowed eyes, making sure the Laotian hadn't been followed by a curious detective or local busybody. He relaxed and put his gun away when Mansay was safely back inside the car.

"What is it?" he demanded.

"Someone came in shooting," Mansay replied, "and throwing hand grenades. It sounds like triads, maybe something drug related."

"Did you see Mahmoud?"

"He's dead," the Laotian said. "With nine or ten others, if you believe the talk."

"Are you sure? I mean about Mahmoud?"

Mansay shrugged, frowning. "I didn't see him. You told me not to ask the pigs."

"Damn it!"

"It's not my fault."

"Shut up and let me think a minute!"

It took less than that, in fact. Mahmoud Safi was their conduit, now he was gone. The motive for his murder was a problem for another time. It might turn out to be irrelevant, but Nguyen didn't plan to bet his life on that idea. Right now he knew what he had to do.

He had to speak with Lee Sun.

"YOU WANT MY TRUST, but honestly, what have you done for me?"

"We saved your life," Mack Bolan replied tersely. "That ought to count for something."

"*You* saved *me?* How many times must I tell you—"

"You had the situation under control," Bolan said. "We've heard it, and it's getting old. Would you rather talk or walk?"

Hirawa Sachiko—she had told them her name at least—peered out the window as they navigated through another blighted slum. "You'd leave me here?" she asked.

"It shouldn't be a problem," Bolan said, "the way you take care of yourself."

"Americans," she said sarcastically. "Why are you all so threatened by strong women?"

"I can't speak for everyone," Bolan replied, "but personally, I have zero tolerance for drama queens." He turned to Yun, behind the wheel, and said, "Pull over. This is fine, right here."

"All right!" Hirawa snapped. "I'll tell you what I wanted from Mahmoud, but only if you'll do the same."

"You first," Bolan said. Yun was visibly relieved as he drove on.

"Nine weeks ago," the woman started, "my parents were returning from a South Seas cruise aboard their yacht."

"You come from money, I take it?"

"My father is—was—the third executive vice president of Mitsubishi Corporation. He's invested wisely through the years in new technology and so forth. Are you also threatened by material success?"

"Just tell the story."

"I was doing so until you interrupted me. My parents and my younger brother were returning from a tour of Melanesia and New Guinea when they were attacked by pirates in the Philippine Sea. My brother leaped overboard to save himself. Our parents...didn't survive."

"I'm sorry, Sachiko."

"I have not asked for sympathy," she answered stiffly, but the pain was audible beneath her tough veneer. "A fisherman rescued Hideki, my brother. He was near death from exposure, but survived. From what he said, and from what I discovered later, I've pieced together what I could about our parents' fate."

She paused and Bolan guessed that it would only cause another flare-up if he prodded her. The lady ranked as volatile on any scale, but she would tell the story in her own way if he gave her time. He'd heard enough already to know they had something in common.

Like pirates, for instance.

"My father's yacht was found four weeks ago in Manila," Hirawa resumed. "Police seized it with a drug shipment aboard. It had been repainted, but the thieves were clumsy. They forgot to change the engine's serial number."

"What did the authorities say?"

There was a brittleness about her shrug. "They sent us photos of the smugglers found on board, but Hideki saw no faces or remembers none during the hijacking. His condition is...fragile. The smugglers claim they bought the boat from a friend on Penang, no questions asked. I'm inclined to believe them."

"Because...?"

"First of all, they're drug dealers, not pirates. They trust in money to provide all their needs. I doubt they have the energy or initiative to capture boats for themselves."

The logic didn't track for Bolan, based on personal experience, but he let it go and asked, "What else?"

"Also," she said, "their so-called friend on Penang is a known dealer in stolen merchandise, including cars and boats, sometimes an airplane. He's apparently protected by corrupt police."

Hirawa's final comment was accompanied by a sidelong glance at David Yun. Yun kept his eyes on traffic, but his shoulders slumped a little, as if from the weight of her indirect accusation.

"So you found the dealer," Bolan said. "What brings you from Penang to Kuala Lumpur and the Happy Dragon?"

"The dealer on Penang is what you'd call a front man," she replied. "His silent partner in the business, as I found out for myself, is Mahmoud Safi."

"Past tense," Bolan said.

"Thanks to you," she retorted.

The soldier wasn't going down that blind alley again. He ignored the remark, shifting gears. "You must've set off some alarms, poking around the capital, for them to haul you in that way."

"I visited Safi once before," the woman said.

"And told him who you were?"

"Of course not!" The idea made her indignant. "He believed I was a journalist from Tokyo."

"And naturally he wouldn't check that out."

She frowned at that but offered no reply. "In any case, he denied any knowledge of illegal actions by his partner on Penang. He even promised to investigate and let me know what he found out."

"You swallowed that?"

She swiveled in her seat to glare at Bolan. "I took everything he told me as a lie, of course. I wanted him to worry and reach out to his suppliers."

"But he reached for you instead."

"I may have underestimated his resourcefulness."

Or his willingness to scrub out a problem with bloodshed, Bolan thought. "Anyway," he said, "there's still the dealer on Penang."

"Exactly!" For the first time since their meeting, Bolan thought Hirawa sounded eager. "I intend to question him most forcefully this time."

"Forget about it," Bolan said.

"Excuse me?"

"You've already blown your cover, and I'm betting you gave up this dealer's name while you were at it. Am I right?" Dead silence told him that he'd scored. "In which case, you'll find more guns waiting for you if you go back to Penang and start nosing around."

She turned to face him once again. "Are you prepared to offer an alternative?"

"I am," he said. "Give us the name. We'll shake him down and go from there."

"While I do what, exactly?"

"Nothing. You go home and take care of your brother. Stay alive."

"My parents were murdered. You think I can forget that?"

"No one's asked you to," Bolan replied. "But you're not helping, standing in the line of fire."

"Your plan is unacceptable," Hirawa stated. "I go with you, or else I go alone."

"You overlooked Plan C."

"What's that?"

"You go to jail and cool your heels until we're done. It shouldn't be that hard to get the dealer's name through channels."

"And who's going to arrest me?" Hirawa inquired. She

turned to Yun again. "This one? I don't think so—unless he wants his superiors to hear all about what happened tonight."

Bolan saw Yun's glare reflected in the rearview mirror. He was already thinking past the problem, wondering how they could cut a deal and still keep the lady out of harm's way.

"If you go with us," Bolan said, "you follow orders and you stay out of the way. We can't accomplish anything if we're tied up around the clock, protecting you from yourself."

Hirawa studied Bolan's face, plainly considering a sharp retort, but she finally thought better of it. "Agreed," she said at last, and offered him her hand. "Shake on it, then?"

"Why not?" the Executioner replied, deliberately ignoring all the reasons that came instantly to mind.

Surabaya, Indonesia

LEE SUN THOUGHT modern technology was a wonderful thing. Without it—and more specifically without the prototype scrambler installed on his cellular phone—how could he have spoken in perfect security to Nguyen Tre Minh, a thousand miles to the northwest in Kuala Lumpur? There were no cables to restrict his movement, yet eavesdroppers still couldn't decode the conversation, since Nguyen had a scrambler built into his phone, as well.

Thanks to space-age technology, the bad news came through loud and clear.

"What do you mean, he's dead?" Lee demanded.

"I mean he's *dead,*" Nguyen replied. "His heart's stopped beating and he isn't breathing anymore."

Lee spoke between clenched teeth. "I'm in no mood for stupid jokes! Tell me what happened, and omit nothing."

"I'm not sure yet," Nguyen said, more subdued. "From the reports, it seems a gang of gunmen came into the club and shot Mahmoud, along with several of his men. Some others tried to stop them, but they set off hand grenades and got away."

"What did they want?"

"Nobody knows," Nguyen replied. "At least, nobody still alive."

"A gang, you said?" Lee was thinking of the enemies Safi had made throughout the Far East, with his penchant for backstabbing when he reckoned he could get away with it. Who hated him enough to mount an armed assault in the Malaysian capital?

"Perhaps a gang," Nguyen repeated. "There's some disagreement on the number. Two or three shooters, at least. One man says five."

"Assume it's two or three," Lee said. "I don't call that a gang."

"Contractors, then. Somebody had to send them."

"And we need to find out who that was."

"You know Mahmoud. His mother wouldn't trust him. He had enemies from here to Vanuatu."

"Even so," Lee said, "we need to make sure these were enemies of his, not ours."

There was a momentary silence on the line. "You think it has to do with—?"

"Never mind," Lee interrupted him. "Just check and see."

"But how? Mahmoud is dead."

"Talk to his people. Find out what he was up to. Hold a séance if you have to. I trust you to think of something."

"But—"

"Don't disappoint me, Minh. It would be a serious mistake."

"No, sir."

"Don't call again until you have the information."

"I wo—"

Lee broke the connection, folded the compact telephone and slipped it back into the soft leather pouch on his belt. He didn't care if Nguyen was insulted, angry, worried. All he had to do was follow orders and get results. If he couldn't do that, then Nguyen wasn't worth the bullet it would take to end his life.

But Lee would kill him anyway.

Lee Sun was one of the South Pacific's most successful pirates, but he hadn't won that title—and he wouldn't hold onto it—by coddling peevish subordinates. Nguyen Tre Minh was the seventh man in three years to serve as Lee's second in command. One of his six predecessors was serving life without parole in a Philippine prison; two others had been killed in action, either on a raid or fighting with police. Lee had killed the other three himself, and he'd seen to it that a number of his sailors were on hand to watch each execution.

Two of his late associates had been condemned for skimming cash or other valuables they'd stolen from ships at sea before the loot was presented to Lee for proper division. The items were trivial in each case and could've been theirs for the asking, but they hadn't asked, and that had sealed their fate. Lee had beheaded each in turn with an antique samurai sword, first severing the hands that had offended him, then banishing their scurvy souls to Hell.

The third had been a somewhat different matter. His lieutenant had been rash enough to rape a female captive after Lee had promised her return—intact—on payment of a $750,000 ransom. Belated discovery of the assault had so embarrassed Lee that he'd returned half of the money and spent the next three days extracting it from his randy subordinate's hide, one bloody inch at a time.

Lee Sun was a harsh master, but his men always knew exactly what to expect: a fair reward if they obeyed him and survived, a rousing toast if they were killed obeying his commands, and screaming death if they betrayed him in the smallest thing.

Right now, he hoped Nguyen Tre Minh was frightened—but not paralyzed. Lee needed him to find out what Mahmoud was doing when he died, and whether it had anything to do with the reports of a young woman asking pointed questions around Kuala Lumpur. Above all, he wanted to know where that young woman was.

And to silence her forever.

HIRAWA SACHIKO worried that she'd made a bad bargain for herself. Two weeks in Malaysia, and she knew enough already to distrust *all* native lawmen until they were proved honest beyond the shadow of a doubt. David Yun was a stranger, and while he seemed to take offense at implications of dishonesty, that proved nothing. He could simply be a thief with an ego.

As for the American, Mike Belasko, she had no clue what to make of him. He claimed to serve the U.S. government indirectly, but what did that mean? Was he a CIA agent? A mercenary? Simply another in the long parade of liars she'd confronted so far in her quest for the truth?

He had saved her life, though she'd never admit it. Mahmoud Safi would certainly have shot her at the Leung Chung Club, and despite all her bluster Hirawa knew she couldn't have reached him in time to kick the pistol from his hand before he fired at least one shot. She hated owing so much to a stranger, reckoning—correctly—that it gave him an advantage she could never match unless she saved his life in turn, or put her own at risk on his behalf.

What were the odds of that?

It was apparent that the American meant to keep her safely on the sidelines of whatever happened next. She'd done the groundwork, first on Penang, then in Kuala Lumpur, and it galled her to see strangers move in, assuming control of her mission, as if their gender gave them preordained authority. Of course, they claimed to have crossed her path by coincidence, but that—if true—only meant they were starting out behind, unaware of the leads she'd discovered.

Until she handed them up on a silver platter.

It was a minor victory for Hirawa when the American agreed to let her join them on Penang, but she still relished the feeling she'd experienced when he caved in. Before much longer, she would prove her value to the new team she'd grudgingly joined—and not only in terms of providing a name or address. If Yun and Belasko thought she'd meekly stand by and let *them* run the show, they were sadly mistaken.

Hirawa's parents had been robbed and killed, not theirs. Her brother had been traumatized to the point where doctors feared he would never recover full use of his mind. She sympathized with the parents of those still held hostage, but her need for revenge was a separate thing, with a will and life of its own.

Hirawa meant to find the men responsible for slaughtering her family and punish them for this one thing, not for a list of sins that spanned decades and thousands of miles. She wanted vengeance for her parents and her brother, not for strangers. If the American couldn't understand that, he'd best take his own advice and stay out of her way.

Hirawa meant to find the men responsible and punish them with her own hands. After the battle with Mahmoud Safi's gunmen, she believed that it was possible. But if she needed help with numbers, Yun and the American were free to kill the rest.

She wasn't thrilled about returning to Penang, but it was mandatory now, after Belasko killed Mahmoud Safi. There was something about the coastal island that struck her as sinister, almost oppressive. She wasn't interested in the Georgetown shops or restaurants, and the gardens and temples held zero attraction for her. Perhaps, she thought, her own morbid turn of mind was infecting her every attitude.

Or maybe not.

There was no way to keep news of Safi's death from preceding them to Penang. His partner there—the boat dealer, Ramli Anuar—would never be mistaken for a genius, but he might be smart enough to flee on learning that Safi had been gunned down. Then again, he might've known the dead man well enough that Safi's passing was neither a shock nor a disappointment. They would simply have to wait and see.

Meanwhile Hirawa wished she'd thought to buy a weapon when she first arrived in Malaysia. Black-market guns were terribly expensive in Japan, and traveling with them was risky at best, but she could've afforded a good pistol in Kuala Lumpur. The fact that she'd never fired a gun in her life had dissuaded her from making the purchase, prompting her to trust the martial arts she'd studied from childhood. But now the stakes were higher, the players more desperate—and she seemed to be the only one un-armed.

Perhaps she could still remedy that situation when they got to Penang, if Yun and Belasko relaxed their guard for a moment. If not, Hirawa would do her best with what she had: her courage, training and determination to succeed.

Bushido, she thought, almost smiling. It was the spirit of the samurai, supposedly restricted to men who threw their lives away with glorious gestures in wartime. The kamikaze of the last world war had been a prime example, still revered by many in Japan for their sacrifice. Hirawa didn't plan to waste her life, though. If she had to spend it, that was one thing, but she wanted decent value in return.

The blood of mortal enemies to warm her hands.

Their dying whispers in her dreams.

On to Penang, she thought. And let the games begin.

Captivity

JEFF RYAN HAD DECIDED they were on an island. He'd come to the decision over time, working it out from clues that really didn't take much work when they were laid out in a row. It felt like an achievement of sorts—until Kim reminded him that he still had no idea where the island was or how they could get away from it and back to civilization.

When he looked at it that way, Ryan was embarrassed that it had taken him three days to determine they weren't simply caged in some small coastal village, but rather on an island where the kidnappers could come and go at will. They'd been blindfolded during the journey, transported by water and landed in soft, frothing surf, on firm sand. When the blindfolds were removed, inside their squalid quarters, he could still see enough from the one tiny window to pick out palm trees and blue sky. The sound of lapping water was incessant, telling him they weren't far from the beach.

Above all else, the conduct of the pirates indicated that they had no pressing fear of the police or anybody else arriving unannounced to spoil their idle in the sun. A few men stood guard, while others took turns greeting boats, unloading gear, but most of them had leisure time to burn.

That part had worried Ryan at first. It didn't take a novelist's imagination to be apprehensive over what a gang of thugs might try with Kim while they were lounging on a jungle island somewhere in the South Pacific, killing time. He'd waited for it, kept expecting them each time a guard brought in their food, knowing it was a hopeless vigil, still prepared to fight until they killed him. By the sixth day, though, he'd known someone or something held them in abeyance. By the tenth day, even Kim had visibly relaxed.

So, there they were, still waiting, after Ryan had lost count of the days. Or was it weeks? He'd been marking days on the wall at first, little scratches like Robinson Crusoe or something, but then he'd missed a day while quarreling with Kim and his count had gone to hell.

Like it mattered.

All that really counted was the fact that they were still alive and more or less unharmed. But why? And for how long?

The arguments with Kim were preying on his mind. If anyone had asked him earlier, a hypothetical question, he would've said that being kidnapped on their honeymoon would bring newlyweds closer together. It was an adventure of sorts, as long as nobody got hurt, and they still had that first rush of passion, coupled with hatred of a common enemy to bind them.

But it wasn't working out that way. Not at all.

He'd known Kim was spoiled when he met her, but Ryan hadn't minded at the time. Hell, he was a spoiled brat himself and proud of it. The attitude came with the money, a sense of entitlement passed down from filthy-rich parents to infants with bright silver spoons in their mouths.

Except with Kim it never seemed to quit. The kidnapping appeared to piss her off because it was an interruption of their pleasure cruise, not because it had claimed Albert's life or would cost their families a shitload of money to get them safely home again. And speaking of ransom payments, by the way, exactly what in hell was holding up that deal? Ryan wondered.

He had grown accustomed to Kim's moods while they were dating and during their six-month engagement. He'd become adept at soothing her with gifts and sex, but they were out of luck on both counts at the moment. Their credit cards had gone down with the *Valiant*, as far as he knew, and their island prison wasn't big on jewelers or boutiques. As for the nookie cure, Ryan was afraid to touch her, for fear of being seen or overheard and planting notions in the pirates' heads.

So Kim was pissed, and bound to stay that way until they were released. She hadn't built up nerve enough to bad-mouth any of the pirates yet, which meant Ryan was her only whipping boy. He felt like slapping her sometimes, but it would be a while before he sank that low.

Give it a week, the way he felt at the moment.

"So, what's the holdup on the ransom payment?" she demanded for the umpteenth time. "Can you please tell me that?"

"You know as much as I do, babe," he said.

"Don't 'babe' me, damn it! What's ten million lousy dollars, when you think about it?"

What, indeed? It sounded like a chunk of change, but there was twice that in the trust fund that would open up for him next spring. Assuming he was still alive.

"Something's gone wrong," he said, stating the obvious.

"Oh, really? Do you *think* so? God, I didn't figure I was locked up here with Sherlock Holmes!"

"Locked up would be the operative phrase," he said. "I obviously don't know what the fuck they're doing in New York or Washington."

"And so you swear at me about it?"

"Kim—"

"You disappoint me, Jeff. I swear to God, you do."

There's news, he thought. Fed up, he said, "Maybe you'd like it better if I'd fought them on the boat with Albert. Then they could've blown *my* brains out, and you'd be here whining by yourself."

The sudden tears surprised him, after everything. One second she was glaring daggers at him, and the next she'd broken down, sobbing. Feeling suddenly guilty, he moved to sit beside her on the woven mat that was their combination rug and mattress in the prison hut. Ryan slipped an arm around her shoulders, feeling her shudder against him.

"I'm sorry, ba—Kim."

She raised her tear-streaked face to blink at him, and suddenly they were kissing, for the first time since the pirates had stormed aboard the *Valiant*. Kim half turned into his arms, pressing herself against him, firm breasts crushed against his chest. Her mouth opened, tongue searching for his, and he felt as much as heard the little whimpering sound she made in the back of her throat.

Ryan was suddenly on fire with need, surprised by the intensity of the feeling that washed over him. His hands seemed to have minds of their own, gliding over Kim's body, probing and stroking, eliciting murmurs...

Until he caught himself and pulled away, breaking the kiss.

She looked at him, flushed and confused. Her voice was breathless as she stammered, "Wha...what's wrong?"

He jerked a thumb in the direction of the door. "They might walk in, you know? Or hear us. I don't want them to...I mean..."

"You're right," she said, not pouting this time. Simply sad. It nearly broke his heart when she began to weep again.

5

Penang Island

There are three ways to approach Penang. An eight-mile bridge, the longest in Asia, provides access for drivers and pedestrians from the Malaysian mainland. For fliers, Penang's Bayan Lepas International Airport is located twelve miles from the island's capital city of Georgetown. By sea, for those who don't possess their own boats, round-the-clock ferry service is available from Butterworth, on the mainland.

Bolan and Yun had decided to drive. They'd traded in Yun's official sedan for a four-door Perodua Kenari borrowed from one of his civilian friends. The vehicle resembled a sawed-off Chevy Blazer, with a hatchback in place of a trunk, powered by a 1000 cc 12-valve engine. Bolan left a $5,000 cash deposit with the owner to cover any damage and they motored north along the mountainous spine of Malaysia from Kuala Lumpur to Ipoh and Taiping, swinging west to follow the coast road from there into Butterworth. The two-hundred-mile drive gave them all time to think, and Bolan wasn't pleased with most of what he thought along the way.

For openers, although he trusted David Yun in terms of honesty, Bolan was now aware that the detective was a combat virgin prior to their encounter with Mahmoud Safi's shooters at the Leung Chung Club. For all his years in the police department, Yun had never shot a man before the past night, and Bolan reckoned it was eating at him now, making Yun second-guess himself. That kind of thinking could be fatal if he let it run away with him, producing hesitation at some vital moment down the line. More to the point, if Yun screwed up or froze and got himself killed in the process, he would jeopardize his partners at the same time.

That brought Bolan to his second headache. Hirawa Sachiko. He'd allowed her to ride along as a matter of convenience, to avoid any hassles with the authorities in Kuala Lumpur, but he didn't trust her promise to follow instructions and keep to the sidelines if there was trouble. There would be trouble, of course—Bolan never doubted that for an instant—and he feared that Hirawa's personal mission would compel her literally to jump in with both feet. The last thing Bolan needed at the moment was a kung-fu princess with a grudge against the men he'd traveled halfway round the world to find, when innocent lives depended on precision work.

Granted, he understood Hirawa's rage. The Executioner had been there and done that, at the beginning of his one-man war against the Mafia, avenging the deaths of his parents and sister. Bolan had more in common with Hirawa than the young woman would ever realize. But he hadn't surrendered to the rage, had never let it drive him recklessly along a path of self-destruction, taking others with him to the bitter end.

His struggle was about repaying debts, settling accounts—and in this case, if possible, retrieving hostages intact. It might already be too late for that, but they'd never know if he let Hirawa's private yen for vengeance dictate the agenda. If she broke her word and wouldn't play along, Bolan would have to take decisive action for the mission's sake.

He didn't want to think about that now, but rather concentrated on his final problem, namely, whether he could find Mahmoud Safi's partner on Penang and squeeze from him the information they required to home in on the pirates they were hunting. Hirawa hadn't given up the name yet, but the pitfalls were apparent. If the mark found out Safi was dead, he might take off or go to ground behind a wall of guns. Conversely, if and when they found him, there was still a chance he'd have no useful information that would help them find the pirates they were seeking.

On the other hand, he might know something useful. Bolan didn't hope—or wish—to find the pirates on Penang. The last thing he wanted was a running battle through the crowded streets of Georgetown, but if worse came to worst, he'd take whatever he could get. Ideally, they would find the Ryans still alive and extricate them from captivity. Failing that—and losing them would be a failure, no mistake about it—there was still the vengeance card to play. Hirawa might get her wish, after all.

One thing was definite: He had no ransom to deliver, no cash to pay for the hostages' release. Bolan didn't mind negotiating in bad faith with predators, but when—not if—they called his bluff, it would come down to pure brute force.

As usual.

There would be blood and plenty of it by the time he finished in Malaysia, or wherever the quest finally took him. The best he could hope for was that none of that blood would belong to hostages or innocent bystanders.

The bridge to Penang seemed longer than it was. The drive across open water had a surreal quality about it. Bolan imagined sharks cruising below, waiting for a jumper to put some variety into their all-seafood diet. He wondered how often it happened, if ever. Then, aware that he was putting off the inevitable, he turned to Hirawa in the passenger seat beside him.

"It's time for the name and address," he informed her.

She frowned but offered no further resistance. "All right, but we still have a deal."

"Goes both ways," Bolan said.

"Of course." Her tone was almost smug. Why wasn't he convinced of her sincerity? "The dealer's name is Ramli Anuar. His shop and dock are on the south shore of the island."

"How far out of Georgetown?" Bolan asked.

Hirawa shrugged. "I'm not sure, but it doesn't matter. I can show you where it is."

"Terrific." There were few things less enchanting than pursuing unknown enemies on unfamiliar turf, taking directions from a guide he didn't trust.

"Relax," she said. "I've given you my word to help and I won't let you down."

"Not twice," Bolan replied, and concentrated on the long, straight bridge ahead.

RAMLI ANUAR WAS WORRIED. The news from Kuala Lumpur was bad, the worst that he'd received since his indictment on a charge of pandering in 1986. It might be even worse than that. The indictment had threatened Anuar's liberty, although he had finally beaten the rap. He feared now that the news from Kuala Lumpur might threaten his very life.

Mahmoud Safi was dead. That would've been grounds for mourning in itself, since a large percentage of Anuar's business depended on dealings with Safi and his people, but it was the manner of death that worried him more. Safi hadn't died from a stroke or heart attack. He hadn't eaten a piece of tainted sushi or stepped in front of a bus. Mahmoud Safi had been murdered in his own nightclub, along with seven of his men. Some of the dead were killers with substantial reputations of their own, not that it helped them in the end.

After recovering from the initial shock—a midnight phone call, one of the survivors speaking rapidly in Cantonese before Anuar had calmed him down enough to speak in broken English—Anuar had turned his thoughts to the inevitable question. What did Safi's murder mean to him? Had it sprung from events that would threaten more than Anuar's monthly income? Above all else, was he in danger?

Anuar thought at once of the young Japanese woman who'd been asking questions around Penang two weeks earlier. He'd brushed her off at the time, calling ahead to warn Safi of her prying, and Safi had informed him of her subsequent arrival in Kuala Lumpur. What was her name? Anuar couldn't remember, but it seemed unlikely that she'd be involved with Safi's murder.

Her parents had been killed by pirates. They were Japanese.
But suppose they had connections to the dreaded Yakuza!

Anuar felt his blood pressure spiking before he caught
himself. It was ridiculous to think that the Japanese crime syn-
dicate would send a woman to Malaysia seeking information.
If the victims had been Yakuza, Anuar knew he'd have been
confronted by a team of hardmen who asked pointed questions and brooked no denials. In fact, he'd probably be dead
already, rotting in a shallow grave or feeding fish a mile offshore.

Not Yakuza. Then who?

Anuar was no believer in coincidence. It was clear to him
that Safi was a man with enemies. They'd caught up with him
in the end, but it didn't have to be Anuar's problem—unless
the trouble sprang from their joint venture with Lee Sun.

That thought was troubling in itself because Lee's pirates
were a ruthless lot, capable of squashing Safi like an insect
if they thought he'd cheated them or otherwise transgressed
their strange and savage code of honor. The risk to Anuar, in
that case, was that Lee's men might think *he* was involved in
whatever had driven them to kill Safi. And it was true, he
might have been. How could he know, until it was determined who had killed Safi, and why?

Anuar considered that it might be wise for him to take a
short vacation, leave Penang behind and spend some time at
his country retreat on the mainland. He had associates who
knew the business as well he did, and who would steal no
more than usual in his absence. A week or two should be
enough to let it all blow over—or at least to find out what had
led to his partner's death. If it didn't concern Anuar, so much
the better. If it did...well, then perhaps a bargain could be
struck with those responsible to spare his life.

Or he could simply disappear.

Ramli Anuar was the first to recognize his own shortcom-
ings as an intellect and businessman, but he wasn't as foolish as some might believe. He had plenty of money laid aside
to tide him over in an emergency such as this one. If he had

to vanish for six months or a year, Anuar could afford it. If he had to reestablish himself in new quarters elsewhere for good, he could afford that, too.

Anuar decided there was no time like the present to begin his getaway. He took his briefcase to the backroom of his office, closed and locked the door behind him to forestall intrusions, and opened the wall safe hidden behind a calendar featuring nude photographs of teenaged girls. In truth, his taste ran more toward teenaged boys, but there were still proprieties to be observed, facades to be maintained.

The safe held cash and travel documents, in addition to various legal papers concerning Anuar's business. He left the deeds and contracts where they were, removing the currency and his three passports in different names. Each would support the purchase of international airline tickets where photo ID was required, leaving Anuar free to travel the globe at will. He didn't plan to go that far, just yet, but it was good to know the means were at his fingertips.

Just in case.

Satisfied with his choices, Anuar latched the briefcase, closed the safe and spun the dial, then returned the calendar to its place on the wall. He was smiling as he exited the backroom—but the smile disappeared when he saw the young Japanese woman standing beside his desk.

"You're back, Miss...ah...forgive me."

"Hirawa," she reminded him. "Hirawa Sachiko."

"Of course. My apologies, but I'm a busy man."

"I understand," she said. "I need a few more minutes of your precious time."

Anuar disliked the sound of that, and he disliked the timing of her visit even more. "Unfortunately," he replied, "you've caught me at an inconvenient moment. I'm just on my way to the airport."

"This shouldn't take much time," she said.

"As I've explained—" Anuar never finished the sentence. He felt the men behind him before he turned and saw them. One was Malaysian, the other a tall white man, perhaps Amer-

ican or British. They had to have been standing in the corner
where he couldn't see them when the backroom door was
opened outward.

"Like she said," the white man told Anuar, "this shouldn't
take much time."

HIRAWA SACHIKO WAS SILENT as they walked Ramli Anuar
from his office to their waiting car. He'd been warned to re-
frain from alerting his employees, and he played his part well
enough, despite a certain nervous air that he couldn't control.
At the car, Anvar was ordered into the back seat and Bolan
crawled in beside him. Hirawa took the front passenger's
seat, while Yun slid behind the wheel.

They drove across Penang Island to the west, following a
two-lane coastal road until they were well removed from
Georgetown and any other settlement. Yun chose an unpaved
access road, seemingly at random, and followed its winding,
climbing course into the hills that overlook the Strait of
Malacca. Trees soon blocked their view of blue water, leaving them cut off from the world outside.

Anuar had begun to ask questions. "Where are you taking
me? What's the meaning of this? Who are you people?" When
the questions brought no answers, he appealed to Hirawa directly. "I've told you everything I know, Missy," he said. "I
never saw your parents. I have no idea what happened to
them."

Cold inside, she answered, "There's no mystery about
what happened. They were robbed and murdered. You're the
pig who sold their boat. We mean to find out your supplier's
name and where he lives."

Anuar produced a clucking sound. "I've told you twice,
already—"

"You were lying," she said, interrupting him. "You either
forged the bill of sale or took it as it was presented to you.
It's ridiculous to think you purchase custom sporting yachts
from strangers."

"But I—"

"Save your breath," Hirawa said. "You'll need it soon, for squealing."

It pleased her to threaten him, see the fear in his eyes, after long weeks of being ignored or diverted. Some of those she'd spoken to had lied to her face, others made it plain that they had no time for her private crusade. Across the board, they had dismissed her as a woman and a foreigner.

But not this time.

This time she would have blood or answers, maybe both.

Yun stopped the vehicle at a wide spot in the road, pulling well off the shoulder under cover of trees. Silence fell as he switched off the engine. Hirawa guessed they would hear traffic coming before it was visible, but the road was quiet now. They'd seen no other cars since leaving the highway, and few in the hour before that.

They got out of the car, the American prodding Anuar ahead of him, showing their hostage a pistol. Anuar clung to the briefcase he'd brought with him, as if it held some kind of talisman that would protect him from harm. Hirawa wondered what was inside it and how Anuar thought it could help him.

"We'll be asking you some questions," Bolan told the dealer. "You'd be wise to answer honestly. Deception carries penalties." He punctuated the warning with a flourish of his pistol.

"There's been some mistake," Anuar replied, a tremor in his voice. "I know nothing of this woman's family."

"No one claims you led the raid yourself," Bolan said. "You wouldn't have the guts for that. You *can* tell us who palmed the yacht off with a phony bill of sale, and while you're at it, let's hear all about your dealings with Mahmoud Safi."

"Poor Mahmoud!" Anuar replied. "He's dead, you know."

"Keep that in mind," Bolan said. "He might want company."

"You—*you* killed him?"

"Let's just say he didn't answer questions in a timely manner. You could learn from his mistake."

"But I know nothing!" Anuar wailed.

"Let's call that lie your first and last freebie," the American answered. "Everyone knows something, wouldn't you agree?"

"I meant to say—"

"Careful." Bolan cocked his gun for emphasis.

"I want to help, of course!"

"I never doubted it. Let's start with the Hirawa deal and go from there. Who brought their yacht in to your shop?"

Anuar considered lying but thought better of it. "There were two men," he replied. "One I have never seen before. The other calls himself Nguyen Tre Minh."

"Pirates?" Bolan asked.

"I've purchased boats from Nguyen in the past," Anuar said, avoiding the question. "His paperwork always appears to be in order."

"Meaning that what you don't know doesn't cost you any sleep."

"The law requires—"

Bolan interrupted him. "What's the connection between Nguyen Tre Minh and your buddy Mahmoud?"

"I believe they've done business on occasion."

"You believe or you know?"

"I never saw them together," Anuar hedged, "but I take it for granted they were partners of a sort."

"Mahmoud moved stolen property, the same way you move boats," Bolan said.

"My business is—"

"A simple yes or no."

"Mahmoud wouldn't require a bill of sale for any merchandise," Anuar replied. "He dealt in currency, jewelry, such items as are easily transferred."

"Provided by your friend Nguyen."

"And others, I assume."

"Does Nguyen call the shots?"

Anuar looked puzzled. "Shots?"

"Is he in charge?" Bolan said in clarification.

A shadow crossed the dealer's face and left him trembling. "Nguyen works for Lee Sun."

"And where would we find Mr. Lee?" the American asked.

"I've never met him," Anuar said. "I know him only by his reputation."

"But you've heard things."

"Idle rumors, I suppose."

"So, share."

"I'm told Lee operates from Indonesia."

"That's a lot of territory. Pin it down."

"There is an island called Wewak, south of Ceram. It's said he has headquarters there."

Bolan glanced at David Yun, a question in his eyes, and the policeman nodded back. "What else?" the tall man asked Anuar.

"Nothing, I swear."

"I hope you're right."

"There's nothing more, I promise you."

"Okay," Bolan said—and shot him in the face.

Hirawa staggered, reeling, as she turned back toward the car, surprised by sudden tears.

Kuala Lumpur

DAVID YUN WAS TROUBLED as he packed his bag for the flight to Ceram. So many things had happened in the past two days, none of them good. He'd been forced to kill for the first time in his life, and more than once. His superiors had excused the killings in Kuala Lumpur, glad to be rid of Mahmoud Safi and his thugs, but Penang had put a new color on things.

With Mike Belasko's execution of Ramli Anuar, Yun had become an accessory to kidnapping and murder. He'd even helped to dispose of the corpse, thereby eliminating any chance to plead ignorance of the American's intentions. There was no question of claiming self-defense in Anuar's case, nor any hope of passing his abduction off as a legitimate arrest. Accordingly, Yun took what seemed to be the wisest course of action in the circumstances.

He had lied to his superiors.

In Yun's report of the Penang excursion he'd omitted any reference to Ramli Anuar, explaining instead that confidential informants had been interviewed and had provided tentative directions to the lair of pirate Lee Sun on Wewak, a presumed island in the vast Indonesian archipelago. Yun had never heard of it, but twenty minutes with an atlas showed him where it was—a flyspeck a hundred miles southwest of Ambon in the Banda Sea.

Yun had consulted his captain and received the expected response. He was free to accompany Mike Belasko to Wewak, on full pay, with the understanding that his downtime would be treated as a leave of absence, strictly voluntary and without official sanction. There could be no question of Malaysian officers invading Indonesian territory on an errand for America. If anything went wrong—meaning, of course, if Yun was killed or captured in the course of his adventure, either by the enemy or by Indonesian authorities—Kuala Lumpur would deny any knowledge of his purely private actions. In the event that Yun survived capture, no effort would be made to rescue him from pirates or to interfere with the natural course of Indonesian justice.

In short, Yun would be set adrift from the moment his aircraft took off in the morning until he returned from his jaunt. If he returned.

Survival was a definite consideration of the plan his partner had in mind. Yun knew the pirate Lee by reputation, though Lee hadn't been arrested since Yun joined the police force. A hasty review of his rather slim file at headquarters described a thirty-six-year-old career criminal who had served prison time as a juvenile and in his early twenties, then miraculously managed to avoid both capture and indictment for the past ten years. He was "presumed" to be involved with bad companions, "strongly suspected" of piracy and other crimes, but no Malaysian officials had bothered to collect hard evidence against him in a decade.

The reason, though unstated in the file, was obvious to

David Yun. Lee had learned to pay his way with well-placed bribes, thereby avoiding interference until his most recent transgression elicited protests from Washington, D.C. Even now, Malaysian cooperation with America's chosen man-hunter remained unofficial, thus avoiding the dual pitfalls of diplomatic conflict and exposure of Lee's prior graft payments. Whatever happened to Mike Belasko—and now, by extension, to Yun and Hirawa—the Malaysian government would emerge unscathed.

Yun was on his own, except for his two companions in crime.

And there could be no doubt about it now. They were embarked upon a criminal endeavor. Even though their goal was justice of a sort, and liberation of two kidnapped hostages, the course they'd chosen set them in direct opposition to every known criminal statute.

He had armed himself in preparation for the journey, lifting a confiscated AK-47 and spare magazines from the police evidence locker to back up his Daewoo pistol. Yun calculated that since his superiors were closing their eyes to his enlistment in an international vigilante campaign, they wouldn't mind the small matter of an arms theft from headquarters. Record keeping in the property department was a joke, in any case, the officers in charge too busy losing drug shipments to worry about one assault rifle and a few boxes of ammunition.

At one time, not so very long ago, the theft would have weighed heavily upon Yun's mind. He thought his overall perspective had to be changing because it didn't bother him at all.

He was preoccupied with wondering how many more men he would have to kill before the job was done—and whether he would live to see the end of it.

Ceram Island

THE FISHING BOAT was a private charter. Bolan paid the captain double his usual fee to leave his mate at home and let his

three paying passengers take up the slack. The fewer witnesses who came along for the ride, the better Bolan liked it.
He'd have gladly ditched the captain, too, but that would've
meant buying the old boat outright, dealing with navigation
and any mechanical foibles simultaneously, while he had
other things on his mind.

Like staying alive.

It could be dicey, facing unknown odds on unfamiliar turf,
and Bolan wasn't sure either one of his companions was up
to the challenge. David Yun, at least, had police training and
a familiarity with weapons to fall back on, and he'd proved
himself capable of killing at the Leung Chung Club in Kuala
Lumpur. It clearly didn't sit well with him, but Bolan believed
Yun could pull his own weight, to a point, when the going got
rough.

Hirawa Sachiko was a different story altogether. She'd
proved an ability to hold her own in unarmed self-defense,
but Bolan cringed at the thought of giving her a weapon and
putting her on the firing line against career felons. At the same
time, there was no way to lose her before they hit Wewak, as
she'd made amply clear from the beginning.

They'd chartered a flight from Kuala Lumpur to Ceram,
thereby facilitating transport of their arms without passage
through airport terminals. There was a Customs man to deal
with on arrival, but David Yun handled the formalities, showing his badge and making up a story that omitted any mention of pirates or Lee Sun. He told the man their mission
involved the search for a wealthy missing person who had disappeared while sailing from Papua New Guinea to Kuala
Lumpur. Family assets were involved, no foul play was suspected and the searchers anticipated no conflict with Indonesian authorities. In fact, Yun led the Customs man to believe,
they were basically spinning their wheels as a means to pad
a fat expense account. No search of their arms-laden baggage
was required, once a nominal bribe had been paid. For a
slightly higher fee, one of the blue-suited officials suggested,
various official stamps and signatures could be attached to

Yun's final report, making the bogus search seem more impressive.

They were on their way three hours later, having driven forty miles across the island in a rental car to find a smallish port and choose a captain who would sail with them alone, no questions asked beyond the price. His name was Pangeran, and he'd christened his aging trawler *Victoriana*. The boat was seaworthy, complete with a pervasive smell of overripe fish that clung to the cabins. So much the better for Bolan's purposes, since he wanted nothing to attract naval patrols or pirates on the run south from Ceram to Wewak.

Their captain knew the island they were seeking and promised them a quiet landing, unobserved by hostile inhabitants, in return for payment of a minor additional fee. Bolan paid out of pocket without protest, but made it clear to Pangeran that any failure or betrayal on his part would send him, with *Victoriana,* to the bottom of the Banda Sea. The captain only nodded, grinning, as if such terms were expected in his line of work.

So they began the long journey southwestward, making twelve knots maximum, at least one member of the team awake and on guard at all times. Pangeran preferred the woman, smiling ear-to-ear at her approach and waxing eloquent in pidgin English that included at least one good-natured proposition per hour. Hirawa didn't seem to mind, doing her part to keep the captain jovial and watching out for any move he might make to betray them.

Bolan had no illusions about what would happen if Lee's pirates surprised them at sea. They could defend *Victoriana* to a point, but it would be difficult—more likely impossible— to outrun faster vessels on the open water, and any pirate craft armed with weapons heavier than Kalashnikov assault rifles could lie back out of range, riddling Pangeran's trawler until it went down with all hands. It was crucial, therefore, that the captain sent no messages before he landed them on Wewak, at which time Bolan intended to add a cash bonus and disable *Victoriana*'s radio for the return trip to Ceram.

Short of killing Pangeran at the drop-off point, it was all they could do to insure his silence. There was no nonviolent way to stop him from putting them ashore, then sailing back around the island in search of pirates to warn, but Bolan didn't think Pangeran would try the personal approach. Lee's buccaneers were as likely to kill him outright, after testing his story by torture, as they were to pay him for information on trespassers, and Pangeran would know that in advance.

Whatever else he might be, when their backs were turned, Pangeran didn't strike Bolan as a man who risked his life foolishly.

That decided, Bolan settled in to make the best of their cruise, resting as much as possible against the time when there would be no rest, nothing but fire and blood to pass the time. He didn't know if they would find the hostages they sought on Wewak, but he trusted they would find someone who had more information on their whereabouts.

All Bolan and his allies had to do was bag that person, capture him alive and then persuade him to share whatever he knew. All that, without losing their lives in the process.

Should be easy, Bolan thought.

Like falling off a cliff.

6

Wewak Island

The island was what Bolan had expected, more or less. It measured ten kilometers from east to west and six across its widest point, from north to south. Its highest ground was at the eastern end, where a dormant volcano thrust its silent cone six hundred feet above sea level. From a distance, Wewak looked green and inviting, but appearances could be deceiving.

Bolan brought no expectations to Wewak, beyond the reasonable certainty that people would die on the island this day. Who those victims were, and how many went down, were questions that could only be answered when the fighting ended and the battle smoke began to clear. Nothing was guaranteed before the shooting started, and survival least of all.

Pangeran, as expected, didn't mourn the passing of *Victoriana*'s radio after he pocketed another wad of currency. They had circled the island, adding another hour to the journey, before he wished them well and watched them board a rubber dinghy for the silent run to shore. They saw him waving as *Victoriana* pulled away and gradually disappeared around the headland, steaming to the east.

"I still think we should've had him wait for us," Hirawa said. She wasn't pouting, but the lack of guaranteed return-trip passage plainly had her worried, even after they'd discussed it on the last leg of the trip down from Ceram.

"We'll find another boat," Bolan told her.

Then, to Yun, he said, "Keep that in mind when it gets heavy. We'll need one boat left to get us out of here."

"I'll see if I can manage to control myself," Yun answered, frowning through the sarcasm.

They got wet on the landing, soaked below the waist—or the chest, in Hirawa's case—as they waded in, dragging the dinghy. They landed unopposed in a well-sheltered cove, with no more than thirty or forty feet of clear beach between tumbled boulders on both sides. The surf broke, foaming, on pristine sand that was gray under starlight, no moon to betray them. After they'd hidden the dinghy in jungle above the high-tide line, Bolan consulted his compass and led the team inland, making for a point Pangeran had indicated on the north shore of Wewak, where Lee's pirates had their base camp.

Make that supposedly had their base camp.

It could still be a trap, Bolan thought, but they were doing what they could with what they had. Beyond that, it came down to guts, improvisation and a fair measure of luck. Survivorship would be determined as much by speed and courage as by planning.

Bolan had grown up vaguely believing in a master plan for the Universe, and he still believed to some extent, in spite of everything he'd seen and done, all that was done to him and those he loved. He'd given up on hoping for the Universe to lend a helping hand, however. When the chips were down and life hung in the balance, every living creature on the planet still had to fend for itself. Win or lose, prevail or perish, it was each man for himself—or woman, as the case might be.

That brought his mind back to Hirawa and a promise that he'd made to let her take the final risk with no special favors asked or granted. Bolan would watch out for both his allies under fire, if he could, but it wasn't his primary mission.

The camp, when they found it, was situated a hundred yards inland from the north-shore beach, mostly screened from the seaward approach by palm trees and undergrowth. Lit with a combination of bonfires, storm lanterns and electric lights powered by a portable generator, it would've been visible from the north as illusory flickers of brilliance, there and gone among the trees. Superstition and good, honest fear would keep passing ships from drawing close to investigate after nightfall, and daylight would conceal all but the occasional wisp of smoke from cooking fires.

The pirates had no guards posted to the south of their camp or anywhere else that Bolan could see. With no history of raids or interference on the island, they'd grown lax and complacent about security.

It would soon be revealed as a fatal mistake.

Crouching in darkness outside the camp, Bolan directed his troops. Hirawa had scrounged a .30-caliber M-1 carbine from some unknown source, as well as a change of clothes, prior to flying out of Kuala Lumpur, and she'd demonstrated a fair proficiency with the rifle on the trip south, shooting bottles the captain threw overboard to test her marksmanship. It was nothing close to combat, but Bolan wasted no breath telling her to wait on the sidelines. Instead he gave her the west end of the camp, with instructions to raise hell once the firing started and try to make their enemies believe escape was cut off in that direction.

Bolan and Yun would close the pincers, wreaking as much havoc as they could without getting killed in the process. They might find Jeff and Kim Ryan confined in one of the compound's various buildings or they might not. At the very least Bolan meant to finish the night in possession of leads to their fate—and to their location, if one or both were still alive.

And if he failed in that, there would be hell to pay.

DAVID YUN FOUND his position at the east end of the pirate camp and moved in as close as he could to the clearing. It still surprised him that no guards were posted, but he took the arrogance of their targets as a hopeful sign. Whatever happened in the next few minutes, Yun had to do his best to stay alive and uninjured, protecting himself first and his comrades second, before finally turning his attention to the location and rescue of kidnapped Americans.

The more time he spent with Mike Belasko, the more he hoped to find the young Ryans alive. At first, it had seemed a pipe dream, wildly improbable, even with a ransom demand on the table. Discovery of ruthless Lee Sun as the leader of the pirate band responsible for their kidnapping made a safe rescue even less likely, given Lee's reputation and the current stories that placed his total force at some fifty or sixty vessels, manned by two hundred or more fighting men. Why would Lee not simply murder his hostages, and thus save the minor cost of feeding and housing them while he waited for the ransom drop? Such crimes weren't unknown in the Far East. If anything, they were almost routine.

After Yun had seen and risked so much, it seemed important for the honeymooners to be found alive and reasonably well. His partner's exertion on behalf of total strangers seemed to validate and sanctify his quest. Overnight Yun had switched from believing the Ryans were probably dead to a whole new attitude, assuming they lived until he saw the corpses for himself. It wasn't strictly rational, Yun realized, but it made him feel better about what he'd done—and about what he still had to do in pursuit of their goal.

The largest structure at his end of the pirate camp was a makeshift tent patched together from camouflage fabric, supported on stout bamboo poles to create an open-air mess hall. Sweaty cooks were busy cleaning up after dinner and a few stragglers were still scraping tin plates at two of the tent's three long tables constructed of planks and breeze blocks. The entrée looked like stew and smelled like something better left untouched by human hands.

Yun chose a target, singling out one of the diners who wore a long knife on his belt and Skorpion machine pistol slung across his back. That way, when the shooting started, at least Yun could tell himself he'd killed an armed man first.

Unless he missed.

Unless it fell apart and he was killed within the first few seconds of the fight.

I won't be, Yun thought stubbornly. There was no guarantee that he'd survive, of course, but confidence—at least in moderation—was a benefit to fighting men.

He waited, rifle at his shoulder, staring at his target over open sights. Time dragged. Yun sweated through his shirt and felt more perspiration beading on his forehead, trickling down to sting his eyes. In just another moment...

Someone started firing from his left, close by the midpoint of the pirate camp. Yun squeezed the trigger on his stolen AK-47, riding its recoil as his first rounds streamed downrange.

JONG FANG WASN'T intoxicated, but he had reached the twilight between relaxed and drunk where many people failed to recognize the difference. Three pints of homemade brew had brought him to his present state, and he believed at least two more would be required to let him sleep.

The problem wasn't tension; quite the opposite, in fact. Jong was bored, a circumstance that always made him crave some kind of action, even if it turned out to be self-destructive. The young pirate lieutenant wasn't big on patience at the best of times, and sitting idle for two weeks made him itch to take the boats out on the open sea and race the wind until they found a proper prize.

Instead Jong would follow orders and remain in camp, riding herd on a group of thirty pirates who shared his lust for action, using a mixture of threats and cajolery to keep them in line. It grew more difficult by the day, since his heart wasn't in the task assigned, but he wanted to impress Nguyen Tre Minh with his efficiency, perhaps even rate a moment's notice from Lee Sun himself.

If he could only get through one more night without a mutiny, then focus on the next—

The sudden sound of gunfire brought Jong Fang to his feet, wobbling a bit on legs that weren't as steady as he'd thought.

His head swam and his vision blurred, clearing reluctantly. Before he could imagine that he'd dreamed the gunfire, another weapon sounded, then another. Three at least were firing now, while pirates shouted back and forth across the camp, scrambling for cover.

Jong lurched toward the exit from his quarters, pausing en route to grab a British Sterling L-2 A-2 submachine gun that hung from a wall hook by its shoulder strap. He didn't cock the weapon yet, knowing his hands were shaky, but he clutched it tightly as he stepped into the night.

Jong had no idea where the initial shots had come from, much less why they'd been fired, but a dozen or more guns were blazing now, his men finding cover where they could and burning ammunition as they hosed the night with panic fire. Glancing in the direction of the mess tent, Jong saw one of his pirates stretched out on the ground, blood soaking through his shirt. Before he had a chance to turn away, incoming fire took down one of the scrambling cooks and doused his fire with water spouting from a punctured pot.

We're under attack! Jong thought, and caught himself before shouting the words aloud. Instead he started barking orders to his troops as he ran through the heart of the killing zone, bawling at them to stand fast and give no ground.

And all the while he wondered whether he would have the strength to stand himself.

PERSONAL FIREARMS were rare in Japan, and Hirawa had never fired a gun before they set out from Ceram aboard the *Victoriana*. Even so, the M-1 carbine was easy to handle and she took to it naturally, enjoying the feel and sound of the lightweight military rifle—and the vision she nurtured of using it against her parents' killers.

Now that it counted, though, Hirawa found her hatred tempered by fear. In the past two days she'd seen several men killed and had nearly been murdered herself. As Belasko and Yun started firing into the pirate camp, she was suddenly part of a pitched battle, wondering how she'd come so far from home and her settled life in Japan. Where would she find the nerve to risk her life against professional killers?

The confusion lasted only for a moment. After the first crackle of gunfire, men were rushing toward her position, fleeing the guns of her comrades, and Hirawa's anger took over. Some of these pirates might've been involved in her parents' murder—and if not, they almost certainly knew those who were. In any case, they were vermin who deserved extermination by any and all means available.

She fired the first few shots from her 30-round banana clip without aiming precisely, surprised when one of the men racing toward her collapsed on the ground, clutching a bloody thigh. It wasn't the best of all possible shots, but it was a start. The wounded pirate's three companions scattered, veering off in different directions, firing wildly toward the outer darkness as they ducked and dodged.

Hirawa tracked the nearest of them, leading him as Yun had instructed, so that her bullets wouldn't pass behind him, through empty air. Even so, it took three shots to bring him down, but one was a solid hit to the chest, her target twitching as he fell, making no effort to scramble away.

A wave of nausea surprised Hirawa, but she fought it down and swung the M-1 toward the next-nearest pirate. He was young, Chinese and armed with a submachine gun that he used to spray the tree line where she lay concealed by shrubbery and a fallen palm. The bullets rattled overhead, missing her by at least three feet, but they were disconcerting and she missed her next two shots before a third round dropped her adversary to his knees.

The young man had a dazed expression on his face. He gaped into the darkness, trying to discover who had done this to him, struggling to hold his weapon level as blood pulsed from a stomach wound. In place of nausea, Hirawa felt a sudden rush of power—the unaccustomed sense that she controlled a total stranger's life and death. Before she framed his pale face in the carbine's sights and put a bullet through his forehead, she understood how that feeling could become addictive, driving men to commit fearsome deeds.

One runner left. Hirawa swung around to track him, felt a moment's hesitation as she sighted on the man's retreating back, then thought of how her parents had no chance to run away and squeezed off three quick rounds to make sure that he wouldn't rise again.

DAVID YUN REPLACED his AK-47's empty magazine with a fresh one before he broke cover, running in a zigzag pattern from the tree line to the mess tent where he'd scored his first kills of the night. No one moved underneath the canvas, but he double-checked the bodies anyway, taking nothing for granted. He recalled the training lecture wherein his firearms instructor at the police academy had cautioned against letting "dead" men come up shooting when his back was turned. If necessary, Yun had been advised to blast the corpses from a distance, thus insuring that they didn't rise again.

So far he'd had no problem with the dead. The pirates he'd shot remained where his bullets had dropped them, leaking blood and other bodily fluids into the thirsty earth. It troubled Yun that killing had grown easier, almost an automatic reflex, and that it troubled him so much less this night than it had two days ago.

He was changing, Yun realized—and not necessarily for the better. Still, this wasn't the time to think about it, when his life was riding on the line.

There were half a dozen buildings in the camp where hostages might be confined, but as far as Yun could tell none of them were under guard before the shooting started. He'd initially hoped to find the Americans there, and thus end the mad quest, but now Yun had his doubts. For all they'd risked to come this far, he'd begun to suspect that the trip had been wasted.

It was too late for turning back. Retreat was nothing short of suicidal while their enemies lived. Yun knew he had to do all he could to remedy that situation before he could escape the waking nightmare that his journey with the American and the woman had become.

Nearing the closest of the several buildings they would have to check before they cleared the camp, Yun saw three pirates emerge from the structure, leaving the door agape behind them. He hesitated no more than a heartbeat before raking them with a burst of autofire from his Kalashnikov and dropping them together in a twitching heap.

Yun rushed the hut, hurdling three bodies as he crossed the threshold—to discover there was no one left inside. It was a one-room building, in the manner of a makeshift office, with no hiding places anywhere. If there were hostages in camp, nothing suggested that they'd ever been confined to this room.

Increasingly disheartened at their prospects for finding the Ryans in camp, Yun cautiously emerged from the hut, freezing in place as two pirates ran past him, heading east to west. They were a dozen strides beyond him when one of the runners stopped, did a double take and swung around to aim a shotgun in Yun's direction.

Too late.

Yun's AK-47 stuttered, bullets ripping into both men before they could bring him under fire. They jerked and staggered, falling as he lifted his finger off the trigger and nervously checked his blind side. Yun had improved at killing, but it only heightened his own sense of mortality. What he had done to others, they could do to him.

Unless he did it first and fastest, time and time again, until no living enemies remained—or only one, for questioning. Yun left the capture of a prisoner to Mike Belasko, focused on self-preservation as he jogged toward the heart of the camp.

BOLAN LOBBED a grenade toward what passed for the camp's motor pool, rewarded seconds later by a blast that toppled half a dozen dirt bikes, capsizing a late-model all-terrain vehicle. The pirates weren't marooned yet, but at least they wouldn't get away on wheels.

Three speedboats and a dinghy were moored to a fifty-foot pier north of camp; the pier pointed like an accusing finger toward a larger cabin cruiser anchored offshore. No lights were showing on the cruiser, but pirates were scrambling for the other boats now, looking seaward for security they couldn't find ashore.

Bolan strafed them as they ran, ducking and weaving when a pirate found the nerve to stand and fight a rear-guard action. None of them were very good at it, convincing Bolan that they were used to sitting targets, unarmed and unable to defend themselves. They were jackals more than sea wolves, but he knew they'd still fight like cornered rats to save themselves.

Bolan caught a glimpse of Yun fighting his way from one building to the next, near the heart of the compound, apparently unscathed after several minutes of engagement with the enemy. There was none of the hesitation he'd noted previously in Yun's movements when it came to using deadly force. The change was beneficial, if not entirely welcome. It would help Yun stay alive, but Bolan took no pleasure in causing others to touch base with their primitive side.

Returning his focus to the enemy, the Executioner dropped two more pirates on the run, then shot a third who turned to spray the trees with submachine-gun fire. It was almost too easy, as disorganized and frightened as his targets were, but Bolan never complained when the predators made his work easier. Some two-thirds of the pirates in camp were already down and out. With any luck, the rest would follow soon, cut down before they managed to coordinate a strategy for self-defense.

Still Bolan needed one of them alive. He'd known that going in, and barring rescue of the Ryans on the spot—which now appeared unlikely—questioning a prisoner was his top priority on Wewak. Someone who was likely to possess the information he required, yet who was weak or cowardly enough to give it up without resisting to the death.

Scanning the pier, he spied one pirate shouting orders at

the others who remained, directing them to first one speed-boat, then another. Bolan took a chance and slammed a bul-let through his shoulder, dropping the man in a shuddering heap on the pier.

That done, he swept the dock and speedboats, picking off the pirates one by one, or in small groups where they huddled together, accepting the illusion of safety in numbers. A cou-ple of them sighted Bolan's muzzle-flashes and tried to return fire, but their efforts were halfhearted and clumsy. The next-to-last pirate alive on the pier was running flat-out for the dinghy when Bolan shot him from behind, a 3-round burst be-tween the shoulder blades that pitched him headlong into the sea.

That left one, and the wounded pirate on the dock wasn't going anywhere, as Bolan turned his weapon and attention to-ward the camp that had become a bloody killing ground.

"DO YOU SPEAK English?"

Jong Fang was drowning in a restless sea of pain when the voice reached out and pulled him to the surface. He resisted it at first, preferring the escape hatch of oblivion, but rough hands shook him back to consciousness.

The question was repeated, this time with a stinging slap across the face that made him answer. "Yes, I speak English!"

"You won't believe it," said a stranger, looming over him, "but this may be your lucky night."

Lucky? The notion nearly made Jong laugh, but a new flare of pain from his wounded shoulder choked off the sound in his throat. He waited grimly for another bullet—or for some-thing even worse.

"We're looking for the hostages," his nearest captor said. "Americans. Where are they?"

Jong Fang saw his first ray of hope since he was shot. He didn't know how many of his men were still alive or whether any had escaped the trap. He smelled smoke from the camp and knew it wasn't from the evening's cook fires. There was no sound from the water to mark passage of escaping boats.

They were defeated, and for all Jong could tell, he might now be the only pirate left alive of the thirty who'd been safe in camp before the shooting started. Still, he was alive, albeit bleeding from a major wound, and he could always try to barter for his life.

"Americans," he said. "Not here."

"We know that," said the man who gripped his bloody shirt. Another shake sent bolts of misery shooting through Jong's upper body. He was suddenly light-headed, whether from the pain, the loss of blood or both, he couldn't say. "Where are they?"

"Gone."

"He's wasting time," a second voice remarked.

"Once more," the first voice told Jong. "And try to bear in mind that if you can't be helpful, then you're just dead-weight."

"He should be dead." A woman's bitter voice commented.

"Americans were here," Jong said truthfully. "All gone now."

"Where'd they go? When did they leave?"

"One week," he said, taking the second question first. "Nobody tell me where they go."

"If that's a lie, you'll take it to your grave."

"No lie!" Jong insisted, willing those around him to know that he spoke the truth.

"He's useless," the woman said.

"Not necessarily," the first man answered.

"He can't help us."

"He can't *guide* us. They're two different things." The big man leaned in closer, lowering his voice. "You've got one chance to live. It's your choice."

"Yes, I live," the pirate said.

"We have a message for your boss, Lee Sun." The name still had its power to frighten Jong Fang, but he was more afraid of Death, who held him by the shirt and shook him like a child.

"Message. I give to Lee."

"Tell him we want to pay the ransom, but we need proof that the hostages are still alive. You hear that? Proof of life, and that means visual. No voices on the telephone we've never heard before. No Polaroids with newspaper headlines."

"Prove they are alive, in person."

"That's the deal." A slender plastic shape was pressed into one of Jong's trembling hands. "Your boss can use this to make contact. Got it?"

Jong hoped he had it. If he didn't, he would be as good as dead. "I understand."

There was sudden pressure on his wounded shoulder, and a bolt of pain that forced a cry from Jong's lips. He felt his grip on consciousness falter, sweet darkness closing in around him as his mind repeated endlessly, I understand.

7

Ambon, Indonesia

Nguyen Tre Minh disliked hospitals. If asked, he couldn't
have explained the feeling that verged on a phobic reaction,
but everything about healing places set his teeth on edge—
from their pervasive antiseptic smell and the squeak of nurses'
rubber-soled shoes on waxed linoleum, to the muffled moan-
ing sounds that issued from behind closed doors. Each time
he crossed the threshold of a hospital, Nguyen was moved to
wonder whether he'd escape alive and in one piece.

Ambon's small infirmary wasn't much to look at, as hospitals went. It handled trauma and disease that didn't call for
specialists or exotic life-saving surgery, holding its own
against a variety of fevers and infections, snakebites and scor-
pion stings, abrasions and fractures, sunstroke and near
drownings. The doctors also knew their way around a simple
bullet wound, which brought Nguyen to the bedside of his
comrade Jong Fang.

Jong looked like death warmed over, but the doctors said
he would survive, assuming that he changed his dressings reg-
ularly and abstained from any strenuous activity that might
reopen his wounds. He was lucky, the lone survivor of a thirty-
man garrison on Wewak, clinging stubbornly to life—and to
a secret message—while the pirates under his command were
being stripped and washed in preparation for their funerals.

Get FREE BOOKS and a FREE GIFT when you play the...

LAS VEGAS GAME

Just scratch off the gold box with a coin. Then check below to see the gifts you get!

YES! I have scratched off the gold Box. Please send me my **2 FREE BOOKS** and gift for which I qualify. I understand that I am under no obligation to purchase any books as explained on the back of this card.

366 ADL DVFD

166 ADL DVFC
(MB-04)

FIRST NAME

LAST NAME

ADDRESS

APT.#

CITY

STATE/PROV.

ZIP/POSTAL CODE

7	7	7	Worth TWO FREE BOOKS plus a BONUS Mystery Gift!
🍒	🍒	🍒	Worth TWO FREE BOOKS!
🔔	🔔	♣	TRY AGAIN!

Offer limited to one per household and not valid to current Gold Eagle® subscribers. All orders subject to approval.

© 2001 GOLD EAGLE

The Gold Eagle Reader Service™ — Here's how it works:

Accepting your 2 free books and gift places you under no obligation to buy anything. You may keep the books and gift and return the shipping statement marked "cancel." If you do not cancel, about a month later we'll send you 6 additional books and bill you just $29.94* — that's a saving of 10% off the cover price of all 6 books! And there's no extra charge for shipping! You may cancel at any time, but if you choose to continue, every other month we'll send you 6 more books, which you may either purchase at the discount price or return to us and cancel your subscription.

*Terms and prices subject to change without notice. Sales tax applicable in N.Y. Canadian residents will be charged applicable provincial taxes and GST. Credit or Debit balances in a customer's account(s) may be offset by any other outstanding balance owed by or to the customer.

If offer card is missing write to: Gold Eagle Reader Service, 3010 Walden Ave., P.O. Box 1867, Buffalo NY 14240-1867

BUSINESS REPLY MAIL

FIRST-CLASS MAIL   PERMIT NO. 717-003   BUFFALO, NY

POSTAGE WILL BE PAID BY ADDRESSEE

GOLD EAGLE READER SERVICE
3010 WALDEN AVE
PO BOX 1867
BUFFALO NY 14240-9952

NO POSTAGE
NECESSARY
IF MAILED
IN THE
UNITED STATES

It was the message that brought Nguyen to speak with Jong Fang. He didn't really care about the man laid out in bed before him or about those who'd died on Wewak, come to think of it. The attack itself was an affront to Nguyen and to Lee, but there were always more pirates in waiting, anxious to ship out for wealth and adventure with a bloodthirsty crew.

Nguyen wasn't concerned as to the state of Jong's health, whether he lived or died. It mattered only that his message be conveyed in timely fashion to Lee. The doctors had reported the man's eagerness to share some bit of information that he held in confidence for his superiors, and they believed the strain of holding it inside might jeopardize his ultimate recovery. Word of the Wewak raid, Jong's survival and his message was relayed to Lee, who then ordered Nguyen to board a seaplane and discover what the fuss was all about.

Jong was red-faced and sweating when Nguyen entered his hospital room, flanked by two bodyguards. He would've brought more, in the circumstances, but the seaplane was a small one and Ambon Island was far enough removed from Wewak that Nguyen believed he was safe from attack. If not, his bodyguards both carried Skorpion machine pistols under their baggy jackets, while Nguyen himself wore a Browning Mark 3 semiauto pistol holstered at the small of his back.

Jong visibly relaxed as Nguyen and his soldiers entered the hospital room. Lee had ordered private quarters for his wounded lieutenant—at least until Jong spilled his secret about the attack. Now, with Nguyen and the others standing over him, the wounded pirate seemed to release pent-up tension, abandoning some measure of resistance to fatigue and the sedative dribbling into his veins from an IV rig mounted beside his bed.

Nguyen wasted no time on preliminaries. "You have something to tell me," he said.

Jong launched into his story, haltingly at first, then with greater confidence. Nguyen listened without interruption to his tale of a surprise assault by night, automatic weapons raking the camp, killing all who stood before them. All except Jong.

"I alone was spared," Jong proclaimed, "to tell you what the raiders want."

"Which is?"

"They came for the Americans. The hostages."

Nguyen had feared as much. No matter how he racked his brain, the only alternative he could think of was a raid by rival pirates—but who among them would be fool enough to challenge Lee so flagrantly? Perhaps the Filipinos led by Sanchez, but they operated mostly from Luzon, better than twelve hundred miles north of Wewak. Malice alone wouldn't lure them so far from home to risk their lives in hostile waters.

"How many were there?" Nguyen asked.

"I can't be certain," Jong said. "In the confusion, with my wound—"

"An estimate."

"I saw three. Two men and a woman."

"All white?"

"One, I think. The woman may have been Japanese."

That stirred a memory in Nguyen's mind and made him think of Mahmoud Safi and Ramli Anuar on Penang. A Japanese woman had wandered into their affairs before Safi was killed and Anuar disappeared. Asking questions about...

"What did they say?"

"The white man asked me where the hostages were kept. Of course, I didn't say."

Because you didn't know, Nguyen thought. There were reasons why he kept subordinates in ignorance. "Go on."

"They'll pay the ransom," Jong said. "The white man waits to hear from someone in authority, with terms for the exchange."

"And how am I supposed to contact him?"

Jong fumbled beneath his pillow, wincing as the movement

caused him pain. A moment later he withdrew his hand and held a slender cell phone out to Nguyen.

"With this," the smiling pirate said.

The Timor Sea

THE LIBERATED CABIN CRUISER—*Adamant* by name—was a Rinker 342 Fiesta Vee, powered by twin 350 MPI Horizon diesel engines with a top speed of thirty-five knots per hour. It measured thirty-seven feet in length, with a twelve-foot beam, and slept six belowdecks in relative luxury. The galley was well stocked with food, and the 235-gallon fuel tank was nearly full.

Best of all, the whole setup was free.

After leaving an extra, programmed cell phone with the wounded pirate on Wewak, Bolan and his two companions had helped themselves to one of the speedboats, using it to access and claim the cabin cruiser. There was no one aboard to contest their move, and the Fiesta's controls were simple enough for any first-timer to handle. Bolan assumed the craft was stolen, its name and registration numbers altered, but he had no time to spare thinking about the original owners. If they were still alive, they could count themselves lucky. If not, then they had no more use for the cruiser.

Yun and Hirawa were trying to relax in the *Adamant*'s wheelhouse, sipping chilled drinks prepared with the built-in ice maker and blender, while Bolan piloted the boat. He'd settled for soda on the rocks, but didn't argue when his two companions went for alcohol. They were still keyed up from the firefight, fast-talking and punctuating their conversation with jerky hand gestures, but two hundred miles of smooth water lay behind them, separating them from Wewak's killing ground, and Bolan could feel them starting to relax a bit.

As for himself, he thought about the cell phone on the console in front of him, wondering when—or if—it would ring. He'd gambled on the wounded pirate to survive and to recall their conversation in sufficient detail that it would still be coherent when he passed it on. An anonymous call to the Indonesian coast guard had improved the thug's odds of living through the afternoon, but that still didn't mean he'd deliver the cell phone to someone who mattered. If it was left behind or lost in transit, maybe lifted by a sticky-fingered cop or ambulance attendant, Bolan would never know the difference. Silence could mean anything from a simple breakdown in communication to a death sentence for Jeff and Kimberly Ryan.

The ransom line was another gamble—and a desperate one, at that. Bolan had ample cash on hand, but nothing like ten million dollars and no hope of raising any such amount, even if he'd been so inclined. It was a lure, plain and simple, or maybe not so simple, if the bottom feeders he was trolling for rejected the bait. Still, he had to try something, and until he knew where the Ryans were held—or if they were even still alive—negotiation seemed to be the only game in town.

Hirawa's voice distracted Bolan from his thoughts and from the task of piloting the cruiser westward. "Tell me," she ordered, "do you do this often?"

"What's that?" Bolan asked her. "Joyride in a stolen boat?"

She sobered, knuckles blanching where she gripped her frosty glass. "I was referring to the massacre of perfect strangers."

"Were they perfect?" Bolan challenged her. "I thought they were a gang of thieves and murderers."

"Of course," she said. "Don't take offense. There is a certain pleasure in it, I admit."

"Speak for yourself," the Executioner replied. "For me, it's just a job."

That wasn't strictly true, of course. There'd been times when Bolan reveled in the violence, drawing strength and solace from revenge, but a professional either controlled those feelings or he didn't last. Distractions were a lethal liability in Bolan's line of work, and that included taking too much pleasure from a kill.

He'd known war lovers, from his days in uniform and later. In the Army, some of them had lived to win promotion and were thus removed from front-line combat, but it only seemed to make them worse. Instead of risking their own lives in the pursuit of thrills, they were compelled to play with others, risk spilling the blood of those they didn't even know.

"I came here to avenge my parents," Hirawa said. "What draws you?"

"We covered that already," Bolan replied.

"There's more, I think. To fight so hard and kill so many must require—"

The shrilling of Bolan's cell phone interrupted her. He picked it up and answered midway through the second ring. "Hello."

The voice in his ear was masculine, melodic, self-assured. "I must speak to the warrior," it said.

Surabaya, Indonesia

"SPEAKING."

Lee Sun frowned. He didn't recognize the voice, but there was no good reason why he should. "Is this the man," he asked, "who left a message recently with one of my associates?"

"We had a little chat. You got my present."

"It was thoughtful," Lee said, "but it poses a problem."

"You've had time to take it apart," Bolan replied. "If your crew is any good, you know it isn't bugged. They should've found the built-in scrambler, too."

They had, but that discovery had only solved half of Lee's problem. "You're correct," he said, "but since the instrument includes no video connection, you retain the advantage. How am I to know who may be listening, or even recording our conversation?"

"To what purpose? No one's building a case here."

"That's easily said."

"What does it take?" Bolan asked.

"A balance of jeopardy," Lee said. "You seek declarations

from me. I need something from you, for anyone who may be listening."

"Such as?"

"A number of men were killed the past night on Wewak Island. The telephone I'm holding now was left behind by one of those who killed them. I must know if you're that man."

The hesitation lasted no more than a heartbeat. "Yes, I am."

"And do you represent a law-enforcement agency?"

There was no hesitation this time. "No, I don't."

"It's murder, then. Your name?"

"I haven't asked for yours."

"But you're aware of it," Lee said, "unless the Wewak raid was mere coincidence."

"It wasn't."

"In that case...?"

"Look, we're wasting time. I heard you may be able to negotiate the return of certain merchandise. Two packages, to be precise. I understand there'll be a finder's fee involved."

"Last night's adventure indicates bad faith," Lee said. "If all you want is the return of merchandise intact, the raid was both dangerous and counterproductive."

"It was worth a shot."

"More than that, I'm afraid. The finder's fee you mentioned now must be increased to compensate for damages."

"What kind of compensation did you have in mind?"

Lee thought about it for a moment, smiling to himself. "The price has tripled. Make it thirty million for the safe return of what you seek."

"That's not a problem," came the swift reply.

"Indeed?" Lee lost his smile. It seemed too easy. "You may wish to speak with your employer before extending your commitment."

"I have full discretion. Do you want the cash or not?"

"I want it all," Lee said. "If you have insufficient funds on hand—"

"It's covered."

"The penalties for fraud are very strict," Lee said.

"You worry too much. It's a simple business deal."

"Of course." Lee's smile was back. "In that case, all that's left is to negotiate a mutually acceptable venue for the exchange."

"Not quite."

"Excuse me?"

"Thirty million is a hefty price. Before I part with it, I'll need some proof the merchandise is still intact."

"Ah, yes. The proof of life."

"That's it."

"But surely, presentation of the merchandise at the exchange—"

"Won't do me any good if you show up with guns instead of goods," the stranger said, interrupting him.

He wasn't stupid, Lee decided, even if he did take suicidal risks. "You want to see the merchandise before you purchase it?"

"I do."

"Such an arrangement complicates the matter," Lee replied.

"I need a look, that's all."

"And you shall have it—for ten million dollars. I'll accept the other twenty on delivery."

"You've got a deal."

A faint alarm was going off in the back of Lee Sun's mind. It all seemed too easy, his nameless adversary too agreeable. He smelled a trap, but shrugged it off. Two could play that game, and Lee was a master.

"The exchange point?" he asked.

"Your call. I may need time to get there."

"Certainly. Shall we say Singapore?"

"It's doable."

"How soon can you arrive?"

"This time tomorrow."

"Excellent." There would be time to plan. "Tomorrow, midnight. At the Empire Dock?"

"We're on."

"How will my people know you?"

"I'll know them."

The line went dead. Lee closed the folding telephone and handed it to Nguyen Tre Minh. "We have them," he declared.

"Why Singapore?"

"Why not? We have friends there. It gives you time to organize a welcoming committee."

Nguyen smiled at the news, but something in his expression struck Lee as forced. There was a hint of stiffness in his tone as Nguyen said, "I will look forward to destroying them."

"Save one, if possible," Lee said. "I want to know who sent them after me, so that we may repay the favor."

"What about the hostages? You promised him—"

"I have a plan," Lee told his first lieutenant. "Never fear."

The Timor Sea

"WHY SINGAPORE?" David Yun asked.

The American shrugged and said, "Why not?"

"The trip will take another twenty hours at top speed," Yun said, "and we'll be forced to stop for fuel."

"I don't think so," the tall American replied.

"You have a plan?" Hirawa asked.

"I'm hopeful. But we'll need a contact with a private plane."

Yun thought he saw where his partner was going. A charter flight would save them precious time. If it could be arranged without untoward delay.

"I know someone," he said. "A smuggler from Keluang. He owes me a favor. If I can reach him, and if he's available—"

Bolan tossed him the cell phone. Yun was pleased to catch it deftly, without fumbling. "Give him a call," the American said. "See what you can negotiate."

It took three tries for Yun to reach Shazril Hadzrami. The smuggler was surprised to hear from him, much less at the Keluang whorehouse where Yun finally tracked him down.

Hadzrami didn't appreciate the interruption, but he was in no position to argue. Yun had given him a pass on smuggling charges twice—the first for hashish, and again for ancient artifacts of suspect origin—because Hadzrami supplied information on his more successful competitors, and because he had a certain boyish charm that never failed to make Yun smile. Their near-friendship aside, however, Yun never let Hadzrami forget who wore the badge in their relationship.

"I can't come now," Hadzrami said. "It's late, and anyway, the plane needs gas."

"Fill it," Yun said. "I want you airborne in an hour, or I'll have your ass in court first thing tomorrow."

"For what?" Hadzrami asked him, playing innocent.

"For twenty years on the hashish, to start with," Yun replied. "And the Chinese may not be so lenient when they learn about your trade in artifacts."

"All right! Suppose I can afford the fuel—"

"You'll manage," Yun assured him.

"We still need to pick a meeting place where I can land without formalities."

"Suggest a place," Yun said.

"You know Flores?"

"I do." It was an island in the Lesser Sunda chain, perhaps 250 miles due west of their position. If their luck held, they could be there in five hours, more or less.

"There's a cove on the south coast, thirty miles west of Ende," Hadzrami said. "I can be there within six hours of takeoff. Call it five o'clock."

"Agreed. And Shazril?"

"What?"

"Don't make me wait."

Yun broke the connection before Hadzrami could think of a comeback. "It's done," he told Bolan.

"When and where?"

Yun described their destination, then pointed it out to Bolan on one of the cabin cruiser's nautical charts. Once they cleared the western tip of Timor, it would be smooth sailing all the way to Flores and their rendezvous.

Or so Yun hoped.

"It gives us downtime, waiting for the plane," Bolan said. "We'll use it working out our plan for Singapore."

"Belasko, do you think Lee Sun will bring the hostages?" Yun asked.

"Maybe. What I don't believe is that he'll hand them over to us without trying something slick."

"A trap, you mean?" Hirawa asked. Her bubbly mood had dissipated. The familiar worried look was back.

Bolan nodded, focused on the open sea in front of them, the long green swell of Timor rising to the north. "Lee won't know if we've got the cash or not, but he'll want payback for the hurt we put on him on Wewak. One way to get it is to kill us, take the ransom, and then either dump the hostages or hold them for a while and try to score a second payoff."

"But there is no money," Hirawa reminded him.

"Same difference," Bolan told her. "Lee wants us dead, either way."

"The authorities—"

"Would only make things worse," the American said, cutting her off. "Lee may have eyes on the police force, since he chose the site himself. If not, you can bet he's got spotters alert to any unusual police activity. Send in the uniforms, and we miss our chance at the Ryans, maybe getting some cops killed in the process."

"But if it's a trap?"

"Put yourself in Lee's shoes," the American replied. "He picked Singapore for a reason. That tells me he's got people there already, or he can move them in quickly before we arrive. At least that's what he *thinks,* calculating our rate of travel from this little beauty." His hands ran over *Adamant*'s polished wooden steering wheel as he spoke. "But he won't know that we've sprouted wings."

"You plan to reverse the trap," Yun said.

"That's the plan in a nutshell," Bolan agreed.

"What if he doesn't bring the hostages?" Hirawa asked.

"Then we're back to Plan B. Grab one of the hit team and squeeze him for leads."

"And if the prisoners are there?" Yun asked.

"We try like hell to bring them out alive."

Captivity

"JEFF? JEFF! Wake up!" Kim whispered. "Somebody's coming!"

He shrugged her off, groggy from fitful sleep, regretting it as soon as he glimpsed the expression on her face. Kim was plainly exhausted, dark shadows painted under her eyes by fatigue. Before the sound of footsteps drew his mind away, Jeff Ryan thought she might've lost about ten pounds since they were captured, though she wouldn't pass for scrawny yet.

"Are you awake?" she asked.

"Do you see my eyes open?"

"You don't need to—"

The sound of a key in the lock shut her up. Ryan rose and drew Kim to her feet after him. He wouldn't look up to their captors again, unless the bastards knocked him down.

The first man through the door had a familiar face. He'd led the team that had attacked the *Valiant,* killing Albert and taking them hostage. Ryan hadn't seen him since that day— how long ago?—but now the man had a big grin on his face, as if he'd just encountered two old friends.

"Good news!" he said by way of greeting. "It appears your families have finally come to their senses."

"You mean they've agreed to the ransom?" Ryan asked.

"Indeed!" The pirate rubbed his hands together, like a man sitting down to Christmas dinner. His smile was wicked as he said, "Someone does want you back after all."

Ryan would've liked to smash his grinning face, but the man wore a pistol on his hip, and two goons armed with some kind of machine guns had entered behind him. It was a measure of the pirate's courage, Ryan thought, that he needed bodyguards to speak with unarmed prisoners.

"When do we get out of here?" Kim asked.

"This very night," the pirate said, still grinning. "But I fear that only one of you may go, at first."

Jeff Ryan felt the angry color rising in his face. "Hey, what the hell?"

"A mere formality," their captor said. "Before the ransom payment is arranged, we are requested to provide a demonstration that you are alive and well."

"You call this 'well'?" Kim asked.

"Hold on a minute," Ryan demanded. "You can't prove we're both alive by showing one of us. It makes no sense."

"A simple gesture of good faith," the pirate said.

"Good faith?" Kim echoed. "You're a kidnapper and murderer. You want to talk about good faith?"

"Kim, please—"

"Please, nothing!" She pulled away from her husband's encircling arm, anger flushing her cheeks beneath the deep tan. "These are criminals, not businessmen!"

The pirate's smile was fading, but he studied Kim with an apparent fascination for her attitude. Or was it just her looks? Ryan wondered. Glancing at the bodyguards, he found them watching Kim as well—but the expressions on their hungry faces left no question in his mind.

"Shut up, Kim!"

"No! I won't shut up! These people think—"

The pirate raised a hand to silence her, and Kim surprised them both by stopping in midsentence, cringing a step as if she thought he was about to strike her. "As you cannot make the choice," their captor said, "I'll make it for you. We take Mr. Jeffrey Ryan to the meeting since he knows how to behave himself."

Ryan felt a fleeting moment of relief before it hit him. He'd been fearful of the pirates taking Kim away, to do God knows what when they had her alone, but now he recognized the obvious. If they took him away to the meeting, she'd still be alone, at the mercy of their keepers. Instead of traveling with three or four pirates, she'd be caged at the mercy of—what? How many? Were there twenty in the camp? Fifty?

The prospect made him sick. Ryan felt his knees go weak. "It's both of us or nothing," he demanded. "You can see that, right? They won't pay off unless you prove both of us are alive and well."

The smile was gone now as the pirate turned to face him. "Prisoners do not negotiate," he said. "If you wish to survive, you'll do exactly as you're told."

"I won't leave Kim!" Ryan said defiantly.

"So be it." Turning to his bodyguards, the pirate told them, "Take the woman."

Blind with sudden rage, Ryan rushed them, knowing that he didn't have a prayer of taking down all three. In fact he didn't even manage one. The taller of the bodyguards lunged forward with a snarl and swung his weapon into Ryan's face. The stunning impact dropped him to his knees, where a kick found his ribs and doubled him over in pain.

The beating went on for several minutes, Ryan conscious only of the jolting agony, his assailants looming over him, and Kim's helpless screams in the background. He was conscious when they left him, dragging Kim behind them, but he couldn't move, could barely draw a breath to fill his lungs.

And still it wasn't pain that made Jeff Ryan start to weep.

Flores Island, Indonesia

THEY FOUND THE COVE on their first try, with Yun piloting the cabin cruiser. Bolan stood ready with his AKMS assault rifle, half expecting an ambush that never materialized. He still wasn't entirely convinced that they could trust Yun's pet smuggler, but at least the man hadn't set them up for a slaughter.

So far.

They'd been waiting for the best part of an hour and a half, sheltered by overhanging trees near the west side of the cove, when Bolan heard an aircraft approaching. He took nothing for granted, keeping a hand on his weapon as the sound drew nearer, knowing it could just as easily be tourists, a bush doctor on his rounds or a coast-guard patrol seeking smugglers. In the latter event they were screwed, unless Yun could badge his way out of the confrontation without resorting to force. Bolan had long since pledged that he would never fire on law-enforcement officers, corrupt or otherwise, and guessed that neither of his two companions had the stomach for a firefight with the law either.

"It's Shazril," Yun said, as the ungainly plane came into view, swooping low on its approach to the cove and touchdown. Bolan recognized it as an ancient Grumman Widgeon, used extensively for sea patrols in World War II, maintained in service for the past half century primarily by pilots short on cash and long on ingenuity. This one had been converted to turboprop engines, but it was otherwise intact and showing its age, rocking gently on the waves as its pontoons made contact and the pilot swung it toward shore.

Seeing the plane, the soldier was glad there were no more than three of them prepared to board. Even with their minimal gear it would be cramped in the Widgeon's passenger cabin, but comfort took a back seat—literally, in this case—to their need for speed. If all went well, the plane would deliver them to Singapore in roughly one-third the time they would've spent aboard the cabin cruiser.

But would it be enough?

Bolan had no doubt that Lee Sun's choice of rendezvous points was strategic. The pirate would look for a home-court advantage, a chance to prepare for the showdown without hosting a battle in his own backyard, where he was bound to catch the fallout. Based on prior experience with human predators, Bolan also calculated that Lee would prefer to take the mythical ransom payoff by force, eliminating any and all witnesses while he had the chance. It was simple logic, and not far removed from Bolan's own plan for the meeting.

There were two major flaws in Lee's thinking, however—

either one could prove fatal. First, there was no ransom to be had. Lee might suspect it, especially after Bolan had quickly agreed to the steep hike in price, but his nature would demand that he check it out anyway. What pirate worthy of his salt could pass on thirty million dollars when it came his way?

The second flaw—at least, if their luck held—was Lee's sense of timing. Bolan had bet their lives on the assumption that Lee thought they were sailing the *Adamant* to Singapore, condemned by its top cruising speed of fifty miles per hour to complete twenty-hour trip and wind up in Singapore exhausted, with barely time enough to make the ransom drop. Lee might send pirates out to look for them along the way, but there were several routes they could've taken, and Bolan didn't think the disappearing act would tip off Lee.

Not yet.

It would be dicey if pursuers found the cabin cruiser, though. That's why he'd pulled the pin on a grenade and taped the spoon down, dropping it into the cruiser's fuel tank just before he boarded the Widgeon. It would take an hour or two for gasoline to dissolve the tape's adhesive, thereby detonating the charge and sending *Adamant* to the bottom of the cove, a burned-out hulk for fish and coral to colonize.

The trick now would be slipping into Singapore unseen. Yun had assured them that their pilot had it covered, but they'd have to wait and see. Meanwhile Bolan would keep his weapons handy, just in case.

Once they were on the ground, the last phase of their mission would begin. They might retrieve the hostages by the next night, but Bolan wasn't counting on it. What he did count on was bloodshed, and with luck, a chance to question one of Lee's men. They'd come this far and he imagined he could smell the finish line.

It smelled like death.

8

Singapore

Nguyen Tre Minh lit his second cigar of the day and drew the smoke deeply into his lungs. He waited for the nicotine to do its work, calming his nerves, and hoped the others wouldn't know he was on edge, dreading his confrontation with the men who'd struck the camp on Wewak Island.

Nguyen told himself that he wasn't afraid, that his jittery nerves were a normal precursor of combat, but he knew that wasn't strictly true. Raiding a ship at sea excited him. This was different. He'd seen what was left of the Wewak encampment and its occupants. The massacre had been complete, except for Jong Fang—and he had been deliberately spared to bear a message.

No, the pirate could admit it to himself, he feared these men.

But he feared Lee Sun more.

Refusal to obey Lee's order was the next best thing to suicide—except that suicide would let Nguyen select a painless mode of death. If he defied Lee, there'd be no option. Lee had specialists on staff who made their living by inflicting pain. Nguyen had seen them keep a man alive and wide awake for days on end, screaming until his vocal cords gave out and could produce no further sound. Still, he lived on, enduring the torments of the damned.

No, thank you, Nguyen thought. He would do as he was told—and keep a sharp eye on the exits, just in case the operation blew up in his face. Lee might command him to arrange the ambush, but he couldn't blame his first lieutenant for surviving if the plan went bad, could he?

Perhaps.

That was the hell of it, trying to out-think Lee Sun. The man was rational—but only to a point. Beyond that point, emotion ruled him and he was as likely to start laughing at some tragic failure, as he was to draw a gun and kill the men he deemed responsible.

Another draw on the cigar helped level Nguyen's mood. He thought the ambush would be perfect. His opponent had permitted him to choose the killing ground, and he had fifteen handpicked men at his disposal. They'd all be armed with automatic weapons, stationed at strategic points around the Empire Dock and primed to strike as one. His targets would be weary from the long trip westward, maybe even seasick. Nguyen had no idea how many there would be, Jong Fang wasn't any help, but Nguyen expected only five or six, if that. More soldiers would've left their mark on Wewak, and his search team had found nothing of the kind.

The Ryan woman was his edge. The bleeding-heart Americans had decided to meet Lee's demands, after their rescue effort on Wewak had failed. Nguyen still didn't understand how they could raise an additional twenty million so quickly, but he supposed anything was possible in these days of wire transfers and Internet banking. The only money he trusted personally was the cash in his pockets, the bills and coins he could hold in his hand.

What if the ransom payoff was a trick? Lee had considered it, discussed it with him, and he didn't seem to care. One way or another, they'd have their vengeance on the Wewak raiders and be done with it. If there was cash, so much the better. If not...

The thought stopped him. If not—then, what?

Could they run the ransom scam a second time, after

killing off the delivery team? Who would be stupid enough to sign on for a second attempt? And if there was no ransom coming, what use were the hostages?

Lee Sun had taken pains to forbid him from harming the woman. She could not be killed or injured, Lee insisted. Anyone who disobeyed was subject to the screaming death. That was enough to hold his troops in check—at least, for now—but it didn't prevent them staring at the woman anytime they got the chance, each man on fire with thoughts of what he'd love to do with her if Lee's protection was withdrawn.

Nguyen wasn't immune to such temptations of the flesh, but he had other pressing matters on his mind. There were a few small details of the ambush that he needed to refine before the meet. He wanted nothing left to chance.

Above all else, Nguyen Tre Minh intended to survive.

No matter who he had to kill to save himself.

THE ARRIVAL in Singapore came off without a hitch. Shazril Hadzrami knew his way around the island and its law-enforcement personnel. No Customs agents were around to see the Grumman Widgeon splash down in the leeward shadow of an island off the southern coast. A powerboat was waiting for them, with a short run to the shore. On arrival, they were met by a second friend of Hadzrami's who stood by with two vehicles—a Volkswagen van for Bolan's team and a battered old Citroën that seemed to be the lookout's personal ride. It meant more money out of the soldier's pocket, but he didn't mind as long as it got them safely into town and helped them stay out of sight for the next eighteen hours.

Bolan waited with Yun and Hirawa while Hadzrami took off in his lumbering seaplane, and his Singapore connections left in the Citroën. When they were gone, he waited a bit longer, testing the humid air to satisfy himself that they'd left no traps waiting to spring. Finally, when no enemies sprang from the forest or swooped from the sky, he faced the others with a curt, "Okay, let's go to town."

Yun drove the van, Hirawa riding in the shotgun seat beside him, while Bolan stayed out of sight in the rear. White faces were a fairly common sight in Singapore, but Bolan guessed their enemies would be on the alert until midnight of the following day. He couldn't stay completely out of sight until that time, and only one surviving pirate knew his face, but minimal exposure still struck Bolan as the wisest strategy.

Yun drove the ten or fifteen miles to town along a road that started out unpaved and then got better as they went along. He made directly for the Empire Dock, to check it out in daylight, while they had a chance. Bolan took time to briefly review what he knew about Singapore, in advance of need. Singapore was a parliamentary democracy with a strict sense of justice that included public beatings with a cane for misdemeanors such as petty theft and vandalism. None of which precluded Lee's pirates from corrupting a policeman here and there or operating quietly under the noses of those officers they couldn't buy.

Bolan wondered how deep the stain of corruption ran in Singapore, and who was infected. It hardly mattered in practical terms, since he planned no dealings with the local law, but it might've helped to know how many local cops were bent, and who were the straight shooters.

Never mind, he thought. The only difference, if it came to that, would be that cops on Lee's pad would only fire on Bolan's team, while straight police would open up on anybody with a gun in hand. Since Bolan didn't plan to have that kind of confrontation with the uniforms in Singapore, he'd settled on the tactic of avoiding one and all.

"Here's Empire Dock," Yun said twenty minutes after they rolled into town. Bolan slid forward to survey the scene and found it unremarkable. It looked and smelled like any other waterfront he'd ever seen from Hong Kong to Manhattan. Faces changed, and signs were printed out in different languages, but even a blind man would've known when he was near the docks. They smelled of fish and tar and diesel fumes. The background noise consisted of voices, machinery and motors with the restless, endless sloshing of the ocean underneath and all around them.

"Well," he said, "it's not the best, but it'll have to do."

KIM RYAN RECOGNIZED the moment when she reached her limit and a measure of the fear that had oppressed her since her capture started to recede. Still terrified, she simply understood that there was nothing more her enemies could do to frighten her.

Unless...

Oh, no, you don't! Don't even think of that!

Of course, she'd thought of little else since being separated from her husband. She'd been disappointed in him for his failure to solve all their problems, and while she'd made no effort to conceal those feelings, Kim regretted it now. There was a world of difference, it turned out, between being held captive and being held captive alone.

Kim was frightened in a way that only women can be terrorized, finding herself at the mercy of men without morals or any apparent restraint. Each time she heard one of them pass the doorway to her tiny room, she cringed and waited for the door to open, the intruder to approach her and start ripping at her clothes. Granted, they hadn't touched her yet, except to shove her, pulling her in and out of boats, cars and rooms, but every breath she took reminded Kim that she was one short step away from rape.

Her only hope lay in the fact that someone—her father? More probably her father-in-law—had finally agreed to pay the ransom demanded by their captors. The thought encouraged her, but Kim knew many things could still go wrong. It troubled her that she and her husband had been allowed to see the pirates' faces. Anyone who'd seen a movie in the past ten years knew it was bad news when the heavies started taking off their masks. It signaled that they didn't care who saw them, since they didn't plan on leaving any witnesses alive.

Don't think that way! she scolded herself. Kidnap victims in the so-called Third World were released every day, more or less in one piece. Abduction was a business to these people. Who would ever trust them with another ransom payment if they earned a name for executing hostages? Still, there was something in the leader's face, the way he looked at her...

That brought back her old fear in spades and made Kim sorry that she'd ever chased the train of thought to start with. Her husband had once accused her of thinking too much, and while her sister Amy laughed aloud at the idea, Kim knew it was true. She was no great intellect—just look at her grades from the past year at Vassar—but she did have a tendency to overthink problems, worrying to death and irritating those around her with incessant harping on subjects that interested no one else.

And lately, she'd been focused on escape.

It seemed impossible, but something told her she should try. She had a grim, oppressive sense that her husband was lost to her, and that she'd never see his smile or hear his laughing voice again. The premonition might be false, some kind of paranoid delusion, but she wouldn't take that chance. It was the first time in Kim's life that she'd been truly on her own, no one to count on for a helping hand, and she was bitterly determined not to fail herself.

And having thought the matter through that far, she didn't have a clue how best to proceed.

The door that served her room was locked from the outside. She'd tried it earlier and couldn't turn the knob. There were no windows, but she guessed it had to be dark outside by now. The night would help her hide, if she could get away. But how was she supposed to manage that?

Brute strength was out, unless she found a way to take one of her captors by surprise. That meant she'd have to lure one in and get him close enough to strike without warning. She knew about hurting men, in theory—a kick to the groin, fingernails to the eyes—and while she'd never used the moves in real life, Kim trusted her desperation to give her strength.

It was the risk that worried her. Once she tried anything, there'd be no turning back. The man she chose would be aroused *and* angry, a bad combination once she'd led him on, then done her level best to cripple him. There would be consequences if she failed, and thinking of them made her tremble, fighting nausea.

Perhaps it was too much. She wasn't Xena, after all. What could she do against a gang of hardened criminals with guns and knives?

Her best, that's all. And pray that it was good enough.

Kim sat near the door to wait, ears straining for a sound of footsteps in the hall outside.

IT HAD BEEN seven years since David Yun set foot in Singapore. On that occasion he'd been sent to extradite a triad prisoner and spent no time of any consequence touring the city or outlying parts of the island. He knew the basics, and memories of three prior visits helped him navigate the teeming streets.

Job one, as Mike Belasko had informed him, was to take precautions against being seen and followed by the enemy. Yun thought they'd done a decent job of that so far, including their first meal in Singapore—cartons of take-out food that they had eaten in the van. Having observed the Empire Dock where they would meet the enemy the next night, their task came down to waiting for the time when it was safe to move, take up positions near the site in readiness and hope they were in place before their foes could lay a deadly ambush.

Yun had been troubled on the flight to Singapore, but he was getting used to it. Specifically, a sense that following the American's lead might prove a surefire means to throw his life away. So many things could still go wrong, and the pervasive risk of injury or death at Lee's hands was only part of it. If Yun was jailed in Singapore, it meant the end of his career. Conviction on a murder charge could send him to the gallows or consign him to a prison cell for life. In any case, the shame would mark his family for years to come.

And yet, despite all that, Yun felt a certain eagerness as he anticipated what might happen next. It was perverse, but on some level he appreciated his partner's methods and results. For years Yun had observed Malaysia's justice system moving at a snail's pace, breaking down more often than it functioned properly. He had turned cynical and stoic in his disappointment, confident that there was no other recourse—until Belasko walked into his life. Now everything had changed, and there were fleeting moments when Yun told himself that it was worth the risk—worth anything—to see the bad men running for a change.

It was the way a lawman ought to feel, but seldom did.

After their meal they spent time cleaning weapons and reloading magazines. The smell of cordite brought back vivid memories of the attack on Wewak Island, startling Yun with the realization that he felt no guilt. There was apprehension—a fear that he might be arrested, stripped of everything he owned—but he felt no remorse for killing men he'd never seen before he framed them in his rifle sights. They had been pirates, thieves and murderers—the scum of Asia, gathered to relax between one bloody crime spree and the next. Yun had done the world a favor by eradicating them.

That thought had barely taken form when it occurred to Yun that after this, if he survived the next few hours, he might be forced to reevaluate his life. He'd seen and done so much in three short days, had changed so much inside, he wasn't sure he could return to what he now thought of as his old ways—watching the system limp along from day to day, case to case, failing repeatedly. Could he be part of that again, now that he knew there was a cleaner, better way?

Enough!

It would be folly to confuse himself with Mike Belasko, after such a short acquaintance. The American had plainly been involved in covert operations all his life. He was inured to secrecy, bloodshed, the almost casual violation of laws David Yun had pledged to uphold. There was a world of difference between them, which had nothing to do with race or nationality.

I can't do that, Yun thought. I can't be who he is.

But he could follow Mike Belasko yet a while, until their mission was completed one way or another. He could do that much, and give it everything he had.

Sachi Hirawa's voice distracted Yun as he was topping off an AK-47 magazine. "We're almost finished here," she said, pinning Belasko with her eyes. "What's next?"

"We wait for dark," the tall American replied. Hirawa shivered when he met her gaze and had to look away.

"I mean, what do we do?"

"Stake out the docks," Bolan said. "Try to make sure Lee hasn't put his men in place ahead of us."

"And if he has?" Hirawa asked.

"I'll take them out as quietly as possible."

She noted that he spoke for himself alone, excluding her and Yun from the action. Hirawa had no problem with that, since she doubted her own ability to kill in cold blood, much less without causing an uproar that would doom their plan.

The American seemed to read her thoughts. "With any luck," he said, "Lee thinks we're still at sea. If he's hunting us out there, so much the better. My guess is, he'll start moving people into the killzone three or four hours ahead of the party, to find their positions."

"But you could be wrong," she said.

"Absolutely. That's why we need to check it out again at dusk, and move as soon as night falls."

A sudden thought occurred to her. "What if we're already in place, ahead of time, and they start moving in?"

"I'm counting on it," he replied.

A sudden twinge of panic made her stomach lurch. "Won't we be trapped?"

He offered her a reassuring smile. "I'm looking at positions far enough outside the optimum perimeter that Lee's men should pick spots between us and ground zero, so we're settled in behind them."

"You said 'should.'"

He nodded. "We've been gambling since day one. The

stakes get higher every time we play. If you'd prefer to cash out now—"

"I didn't say that!" Sudden anger flared inside her, coloring her cheeks. "I simply want to understand the plan."

"It's simple," he replied. "We get there first, hang back and wait for Lee to put his men in place. If there's an opportunity, I'll thin the herd before the main event. Come show time, we put down as many of the heavies as we can and take the hostages away from them."

"Do you really think they'll bring the Ryans here?" Yun asked.

Bolan shrugged. "I'd call it fifty-fifty. If they don't, we fall back on Plan B and take at least one of the shooters alive. Try for whoever's in charge of the crew."

"You make it sound easy," Hirawa remarked.

"We should have fewer men to deal with than last time," he replied. "The downside is police. We won't have privacy or time to spare."

Yun frowned and shook his head at mention of police. "I wish there was another way," he said.

"If you come up with one before sundown," Bolan said, "feel free to share."

Hirawa had another question on her mind. She didn't want to ask it, but it wouldn't go away. "If they do bring the hostages," she said, "how will we keep them safe? With all the shooting, won't they be at risk?"

"They've been at risk since they were kidnapped," he reminded her. "But if they're on display, let me take out the shooters nearest to them."

She swallowed a lump in her throat and asked the next logical question. "What if you can't? What if...something happens to you?"

Bolan took the question in stride. "Evaluate the situation as it stands and use your own best judgment. Nobody will blame you if you have to disengage."

Hirawa had no answer for that. It embarrassed her greatly that she couldn't meet his gaze. The American checked his watch and craned to glimpse the sky outside through the van's windshield. "We've got about three hours before we move," he said. "If anybody wants to catch a nap before the party, now's the time."

Captivity

JEFF RYAN PACED his cage and wondered where Kim was, if she was safe. Scratch that. She hadn't been safe from the moment they'd been captured. His true thoughts were more specific and more dreadful. He pictured Kim in the hands of their captors, tormenting himself with graphic images of what they might be doing to her. For all he knew, the ransom story was a line of crap devised to separate them without resistance on his part. But why would the pirates bother with trickery? On second thought, he guessed they would've told him what they planned to do with Kim—and likely would've made him watch, just for the hell of it.

So there was hope, however minimal. That brought him back to where they might've taken her, and why they had been separated if the ransom was about to be delivered. Maybe it was strategy, he thought. Their captors didn't want to risk losing both prisoners in case there was a double cross. That made a certain kind of sense, but it also planted fresh doubts in his mind.

It suddenly occurred to Ryan that there might've been a problem with the ransom. Suppose only part of it was ready or Kim's family had bargained for her release alone. What, then? It struck him as outlandish, but there'd been a certain tension between himself and Kim's father from the day he started dating her. Milton Stroud had raised no objection to their wedding, per se, but his attitude toward Ryan had always been lukewarm at best. Ryan wouldn't put it past the old man to bargain for Kim's release at a discount, leaving Ryan to fend for himself on his family's dime.

No problem, there. His folks had money to burn and he was their only child, the last of the proud Ryan line.

What if the government had interfered somehow? Ryan

didn't watch the news, unless he counted sports, but everyone on the planet had heard the noises coming out of Washington since the Pentagon and World Trade Center attacks in September 2001. The bottom line on terrorism was no mercy, no negotiation. Uncle Sam would spend billions to avenge terrorist victims, but he wouldn't pay a red cent for ransom.

Jesus!

Did this count as terrorism? Wasn't it really more of a business transaction? Something dreamed up by organized crime, for example. His captors didn't want to rule the world or topple governments. For God's sake, they just wanted money!

Ryan felt himself sliding toward panic again, but he controlled the drift with a new thought. If ransom payments were blocked by the U.S. government, why did the pirates think it was payday? Kim's father worked for the State Department and socialized with the President. Would he buck those powerful connections to save his little girl? Could he?

And if not, who was making the drop?

For most of his life, Jeff Ryan had been quite comfortable with his place outside the loop. His parents made the big decisions, and servants took care of the rest. The biggest, most momentous decision he'd ever made for himself had been popping the question to Kim—and look where that had gotten him.

For the first time in his pampered life, Ryan hated knowing that his future rested in the hands of others, men and women whom he'd never met, scheming in offices and situation rooms halfway around the world. It worried him, because he guessed they'd view him as a problem rather than a human being, and they might be more concerned about appearances than whether he and Kim survived.

More worried now than ever, Ryan hoped they wouldn't drop the ball.

Singapore

SUNDOWN CAME SWIFTLY to the waterfront. Night falls without a whimper in the tropics, and because the docks faced southward, Bolan and his two companions had no view of a brief but spectacular sunset. Undistracted in the sweatbox of the van, they had time to survey the waterfront and search for lurking snipers as the shadows fell.

So far, so good. Bolan had spotted no one lurking on the docks as workers fled to seek the comfort of their homes or favorite saloons. That didn't guarantee the docks were clean, of course—he would've had to watch around the clock for that, and still risked shooters slipping past his scrutiny—but he was fairly confident that they could set up shop before the opposition started to arrive.

There would be killing, but it was all part of the plan—as far as any plan could hold together in the given circumstances. He would take as much of it as possible upon himself, trusting Yun to handle his share and hoping that Hirawa would try to stay out of the worst. Survival was a victory of sorts in mortal combat, but they needed more to make it worth the effort.

They left the van at 6:30 p.m. and fanned out to their preselected vantage points, long guns and extra magazines concealed in duffel bags. Bolan went up a narrow ladder to the flat roof of a warehouse that was closed for the night. Yun crept into the rear bed of a covered truck parked near the northeast corner of the Empire Dock, while Hirawa broke the flimsy back door lock on a deserted fast-food stand to the northwest. They had a fair field of triangulated fire, but Bolan knew the situation might be fluid, calling for mobility and all bets off as far as cover was concerned.

Their adversaries started to arrive at 8:10. They came in pairs, moving along the waterfront on foot from east and west, then splitting up to look for cover on the docks. There were sixteen of them in all, and Bolan tracked each one in turn to his selected hiding place, marking positions in his mind for future reference. When half an hour passed without another pair arriving, the Executioner reckoned it was time to leave his perch and start to even up the odds.

He had no radio communication with his two companions,

and wouldn't have risked it now in any case, but both knew what he had in mind, once the advance team of their adversaries were in place. Yun and Hirawa had agreed to let him deal with it alone, and to retreat if anything went wrong before the scheduled midnight drop.

Descending from the rooftop, Bolan had his targets charted and prioritized. It would've helped to have a sound suppressor for his Beretta, but he would make do with what he had—a five-inch dagger, hands and feet. If he was forced to use the pistol, it would blow their cover and wipe his best chance yet for retrieving the hostages.

Easy does it. He still had the best part of three hours in which to pick and choose his targets, moving silently among them like a killing shadow. If he did it properly, his enemies would never know what hit them, and the drop team scheduled to arrive at midnight would be desperately short of backup when they needed it the most.

That was the up side. On the other hand, one slip could cost the Executioner his life.

9

Nguyen Tre Minh was restless, waiting for midnight. He always felt that way before some violent action, anxious to get on with it, but at the same time apprehensive. This time, even though the odds were clearly on his side, he couldn't help thinking of the pirates on Wewak Island and how they'd been cut down to the last man, with no sign that they'd even wounded one of their killers.

It will be different this time, Nguyen told himself. He had sixteen gunmen in place on the Empire Dock, waiting to spring a deadly trap on his signal. He had twelve more hand-picked gunmen with him in three cars, rolling through darkness as they finally approached the killing ground.

He'd forced himself to wait for the appointed time instead of going early to the meet and idling there. It would've made him look pathetic and exposed him to further risk, sitting around with weapons and a kidnapped woman in his car if the police came by unexpectedly. Local patrolmen had been paid to stay away, but Lee Sun didn't have the whole police force in his pocket yet, and there was no predicting when a squad car might pass by, its occupants intrigued to find three black sedans parked on the Empire Dock at night. If any showed up during the meeting, Nguyen would surprise them with a fireworks show.

Nguyen didn't care much for protocol, but he was no one's fool. Lee might not forgive him if their enemies slipped through his hands, and while he feared few men on Earth, Lee was the first on that short list.

So they would be on time—not early, and most certainly not late. Nguyen would preserve the illusion of compliance with his enemy's demands, at least until he met them face-to-face. From that point on, when they were well within his snare, he could dispense with the charade and take them down. No mercy and no prisoners.

As for the hostage wedged against him in the back seat of his Citroën sedan, she was expendable once Nguyen had the ransom payment in his hands. Lee had ordered that she not be left behind in Singapore to raise unnecessary questions, but that she should simply disappear. Nguyen could always dump the husband later or assign one of his underlings to do the job. He had a fishing trip in mind, trolling for sharks, using the arrogant American as bait.

"How far?" he asked the driver.

"Almost there," the young Malay replied. At the last instant he recalled his place, adding a hasty "sir."

Nguyen took out his Browning pistol, checked it once again to verify a live round in the chamber and replaced it in the holster underneath his left armpit. Its solid weight was comforting, although it sometimes made his muscles stiff and gave him headaches if he wore the shoulder rig too long.

"Be ready," he told the four pirates who shared his vehicle. There was a general shifting, and a couple of them grunted in response, holding their automatic weapons close. They all knew what to do and had his simple signals memorized. Nguyen was worried that his voice might break if he went through the plans again, so he kept quiet.

Empire Dock was mostly dark, except for floodlights mounted on tall poles to the east and west. Nguyen couldn't see his shooters in place, but he wasn't supposed to. It came down to faith at this point—and the understanding shared by all his men that failure would invite swift, devastating reprisal.

"Stop here," he told his driver when they'd reached a point that satisfied him. There was open space on either side, but they were flanked by boats and buildings where his men were stationed, peering over gun sights, waiting for the enemy to show himself.

Soon.

"Get out," he ordered no one in particular, waiting until his shooters were on guard around the car before he made his move. The woman didn't follow him immediately when he took her wrist, but Nguyen gave the arm a twist that made her squeal and brought her scrambling after him.

"We mustn't keep your good friends waiting," Nguyen said, while dragging Kim across the pavement at his side. His jacket was unbuttoned, flaring as he walked, the pistol easily within his reach. Another moment brought them to the center of the area he'd chosen for the trap, as if a giant *X* was marked on the pavement.

The pirate checked his watch and saw that it was 12:01 a.m. He smiled, remembering a fragment of a childhood game in English. "Come out!" he called across the silent docks. "Come out, wherever you are!"

"I'M RIGHT HERE," Bolan answered, emerging from the shadows with a long, even stride. He paced off thirty feet of cracked, weathered concrete, then stopped. There was a tugboat behind him, and off to his left, some kind of storage shed where he could hit the deck in an emergency. Behind him was the icehouse that had sheltered him while he watched the pirates approach.

It wasn't bad, as cover went, but he was in the open now, and anything could happen while they had him there. He kept the AKMS rifle slung across his back and held a bulky satchel in his left fist, right hand free and empty. In place of cash, the bag was filled with folded newspapers in languages he couldn't read.

Kim Ryan stood beside a slender Asian man who gripped her right hand in his left. The two of them were flanked by nine more shooters, leaving each car with a driver at the wheel, their engines running. From the bright smile on the leader's face, he had to have thought he still had sixteen hidden guns trained on the only target he could see.

He was wrong.

Bolan flexed his right hand, slightly stiff from the blow he'd delivered to one shooter's larynx while they were grappling in the dark. He'd done his best to clean the blood off his hands, but traces lingered at the cuticles and underneath his fingernails. It was a sloppy business, killing sixteen men, but it was done.

"You've come alone?" the pirate asked him, dark eyes shifting left and right to scan the dock. The backup shooters were alert, ready for anything.

"Who else was I supposed to bring?" Bolan asked.

"I imagined we might meet your friends from Wewak Island," the Asian replied.

"You know how that goes," the soldier said. "They'd already made other plans. Are we doing business here or what?"

"You have the money?"

Bolan held the bag out to his side and let it drop, both hands now free. "From where I stand, you're short one hostage."

The pirate smiled, lifting Kim Ryan's hand as if he were a boxing referee, declaring her the winner of a title bout. "This is a good faith offering," he said.

"Full payment for partial delivery isn't good faith," Bolan said. "It's bad business."

The pirate's smile hung in there, cocky. "You refuse to pay?" he asked.

"I'll cover what I see," Bolan replied. "Half for half."

The smile slipped a notch. "You test my patience, American. Does this woman mean nothing to you?"

"Never saw her before in my life," Bolan answered. "And I still don't see her husband."

"He is alive and well," the pirate said.

"Uh-huh. And I'm supposed to trust you—why, again?"

The pirate tried to keep it casual, but he was losing out to anger. Maybe he resented Bolan showing up alone, or the defiance in his attitude. Whatever. Lee's front man was on the edge of losing his cool. "Perhaps," he said, "you lack authority to close the deal?"

"You'd better hope not," Bolan said. "I'm all you get."

"And money, yes?" The smile came back.

It was an easy punt. He kicked the bag of newspapers halfway across the space that separated him from Kim Ryan and her captors, deliberately ignoring the young woman's pale, tear-streaked face.

"Half for half," he repeated. "Like I said."

The pirate leader blinked at him, the message soaking in. "That's half the money? You didn't bring the whole thing?"

"Why don't you have a look?" As Bolan spoke, he shifted on his feet and subtly rolled his shoulders, working the AKMS closer to his right side.

The pirate flicked a hand at one of his shooters and the chosen one moved forward, keeping a grip on his weapon as he approached the satchel. The Executioner tracked him, watching the whole group as best he could. He was half turned in profile by now, his right hand encircling the AKMS's barrel.

He watched the gunman crouch and fumble with the satchel's clasp, reluctantly setting down his SMG to use both hands. Another moment and he had it open, rummaging inside. Bolan was ready with his weapon when the man muttered a curse and raised a handful of newspapers skyward. Rock steady, Bolan slid the folding-stock Kalashnikov beneath his arm and found its pistol grip, sending a burst downrange to meet his enemies.

DAVID YUN WAS ready with his AK-47 when the shooting started. Crouched behind the tailgate of the covered truck, he was positioned to the left of his targets and slightly behind them. He tried to watch the American, but the pirates kept distracting him with small movements, restlessly shifting their bodies and weapons. He worried, too, about the three men in the waiting cars, watching to see if they used radios or cell phones to signal reinforcements or search for the watchers his partner had already killed.

The first shots startled him, although he'd been expecting them. Yun flicked a glance across the dock in time to see the American breaking for cover, apparently unhurt and firing as he ran. Relieved, Yun turned his full attention to the enemy, beginning with the nearest of their vehicles. Sighting quickly, he fired a short burst through the driver's open window and watched the man drop out of view as he was hit.

Yun swung his rifle toward the second car in line, uncertain how long it would be before the pirates noticed him. His first shots had been covered by the general firing on the dock, but he couldn't trust distraction to protect him much longer. Whatever he hoped to accomplish before they were on him, he had to do it swiftly and efficiently.

The second driver didn't know what had transpired behind him yet, but he was stepping from his vehicle, drawing a pistol, when Yun strafed him with a burst of 7.62 mm rounds and dropped him thrashing to the pavement. Another burst tore through the sedan's steering column, disabling it, before Yun swept on toward the first car in line.

Kim Ryan and the spokesman for her captors had emerged from this car earlier, but they wouldn't be using it to flee. Yun shot the driver from behind, spraying his blood and brains across the inside of the windshield, then unleashed another burst that tore the left front tire to shreds. Spent casings jingled on the steel bed of the truck behind him, bouncing off the canvas cover overhead.

An instant later they were joined by bullets ripping through the canvas, as one of the pirates spotted his muzzle-flash and returned fire. The rounds were high but getting closer, chewing through the heavy fabric as his enemy fought the recoil of a short full-auto weapon. Yun framed the pirate in his rifle sights before he could control it, ripping off another burst that knocked his target thrashing to the ground, while his weapon skittered out of reach.

More of them had his fix now, converging streams of fire

tearing the canvas to tatters, rattling off the sides and tailgate of the truck. One of the tires exploded from a hit, and Yun's makeshift bunker dipped sharply to starboard. His ears picked out the hollow *thonk* of bullets puncturing the truck's fuel tank, and he could smell the pungent scent of gasoline.

It was time to flee. Yun had provided himself an escape hatch, ready in advance of need. He'd slit the canvas cover near the left rear corner of the driver's cab, and now he used that makeshift exit to evacuate, keeping the bulk of the truck between himself and the pirates who were hosing it with bullets. He was off and running when a slug sparked underneath the truck and kindled fumes to flame, the detonation lifting Yun completely off his feet and flinging him across the Empire Dock like a rag doll.

KIM RYAN DIDN'T realize that she was screaming until the man who called himself Nguyen slapped her across the face. The impact staggered her, but Nguyen wouldn't let her fall, fingers digging painfully into her biceps as he jerked and shoved her back toward the car in which they'd arrived. There was something wrong with it now. She could see that, even through her frightened tears, but Kim didn't know what it was until they stood beside it and she saw the windshield starred with cracks, painted with blood on the inside.

Her stomach twisted, sudden nausea overwhelming her, but there was no release as Nguyen dragged her toward the second car in line. This time they found the driver stretched out on the pavement, leaking viscous crimson from his chest and back. The third car was no better, driver dead behind the wheel, Nguyen's gunmen huddled around it for cover.

Nguyen crouched behind the car, dragging Kim down beside him. He muttered words she couldn't understand—orders or curses, did it matter which—while bullets rattled overhead and members of the escort party leaped up to return fire at their unseen enemies.

Kim bit her lip to keep from sobbing, frightened of the shooting and disgusted that she hadn't found a chance to flee her captors before their trip to the waterfront. The pirate who'd brought dinner to her room that night had been unmoved by her attempts to look provocative. She didn't know if he was gay or simply frightened by his masters, but he didn't take the bait. The next time Kim's door was unlocked, it had been Nguyen and the rest of them together, announcing it was time to go.

A fleeting image of her husband flashed through her mind, but Kim couldn't hold it. Bullets were flying around her, and she was consumed with panic, fearful that a shot might strike her at any moment. It surprised her, after all she'd been through in the past few weeks, that some new peril still had power to steal her breath away and leave her quaking—but it did.

Crouching behind the bullet-riddled car, she tried to pull away from Nguyen, but his grip on her wrist was as tight as a pair of steel handcuffs. When she tried to twist her arm free, he responded without even glancing at her, squeezing with ferocious strength until she felt the small bones in her wrist grinding together and the pain evoked a small, humiliating sob. That made her angry, fear and fury jostling for control of her emotions, but Kim knew instinctively that there was nothing she could do to hurt Nguyen. Not if she wanted to survive the night.

That in itself seemed damned unlikely at the moment. She didn't know who was firing on Nguyen's men from the shadows, but there were clearly several gunmen involved. Kim hadn't recognized the negotiator—he wasn't one of her father's old friends from the diplomatic world—but he couldn't lay down this kind of fire on his own, blasting away from three sides at once and pinning down Nguyen's pirates this way. Kim felt a momentary thrill of hope, imagining a private army had been sent to save her—and her husband, of course—but the feeling evaporated as she realized Nguyen would probably kill her before he permitted a rescue.

That thought had barely formed when Kim heard a wet smacking sound to her left, and warm droplets of liquid stung her cheek. The pirate crouched beside her croaked a muffled grunt and slumped against her, the side of his head sticky-hot where it pressed against her bare shoulder. Kim squealed, recoiling from the grisly contact, using her free hand to fend off the slouching corpse.

Nguyen glanced past her, saw the dead man sprawled beside her and muttered something that sounded like a curse. He'd done a lot of that since the shooting started, and Kim guessed she was better off without a translator for most of it. Too bad if he was angry now, but he had brought this trouble on himself.

Unfortunately, he had also brought it down on her.

Nguyen had come to a decision now. He didn't share it with his captive, simply leaping to his feet and hauling Kim after him, pulling her along with enough force to nearly dislocate her shoulder.

"Wait!" she cried. "What are you doing? Where—"

"Shut up!" he snapped. "Run now as if your life depends on it, before your good friends shoot you in the back!"

HIRAWA WAS GETTING the hang of her weapon. The last shot had been risky, taking down a gunman crouched beside Kim Ryan, near one of the getaway cars. She'd held her breath and squeezed the trigger gently, as instructed, and the .30-caliber bullet had gone where she meant it to go, smashing into the pirate's grim face. The bloody result should've sickened her, but Hirawa supposed she was becoming callused, that she'd seen and done too much since her parents died to suffer much shock from anything.

She wasn't shocked—but she was certainly surprised—when the pirate leader suddenly sprang to his feet and dragged Kim Ryan after him, running headlong away from the cars, breaking for the dark streets and shops bounding Empire Dock on the north. There was nothing to stop them in that direction, except Hirawa herself.

Hunched in the darkness of the empty fast-food stand, she tracked the runners with her M-1 carbine rifle, hoping for a clear shot at the pirate, but he clutched his hostage close to his left side, keeping an arm around her torso and supporting her, making it perilous for any would-be rescuers to fire on him. Hirawa knew she couldn't risk it, but she also couldn't hold her place and watch them slip away.

It meant leaving her meager sanctuary, but she had no choice. Hirawa shoved the back door open, keeping both hands on the carbine as she shouldered through. The pirate and his captive had already pulled ahead of her, running flat-out across the dock. Hirawa could've risked a shot then, but she lacked the confidence. The American would've done it, maybe even Yun, but how could she live with it if she slipped and hit the woman by mistake?

Instead, Hirawa ran after them, pouring on the speed until she cut their lead by half. They were almost to the street, no traffic moving on it at this hour. But how long would it be until they heard the sirens wailing? If they hadn't finished with the pirate crew by then, she could look forward to spending her golden years in a Singapore prison—if she was lucky.

Thirty yards behind her quarry, Hirawa triggered two quick shots into the air, calling out for the pirate to halt. He ran on a few more paces until she fired another shot that chipped the pavement near his feet. He stopped then, spinning to face her in a movement that brought Kim Ryan around in front of him, clutched between himself and Hirawa like a squirming human shield. He held a pistol pressed against her head, his free hand circling Kim's waist and holding her tightly.

"You're not American," the pirate said in English. He was breathing heavily, his accent thick.

"What difference does it make?" she asked.

"What does this woman mean to you?" he challenged her.

"Nothing," she answered without thinking, conscious of the change in Kim's expression, though she focused on the pirate's face. "I came for you, and for Lee Sun."

He blinked at that, plainly confused. "What do you want from us?"

"Justice," she said. It sounded better than revenge.

"I don't know you," he stated. "I've never seen you in my life before."

"You saw my parents," she informed him. "You, or someone like you, watched them die."

"I don't know what—"

"Don't lie to me, you bastard!"

Nearly shouting at him, finger tightening around the carbine's trigger, Hirawa missed the sound of footsteps slapping on concrete behind her. By the time she saw the pirate's eyes flick toward the dock, across her left shoulder, it was already too late. A smooth, hard object slammed into the base of her skull, and sudden darkness swallowed her before she hit the ground.

RELIEF WASHED OVER Nguyen Tre Minh as he saw the woman crumple, her rifle tumbling to the pavement when she fell. One of his men stood over her, a stout Korean named Joon-Hee, aiming his sawed-off shotgun at the prostrate woman's head.

"No, wait!" Joon-Hee glanced up at Nguyen's call, confused. "Bring her along with us," the pirate leader said. "We may have use for her."

Joon-Hee obeyed, albeit grudgingly. The shotgun had a piece of twine secured around its pistol grip and muzzle, as a makeshift sling. He looped the twine across one shoulder now and stooped to lift the woman, tossing her easily over his other shoulder in a crude fireman's carry. Joon-Hee's face betrayed no strain as he rose from his crouch, the bland expression forcing Nguyen to reevaluate his opinion of the man's physical condition.

"Good," Nguyen said. "Come with me!"

But where were they going? *Away* was the obvious answer, with gunfire still rattling behind them. The remnant of his team was catching hell back there—and what had happened to the men he'd sent in earlier to set the trap? As far as he could tell not one of them had fired a shot so far, which told him they were dead or disabled, hunted down before Nguyen arrived on the scene. Neutralized by an enemy who'd antic-ipated his move and beaten him at his own game.

So far, at least.

The Japanese woman, whatever her motives, was part of the enemy team. It was too much to imagine that she'd turned up by coincidence at the secret time and place when others were supposed to be ransoming Nguyen's prisoner. Her ac-cusation lit a spark of memory, but the pirate leader was too distracted at the moment to consider it. He had to concentrate on getting out of Singapore alive, with both his female hostages securely under guard.

Nguyen's first problem was simply escaping from the Em-pire Dock. They needed wheels, and soon, before police started arriving in a mood to shoot first and ask questions later. There'd be no negotiating with the riot squad, he realized, par-ticularly if they caught him and Joon-Hee running down the street at midnight with illegal weapons and two female hostages. Nguyen and his Korean lackey would be lucky to survive in that event, much less avoid a prison term.

They managed to clear the dock proper without being shot or pursued. Nguyen took it as a positive sign and wished the stragglers in his party well. If they were able to defeat the enemy, so much the better. Conversely, if they only stalled pursuit until he could escape, it would be good enough. Nguyen would have to give Lee some explanation of his lat-est failure, but he couldn't think about the details now. He had to first survive the night.

And that was turning out to be no easy task.

Moving along a darkened side street toward the Ayer Rajah Expressway, they found an aged Volvo station wagon parked outside a dark and silent shop. Nguyen had no idea whom it belonged to, and he didn't care. "Can you hot-wire this?" he demanded of Joon-Hee.

The muscular Korean frowned, considered it, then shook his head. "No good," he said. "I'm not mechanical."

Nguyen was ready to berate the pirate for his ignorance, had actually framed the first barrage of insults in his mind, when headlights splashed across his face, dazzling his eyes. A car was rolling toward them, the driver slowing for a closer look at the peculiar curbside scene ahead of him.

Joon-Hee ran into the street, a lumbering figure with the woman slung across his shoulder, leveling his shotgun at the car's startled driver. Barking orders first in Korean, then in fractured English, he routed the driver and a female passenger from the vehicle, sending them back along the street at a dead run.

"Quick! Inside!" Nguyen barked, suiting action to words as he shoved Kim Ryan ahead of him, forcing her into the back seat of what he now recognized as a Proton compact. She struggled briefly, sobbing, until he struck her across the shoulders with his Browning pistol and kicked her across the seat. In front of them, Joon-Hee wrestled his unconscious burden into the passenger's seat, then climbed behind the Proton's wheel with the engine still running and threw it into gear. A shot sounded behind them, but Joon-Hee tramped down on the accelerator and sped away with smoking tires.

BOLAN WAS SLOW in pursuit of the runners, pinned down under fire from three weapons when Nguyen made his break with Kim Ryan. Even then, he glimpsed Hirawa giving chase and gave her points for stubborn courage, even though he wished she'd stayed in place. He had enough dead allies on his conscience, and he didn't need another one to make it any worse.

Two of the pirates chose that moment to display their courage, rushing Bolan in a kind of pincers movement, firing as they came. The closer of the two was on his left, milking short bursts of fire from a long-barreled submachine gun to cover his loping advance. The Executioner swung to meet him with the AKMS, sighting as much by instinct as by effort, triggering a short burst that caught the runner in midstride and spun him like a dervish, twitching with the impact of each round that tore his flesh.

It was a clean kill, but it cost him as the rifle's slide locked open on an empty chamber. He had no time to reload before the second gunner pinned him down, so Bolan dropped the mute Kalashnikov and went for his Beretta 92-F, clearing the holster in a blur of deadly speed.

The second shooter had to have seen his partner fall, but he was already committed to the rush, no turning back. He had a vintage Thompson SMG, considered obsolete but still a killer anywhere within effective range—and that included Bolan as the .45-caliber slugs began knocking chunks out of the tugboat where he'd found cover. Another few seconds of this, and the pirate was bound to get lucky and score with the blizzard of lead he was throwing downrange.

The Executioner beat him to it, squeezing a double tap from the Beretta that jolted his target, throwing the runner off stride. The man wobbled through two more shambling steps, then dropped to his knees on the pier slumping forward, supported on the muzzle of his tommy gun as if it were a crutch. It didn't help him when his index finger spasmed on the trigger and the Thompson sprayed another burst into the pavement, ricochets flying in all directions, some of them ripping into the shooter himself. With a last cry of anguish, the dying man sprawled on his back and was done.

Bolan leaped from the tugboat before anyone else could pin him down, sprinting off in pursuit of Hirawa and those she was chasing. Behind him he heard Yun's AK-47 hammering away at the enemy from a new location, apparently unscathed after the truck explosion that had nearly roasted him a short time earlier.

Bolan was fast, calling on strength and speed he wasn't certain he possessed, but he was still too late. By the time he caught another glimpse of Hirawa and the others, she was no more than a piece of excess baggage draped across a burly pirate's shoulder. Kim Ryan and her captors were at least a hundred yards ahead of him, standing beside a car as Bolan reached the street and paused, snapping a fresh magazine into his AKMS's receiver. Before he could aim and fire the rifle, a car swung past him, accelerating down the block, then slowing as its headlights framed the curious foursome.

Bolan was off and running again as one of the pirates blocked the car's progress and ordered the passengers out. A moment later, still seventy-five yards distant, he saw his quarry pile into the vehicle and slam its doors. The original owners were running his way, gasping, until they saw yet another armed man and veered off toward an alley fronting on the far side of the street.

The soldier ignored them, risking a long shot at the car as it sped away. He aimed for the right rear tire and heard his bullet whine off pavement as he missed. A burst of autofire might stop them, but he was afraid of bullets tearing through the thin sheet metal, striking one or both of the women by mistake.

Footsteps behind him brought Bolan around, the Kalashnikov braced at his hip and ready to fire. David Yun raised both hands, winded as he slowed his pace and joined Bolan in the middle of the street. "Gone?" he asked glumly.

"Gone is right," Bolan replied.

"And Sachiko?" Yun sounded worried now.

"They took her, too."

"What now?" the stunned policeman asked.

"We take off the gloves," Bolan said, "and throw the rule book out the window."

10

Surabaya, Indonesia

"Let us be clear." Lee Sun allowed no hint of irony or anger to pervade his tone. "You went to fetch a thirty-million-dollar ransom but returned without the money. In the process, you've acquired another hostage and lost twenty-seven men?"

Nguyen Tre Minh looked miserable, which was only right. He stood before Lee's desk, hands twitching at his sides, and couldn't meet his master's gaze. Limp hair framed his pathetic face, giving Nguyen the appearance of a dissipated drunkard who had wandered home somehow after a weekend binge. His clothes were torn and dirty, indicating that he hadn't cared enough to change before his audience with Lee.

"I wouldn't put it that way, sir," he said.

"How would you put it, then? By all means, Minh, please enlighten me. I live to know the error of my comprehension."

"Sir, I didn't mean—"

"Let us examine the event," Lee interrupted him. "Did you retrieve the ransom you were sent for?"

"No, sir."

"No. Am I mistaken in believing that you left with one woman and have returned with two?"

"No, sir."

"Again, no error on my part. You were, if I recall, entrusted with twenty-eight soldiers?"

"Yes, sir."

"And how many still live?"

"I'm not sure."

"Because you ran away. Let me rephrase it. Of the twenty-eight, how many have returned with you?"

"One, sir."

"It seems I was correct in all particulars. Is that not so?"

"Yes, sir." Almost a whisper, this time. Nguyen focused on his shoes as if the secrets of the universe were written on the leather toes.

Lee Sun stood and moved around his desk until he was beside Nguyen, immediately on the slouching pirate's left. "You know how I feel about failure, Minh?"

"Yes, sir."

"You've never disappointed me before, but now...I don't know what to make of it, frankly. Perhaps it's time for you to find another line of work?"

That made Lee's first lieutenant lift his head, a sudden flash of panic in his eyes. Nguyen knew very well that there was no retirement from the pirate fleet. The only way he'd leave Lee's service was in death—perhaps a bullet in the head, with burial at sea.

"No, sir!" he said. "I'll make it right, I swear!"

"And how do you propose to do that? I've lost fifty men to these people already, and we still don't know who they are, where they come from, or—"

"The woman!" Nguyen said. "She claims we killed her parents. She was after Safi and Ramli Anuar before the raid on Wewak."

"But the man I spoke to and the one you saw weren't Japanese," Lee said.

"No, sir." Nguyen's eyes flicked back and forth like pinball paddles, reflecting his mental agitation. "They've formed an alliance against us somehow."

"Which still tells me nothing."

"The woman must know who they are."

"Will she tell you, Minh?"

"I'll persuade her, sir."

Lee pretended to consider it. "You're obviously tired," he said at last, "and also quite emotionally involved. I think perhaps someone else—"

"Please, sir! One last chance to redeem myself?"

Bending close, Lee held Nguyen's eyes with his own, letting Nguyen see the death that waited for him if he failed again. "Very well," he declared. "One last chance."

"Thank you, sir."

"And Minh?"

"Yes, sir?"

"For God's sake, clean yourself up. You embarrass us all."

Nguyen Tre Minh bowed his head and departed, scuttling away to his quarters for a shower and a change of clothes. Lee watched the door close after him and shook his head, disgusted with the turn events had taken in the past few days. He didn't understand how everything could suddenly go wrong, when nothing outwardly had changed.

He didn't know yet, but he meant to find out.

Nguyen had a knack for interrogation or rather, he had in the past. Lee hoped the pirate hadn't lost his nerve, but he would give Nguyen one chance to make the woman talk—under close supervision, of course. If he failed, within a reasonable time, that failure would receive its just reward of pain. The new interrogator would have two subjects to work on, one for information and the other for Lee's amusement.

In the meantime he had to think about his enemies and how best to destroy them before they did any more damage. First he had to find out who they were and where they could be found. Lee guessed that scouring Singapore would be a waste of time, but he had men on the island—a few left, at least—with nothing better to do.

He could wait, but not for long. More trouble was coming. He could almost smell it on the wind that wafted through his open office window, drawing closer.

It reminded Lee Sun of the odor from a freshly opened grave.

Johor Baharu, Malaysia

"SHE'S NOT DEAD YET," Bolan repeated his assurance. "If they only meant to kill her, they'd have left her on the waterfront."

"Small consolation," David Yun replied. "It means they're questioning her, even now."

That prospect sickened Bolan, too. He'd seen enough of torture in his time to recognize the scars it left, both physical and mental. Still, he had to tell himself that there was hope, as long as life remained.

"We'll get her back," he said. "We'll get all three of them. Work with me on the angle."

Returning to Malaysia had been relatively simple. Yun had fixed it with a phone call to his office, and a pair of officers were waiting for them at the border with official-looking documents, no questions asked. Bolan had been prepared to pay them, if they needed greasing, but Yun smoothed it over with a handshake and some private words before the escorts split. Now, sitting in a small apartment with their weapons spread around them, freshly cleaned and loaded, Bolan thought he had his second wind.

"Sachiko won't have any answers for them when they question her," Yun said.

Bolan made note of the first-name familiarity but didn't comment on it. Yun had made his point. If Lee's men grilled Hirawa—and they would, no doubt of that—she had no secrets to reveal, nothing that she could trade to save herself a moment's suffering. Aside from names and Yun's police connection in Malaysia, what more could she say? Perhaps she'd buy some time explaining her own vengeance quest, but that would hold small interest for her captors. Bolan pictured her inventing stories, to prolong the intervals between electric shocks or numbing blows, but if the pirates caught her lying it would only make things worse.

Then again, how much worse could it get?

Bolan dragged his thoughts away from images of naked flesh and electrodes, concentrating on their immediate problem. He needed to find out where Lee Sun was or where he kept his prisoners. It was a safe bet those would be two separate places, but he had to start somewhere. If Bolan couldn't liberate the hostages, he might be able to apply sufficient pressure to compel another meet.

Suddenly, he had it—or he thought so, anyway. It seemed too simple, really, and he wasn't sure about the fine points of technology. For that, he'd have to touch base with an expert, and the ones he trusted were halfway around the world from where he sat.

Yun had to have seen his smile. "You've thought of something?"

"Maybe."

"Well?"

"It may not work. I can't be sure. But if it does..."

Yun frowned, impatient now. "Tell me."

"All right, but it's a long shot."

"Just the same."

"I'm thinking we could try Star Sixty-nine."

Captivity

HIRAWA FELT as if she'd fallen down a flight of stairs. Her head throbbed and her body ached, reminding her of the last time she'd drunk too much sake and wound up hungover the next morning. This was different, though, for she had cuts and bruises to explain most of the aches—and a pinprick surrounded by purpling bruises at the crook of her left arm, where a needle had penetrated her flesh.

Drugged, she thought. And beaten, too, from the feel of it. She remembered being struck from behind, but the rest of it had to have happened after she lost consciousness. Rough handling in transit, perhaps, and a dose of sedative to keep her quiet for the long haul.

At least she was fully clothed, nothing about her present discomfort to suggest a more intimate assault. Thankful for small favors, Hirawa stirred on the hard ground, aware of some rough fabric underneath her. Opening her eyes, she focused on a soiled wicker mat that separated her cheek from a simple dirt floor.

She was stirring, trying not to agitate the snarling demons in her head, when she heard someone whisper, "She's awake." It was a woman's voice, immediately followed by a deeper one responding, "Are you sure?"

Hirawa turned by slow degrees to face the voices. She recognized Kim Ryan from the Empire Dock in Singapore, assuming that the fair-haired man beside her had to be Kim's husband.

"We thought you might be dead," the man explained.

Kim jabbed him with an elbow. "No, *we* didn't, Jeff! I told you she was breathing."

"Well, I didn't check to see."

"I wouldn't let him touch you," Kim assured her.

"Thanks," Hirawa said. "I think."

"They shot you up with something on the way back here," Kim said, confirming her impression. "I asked what it was, but Nguyen wouldn't tell me."

"Nguyen?"

"He's the one you tried to shoot," Kim said. "I have to tell you, no offense, I really wish you'd done it."

"So do I," Hirawa said. "Where are we now?"

"An island," Jeff Ryan replied. "That's all we know."

"They make us wear blindfolds," Kim said. "Except for you, because you weren't awake."

Hirawa was already tired of talking, but she couldn't let it rest. Not yet. "How far are we from Singapore?" she asked.

The newlyweds exchanged a puzzled glance before Ryan answered, "Who knows?"

"The blindfolds—" Kim began, until Hirawa cut her off.

"How did they bring us back?" she asked. "By boat or plane? How long between departure and arrival?"

"Um...it was a plane, this time," Kim said. "I haven't got a watch, though—and I couldn't see it if I did. The blindfold—"

"Estimate the time," Hirawa said.

Kim's face went blank. "Well, I don't know. I wasn't paying attention."

Jesus. Hirawa wondered whether it would help to slap the woman's face. Helpful or not, she guessed that it would make her feel better. "Never mind," she said in a conciliatory tone. "It doesn't matter anyway unless we have a means of getting out."

"Good luck with that," Ryan said.

"You've tried?"

"Well...not exactly."

"What were we supposed to do?" Kim challenged, sounding tearful now. "They've all got guns."

Their shared weakness depressed Hirawa, sparking anger which in turn produced a stronger drumbeat in her skull. She closed her eyes and took deep breaths to calm herself.

"Are you all right?" Kim asked. "If you feel sick or something, there's a bucket over—"

"No, I'm fine." Hirawa didn't want to hear about the bucket or its uses. Not just now.

Another moment passed before Kim asked, "What happened to the ransom?"

Hirawa stared at her until the other woman squirmed. She'd heard the story from Belasko and didn't mind sharing it, under the circumstances. "There will be no ransom," she explained. "Your parents have refused to pay. They won't negotiate with terrorists."

"Oh, that!" Kim made a face and fanned the air with one hand. "That's politics," she said. "I've heard it all before. But I'm family."

"In any case, there'll be no payment."

"What?" she almost screamed.

"No money. Nothing. The delivery was a trick, intended to help you escape."

"A lot of good that did!"

"Hold on a second, now," Ryan said. "My father's not in politics, and he's got money coming out his ears. I know he'll pay the ransom."

"No." Hirawa shook her head, enjoying it a bit too much. "They stand together. It's a matter of official policy."

"I don't freaking believe—"

The sound of footsteps drawing closer to their prison silenced him in midsentence. A moment later, after some initial fumbling with a latch, Hirawa saw a face she recognized come through the door.

The man she should've killed in Singapore pointed a finger at her face and ordered, "Come with me!"

Washington, D.C.

HAL BROGNOLA WAS was running late, still tidying up a bit of extra paperwork from a busy afternoon, when the black telephone on his desk shrilled a demand for attention. It was his private line, bypassing switchboards at the Justice building, his one link with the outside world that wasn't filtered through a range of new security devices installed after September 11, 2001. It was the one line he couldn't ignore, no matter how badly he wanted to be left alone, and especially not when he had agents in the field, risking their lives.

Brognola pressed a red button at the base of the telephone receiver, then lifted the handset. "We're scrambled," he said by way of greeting. "Go ahead."

It would be gibberish to anyone who'd dialed the number by mistake—a punk kid playing games, for instance—but he recognized the deep voice on the other end at once. "I've got a question for the guys at the Farm," Mack Bolan said, referring to the ultracovert group located at Stony Man Farm in Virginia.

Brognola heard the tone of urgency. "I'm listening."

"I need to find out whether they can trace a cell-phone call by satellite," Bolan explained, "and if so, how long it'll take. Also, if feasible, I need to know how accurately they can pinpoint a receiver, if the call originates with me, on a known frequency."

"It wouldn't hurt if I knew what you had in mind," the big Fed said.

Bolan gave him the quick version. They'd arranged a meet with Lee Sun's pirates, hoping to retrieve the hostages, but it had gone to hell. Bolan and his Malaysian ally had reduced the odds once more, but Lee still had the Ryans in his clutches, plus the Japanese woman who had attached herself to Bolan's quest. They were short on connections now, and Bolan was gambling on a high-tech long shot to put him in touch with Lee.

"It doesn't sound impossible," Brognola said when Bolan finished. "Interception of the call's no problem, anyway. Cell phones are God's gift to eavesdroppers. I won't know how precise the tracking is until I check with Aaron, though."

"How long?"

"To check?" Brognola shrugged before remembering that there was no one in the room to see his gesture. "Five, ten minutes ought to do it for the verdict. Setting up the link could take more time. We'd have to wait on satellite positioning to make it feasible. It could be several hours."

"I'll check back in fifteen to see if the Bear can make it happen," Bolan said. "We can make arrangements for the rest when that's confirmed."

"Okay. I'll get right on it, then wait here until we've got it set." Brognola could've asked Bolan how he was holding up, if there was anything he needed, but it would've been superfluous. The soldier had already told him what was urgently required. As for the rest it—emotions, the fatigue that came from too many long hours living on a razor's edge and waiting for the pain of that first cut—Bolan had long since learned to let it go, lock it away for study at another time. Distractions in the midst of battle were a fatal luxury.

"I'll be in touch," Bolan said, and the line went dead immediately. Under normal circumstances, Brognola supposed the sign-off might've been considered rude, but he knew Bolan would be cautious about staying on the line any longer than necessary, giving his enemies even the slightest chance to track him.

Brognola didn't need to cradle the receiver, with the dial tone buzzing in his ear. He tapped out the digits for his link to Stony Man and waited while the duty officer relayed his call. He kept his fingers crossed, hoping that Bolan's plan was feasible and they could pull it off.

He didn't want to think about what Bolan might do otherwise. More blood was waiting for him, come what may. Considering the hell that was about to visit them, Brognola almost found it in his heart to pity Bolan's enemies.

Almost.

A gruff, familiar voice came on the line. "Hey, boss. What can I do you for?" Aaron Kurtzman asked.

"Bear, here's what I need."

Captivity

JEFF RYAN HAD a plan—or part of one, at any rate. He hadn't shared it with the women yet, because he knew that Kim would try to talk him out of it and throw a fit if he refused to play along. He wasn't sure about the other woman—Sachiko, he thought her name was—but she might oppose his plan for different reasons. Kim was letting fear dictate her moves, self-preservation overriding any thought of payback or escape. Sachiko, on the other hand, wasn't afraid to fight, but she appeared to think some friends she wouldn't name were on their way to rescue her.

Fat chance, Ryan thought. He'd soon be in his third week of captivity, and no one from the States had found him yet. From what the Japanese woman said, there were no plans to pay the ransom, either. Kim's old man was standing on his principles or politics, which didn't come as any great surprise, but Ryan was stunned to find his own parents holding back on Milton Stroud's behalf. They didn't even like Stroud, though they were courteous enough when holidays brought the two families together.

No ransom, and the half-assed rescue attempt in Singapore had gone down like the Hindenburg. Okay, they'd taken out some of the pirates. So what? What good did that do, as long as he and Kim were still caged? In his opinion, it was a piss-poor sign of progress when the hunters wound up getting captured by their prey.

There it was, long story short. Ryan had decided they could either sit around waiting for someone who might never show, or *he* could make a move to break them out. He knew it would be risky, but he figured that the odds of being killed if he did nothing were right around one hundred percent. Forget about the blindfolds when they traveled. If the pirates meant to let them live, Ryan reckoned they'd be wearing masks.

Having decided to escape, he found himself confronted with the stumbling blocks of how and when. Between the two, *how* worried him the most, since they were heavily outnumbered and they didn't have a stick or pocketknife among them, much less any guns. In order to escape, he'd have to overpower at least one guard and use the pirate's weapon as they made their way— Where?

Another stumbling block, damn it!

When Ryan imagined breaking out, the pictures in his head were like the trailers for an Arnold Schwarzenegger action movie. He was kicking ass and taking names, dropping the heavies left and right, invincible as he led Kim and Sachiko— where?

To the boats, of course. He hadn't heard an airplane since they reached the island, and he couldn't fly one anyway. Not even if his life depended on it. Boats were something else. The rich adored their water sports, but even with a fast boat under him and no psychotic gunmen in pursuit, he'd still require a destination, something in the way of maps or charts to guide him. Otherwise he might head out to sea and cruise

until the tanks were dry, leaving them stranded and drifting
in the middle of nowhere, starving and dehydrated.

Scratch that. He didn't plan to be the Ancient Mariner.
They'd find a way to pull it off, if he could only grab a good,
fast boat. And boats had radios! While he was driving, Kim
or Sachiko could fire up the two-way—

And summon every pirate found within a hundred miles,
unless they caught a break. Damn it!

This hero stuff wasn't as easy as it looked on television. It
required more thought than he'd put into it so far, and possibly more nerve than he possessed. Rushing a scrimmage line
was one thing. Facing a gang of homicidal maniacs was definitely something else.

Just let me think some more, Ryan told himself. There has
to be a way. The more he thought about it, the more it seemed
as if his hypothetical escape routes led him back inexorably
to a shallow grave.

Java Sea

THE CHAPARRAL 200 speedboat was the same one Nguyen
Tre Minh had taken to attack and loot the *Valiant,* when the
Ryans were captured. Less than three weeks had elapsed
since then, and yet he felt almost as if the ordeal had gone on
forever. It had seemed a simple task at the beginning: grab the
rich young people and detain them until ransom had been
paid, then toss a coin to see if they would be released or ex-
ecuted.

Easy.

But it wasn't easy anymore. Instead of U.S. dollars by the
boatload, Nguyen had problems that bedeviled him and
wouldn't go away. His simple raid had backfired badly. More
than fifty men were dead, and he still couldn't see the end of
it. Lee Sun had lost faith in him—perhaps irredeemably—and
Nguyen had one last chance to put it right. He had to squeeze
the Japanese woman until she told him how and where to find

her allies. Then, when he'd destroyed them and reported back to Lee, there was some measure of the honor and respect he'd lost so far.

The island fortress was three hours out from Surabaya, with the Chapparal making its top speed of thirty-five knots. It would've been quicker to fly, but Lee was holding the seaplane in readiness for his own evacuation, if it came to that.

No matter. What else could go wrong in three hours?

The answer to that, conjured in mental images straight from a slaughterhouse, made Nguyen feel sick to his stomach. He snapped at the captain to hurry, aware that the order was pointless. The captain couldn't make their Mercruiser engine do more than top speed, after all, but Nguyen felt better for badgering him. Whenever things went wrong and he was out of sorts, he loved to spread the misery around.

Rank had its privileges, he thought, and nearly smiled.

Lee had questioned whether he could make the woman talk. That was an insult and a challenge he couldn't ignore. Before Nguyen had finished with her, he'd know when and where the woman's great-grandmother gave up her virginity. He would know everything about her, and she'd beg him for the privilege of telling more—or simply for the sweet release of death.

But death would be a long time coming for the bitch who'd threatened him and spoiled his plans, Nguyen thought. There would be no escape for her until he had made her pay for every headache, insult and embarrassment he'd suffered from the moment that his operation went awry. It might take days but he was equal to the task.

"Land, sir!" the captain said, alerting him.

Nguyen stood and faced northward, along their line of travel. He could see the island now, still several miles ahead, but drawing closer by the moment. Grim anticipation made his stomach clench, a painful knot beneath his ribs. Nguyen would rid himself of all that tension soon, when he began to grill the woman and extract her secrets, one by one.

Interrogation was its own reward.

Nguyen took slow, deep breaths as they approached the island, working hard to calm himself. It wouldn't do for him to lose control and go berserk with the woman, perhaps inflicting lethal damage before her tongue was loosened and she told him what he had to know. Nguyen couldn't survive another failure.

Lee wouldn't let him.

By the time they nosed into the cove and idled toward the dock, Nguyen Tre Minh was in control. Good news for him, and bad news for the woman who had tried to make a fool of him. The time had come for her to settle that account, pay for the insult he had suffered.

He was looking forward to the music of her screams.

Johor Baharu, Malaysia

IT FINALLY CAME DOWN to waiting, as so many things in wartime did. The experts at the Stony Man Farm had readily confirmed their capability of tracking down a cell phone via satellite—but only if the party holding it spoke up and stayed online for ninety seconds, minimum. Forearmed with Bolan's frequency and general parameters, a satellite had been selected for the task and programmed to perform on cue. The all-clear signal was confirmed while it was passing over Panama, chasing its orbit over the blue Caribbean, the vast Atlantic, Africa, and on from there toward Bolan's corner of the world.

The soldier sat with David Yun and waited for the satellite to reach him. In the meantime he tried not to think about what Hirawa might be suffering in hostile hands. He told himself again that if the pirates simply wanted blood, they would've killed her on the dock and left her there. That was a good news–bad news situation, since they obviously wanted her for something, but they had no way of reaching out to Bolan for a trade. More to the point, he had nothing which they desired.

It would be grilling, then, and she'd been in their hands for several hours already. Give the benefit of doubt for travel time, and they could still be working on her even as he sat there, staring at the cell phone in his hand and waiting for the minute hand on his wristwatch to give permission for the call.

Closer. He had thirteen minutes left, and that was time enough to make another pass along his mental list of all the things that could go wrong. First up, Lee Sun may well have ditched the cell phone after their last conversation, in which case he'd miss the second call completely and the effort would be wasted. Even if he had the phone, there was no guarantee he'd answer or that he'd stay on the line while Kurtzman's team at Stony Man worked their computer magic, tracing the signal back to his doorstep. Even the best-case scenario had a potential downside: Bolan finding out where Lee was, only to learn that travel time would leave Hirawa to the tender mercies of her captors for a few more hours, long enough for them to finish what they'd started and destroy her, or inflict enough damage to make her wish they had.

It wouldn't be the first time Bolan had arrived too late to save a comrade's life or sanity. On more than one occasion he'd been relegated to the task of finishing what others had started, bringing merciful release where nothing else was welcome or would serve. He didn't want to play that role again, but Bolan knew he'd do whatever might be necessary.

His thoughts were drifting toward the other hostages, no comfort there. When Bolan checked his watch again, he saw that it was time. He switched on the cell phone and pressed the buttons that would hopefully connect him to the telephone that had produced his last incoming call. No sooner had he done it than the thought occurred to him that Lee might employ some kind of blocker on his line. If Bolan couldn't reach his target, it was all in vain.

A distant phone began to ring, the trilling loud in Bolan's ear. He waited, knowing that the count at Stony Man couldn't begin until another party answered and engaged in active conversation.

"Hello?" The voice was cautious. Bolan thought he recognized it, but he wasn't positive.

"Put Lee Sun on the line," he said.

"Speaking."

He felt himself begin to smile and saw it mirrored on the face of Yun. "We need to talk," he told the pirate. "Have you got a minute?"

11

Java, Indonesia

Bolan held the Holden Commodore VT sedan at a steady fifty miles per hour on the two-lane forest road, leaving the five-speed manual shift alone. There was no other traffic visible, and they were making decent time. Beside him, Yun was silent, glowering. It didn't take a psychic charging by the minute to unlock the secret of his mood. He'd been a poster child for brooding anger since they lost Hirawa on the Empire Dock in Singapore.

Bolan was worried, too, but Yun's reaction seemed to go beyond a comrade's natural compassion—and for that matter, beyond the normal sympathy of most men toward a woman whom they'd known less than a week. That recognition gave the Executioner another reason for concern. Romantic feelings between comrades in a war zone—even if those feelings were one-sided and concealed from public scrutiny—could be a fatal weakness. An afflicted soldier might take foolish chances or forget his duty if the object of his personal devotion was endangered. That was no way for a fighting man or woman to survive, particularly when the odds against them were stacked heavily in favor of the enemy.

Bolan counted on Yun for backup, and Yun hadn't let him down so far. A case of lover's nerves could change that in a hurry, though, and Bolan knew he'd have to keep a closer eye on Yun from that point on. It was another handicap, but not as great for Bolan as it might've been for someone else. He'd led a ten-man squad in combat when he wasn't old enough to vote back in the States, and watching out for comrades was a kind of second nature to him now. He couldn't guarantee the life of a distracted warrior, though. At some point, Yun would have to watch out for himself.

And if he failed, he might not be the only one to suffer.

"How much farther?" Bolan asked.

Yun studied the map in his hands as if he'd never seen it before, much less committed it to memory. It was a computer printout generated by the GPS tracking hardware at Stony Man Farm from the trace on Bolan's cell phone. It had been beamed halfway around the world from the Blue Ridge Mountains of Virginia to a cyber-café in Surabaya, spit out by a laser printer there while Bolan sipped a cup of Java that deserved the classic nickname.

"No more than another mile," Yun told him, tapping the map with his index finger for emphasis. "The estate is here."

Bolan didn't have to ask where "here" was. He'd studied the map himself, before setting out on their drive. His question had been meant to break Yun's worried silence, rather than to gain new information. Now, he saw, it would require a bit more effort.

"Stop short or drive by and see what's happening?" he asked.

Yun turned to face him, frowning. "We go in regardless, yes?"

"I'm thinking it's the only game in town."

"In that case," Yun replied, "stop short. It saves us time."

He was considering logistics. Bolan took that as a hopeful sign, while recognizing that the focus of Yun's strategy was Hirawa Sachiko. Kim and Jeffrey Ryan would come second on Yun's short list of priorities—and in the heat of battle, if he had a choice to make, he might not think of them at all. That was the wrong choice for a trained professional, but Bolan couldn't criticize him for it in advance. Yun wasn't military. He'd come to their mission from a job where his primary goal was helping people in distress, not shooting human predators before they had a chance to strike again. All things considered, he'd done well so far, but Bolan was afraid emotion might betray Yun in a crunch and leave him fatally exposed.

In that case, Bolan knew, he'd have to cut his losses and stay focused on their mission's primary objective. He would extricate the Ryans if they lived and then wreak ungodly havoc on their captors. He'd shown the enemy a bit of that already, but they hadn't seen the Executioner in scorched-earth mode.

Not yet.

He spied a narrow, unpaved forest road and turned the vehicle in, grateful to see no recent tracks laid down since the last rain. He couldn't guarantee the car would be secure once they went EVA, but the rarely used road gave him hope it would sit undisturbed. He drove in far enough to reach a curve that hid them from the main highway, then cut the engine and put on the parking break.

"Are you ready for this?" he asked Yun.

"Ready? Yes." He was already rooting in the duffel bag that sat between his feet, extracting lethal hardware.

"Be ready for the worst," Bolan advised.

"The worst. I understand." Yun didn't normally repeat things that were said to him, but Bolan recognized the signs of mental shutters sliding into place. Yun was preparing for a bloodbath, for the sight of Hirawa maimed or worse, and getting ready to react on instinct, doing what was necessary to repay the hurt. It was a warrior's way of bracing for a bloodbath. Bolan knew the trick firsthand and hoped that it would help keep Yun—keep *both* of them—alive.

He locked the car and stood beside it for a moment, listening to peaceful forest sounds, knowing they couldn't last.

He checked the safety switch on his Kalashnikov, then said, "Let's go," and started walking south.

Captivity

HIRAWA'S WORLD was pain. She had absorbed so much of it that she'd imagined she could hold no more, thinking the further efforts of her captors would be wasted. The idea had nearly made her smile—until she found out she was wrong.

There seemed to be no limit on the suffering flesh could endure. She knew that wasn't strictly true, of course. There was an end to everything, if only in the grave. But even in the midst of torture, when her soul cried out for that release, it lingered just beyond her reach.

Three men were present at her degradation. One she knew by sight, the same man she'd pursued in Singapore. Kim had called him Nguyen. He asked all the questions, issued all the threats. A slender lizard of a man took over when her answers failed to satisfy Nguyen. He never spoke—or if he did, Hirawa missed his words while she was screaming. Number Three sat in a metal folding chair, off to her left, and watched as if he found the whole procedure fascinating. Now and then he beckoned Nguyen, whispered something to him, and Nguyen came back with a new question.

She'd held back nothing when they asked about her family, her motives for pursuing Ramli Anuar and Mahmoud Safi. No coercion was required to make her tell that story one more time. She spelled it out in detail, taking credit for the deaths of both men who'd been instrumental in the slaughter of her family, promising worse to those who'd pulled the triggers if they had the courage to release her.

That was where Hirawa's rapport with the three men broke down. Nguyen clearly resented the threats, but he was more angry about her claims that she'd killed Anuar and Safi on her own. Armed men had been seen by survivors at Safi's club in Kuala Lumpur, and her interrogators wanted to know who they were, who they worked for and where they could be found. On those points, she'd been resolute and kept her secrets to herself.

Or had she?

There'd been so much pain and so much screaming, she was losing track of time. How long had it been going on? All night? Two days? Longer? Trying to reconstruct the series of events, her mind shut down in self-defense. Each question had been phrased, rephrased, repeated, hammered home so often that she couldn't swear her answers were consistent and she didn't care. The only thing that mattered was protecting David Yun and Mike Belasko, which she'd done so far.

Unless...

She caught her straying thoughts before they wandered too far down a self-defeating path. Her three tormentors had departed moments earlier, taking a break, the spokesman leaving her with promises of worse to come. Surely they'd have finished with her if she'd told them what they needed, wouldn't they? Or had the torture changed from duty to diversion?

Either way, Hirawa still lay naked, bound to a long wooden table that shook when her body convulsed. Makeshift equipment, but it did the job. So did the hand-crank generator with its cruel-jawed jumper cables and the other instruments they had employed. However else they might be judged deficient in their daily lives, these skills the bastards had, without a doubt.

Hirawa used the private time to test her bond. They were unyielding, but she had to try. Her mind, meanwhile, worked on the matter of her failure like a stray dog gnawing on a bone. She couldn't let it go, knowing that everything she suffered was her own responsibility, that she'd accomplished nothing for her parents, for her brother or for the hostages she'd tried in vain to liberate.

She hoped the men would kill her soon, before she made another error and blurted out some bit of information that betrayed her allies. If the dismal future held a fading glint of hope, she saw it in the fact that she had no idea where her partners were right now. They would be on the move, evading any gunmen who pursued them, possibly preparing for another raid to free the hostages. Hirawa didn't think she'd live to see it happen, but she had a feeling that the American would be ruthless in avenging those he couldn't rescue.

She heard her captors coming back. Nguyen frowned at the sight of her. "You find this pleasant?" he demanded. "It amuses you?"

"I had a vision," she replied, and put another ten watts in her smile. "I saw your death."

ABADI GINANDJAR hated guard duty. It was either tedious or dangerous, and sometimes both. He was a man of action, within certain limits, and he had no tolerance for boredom. Watching empty houses was his notion of a wasted day, and his sour mood wasn't improved by Nguyen's suggestion that a group of strangers might come by to kill him later in the afternoon.

At least Nguyen hadn't left him alone. There were five more men besides himself assigned to guard the grounds of Lee's home until they were relieved. When that might be, no one had deigned to say. Ginandjar guessed that he would be on duty throughout the night and possibly the next day, too. It galled him, but he didn't dare complain.

Ginandjar had a German HK-32 A-3 assault rifle, three spare 40-round magazines resting heavily in the canvas pouch he'd slung across one shoulder. The rifle was one of his favorite weapons, accurate and hard-hitting, with a cyclic rate approaching six hundred rounds per minute, but now he had less faith than usual in firepower.

And he didn't trust his fellow watchdogs at all.

They were slackers like himself, most of them, and while survival in the pirate trade suggested some level of skill at self-defense, that didn't make them reliable guards. It was safe enough for Lee Sun to leave them behind, knowing that none of them would dare to steal from him, but that didn't make them reliable fighters. Assassins were one thing; soldiers were cut from different cloth, with different thought processes, different rules and levels of ability.

Soldiers were like the men who'd killed so many pirates in the raid on Wewak Island, then rebounded to humiliate Nguyen in Singapore two nights later. They were killing machines, professional and dispassionate. They wouldn't spook and run at the first whiff of gun smoke, the first sight of blood.

Abadi Ginandjar had been a soldier once, for nineteen days. The Indonesian military saw enough of him in that short time to offer him a choice: dishonorable discharge with a caning, or a year at hard labor on one of the outlying islands where fever and cobras competed to see which could kill the most men. He had taken the caning and still bore its scars, grateful to be free of the hated discipline and constant shouted orders. Ginandjar still lied to women about it sometimes, calling himself a veteran, hinting at bloody action in East Timor, but he knew he'd never been cut out to lead a soldier's life. It took more dedication and commitment than he'd ever felt toward anyone or anything in memory.

He scanned the lawn and trees, hoping the men he waited for would come by, pursue Lee and leave Ginandjar in peace. He wished Lee no ill, but he hadn't signed on to be a bodyguard, especially not when the body in question had already fled. Fighting—maybe dying—for abandoned houses was a fool's game.

Did that make Ginandjar a fool? He didn't think so, but he hadn't really risked his life yet. Walking on the lawn in bright sunshine, an automatic rifle slung across his shoulder, it was possible for him to feel adventurous, romantic. That was how he felt at sea, as they approached a prize ripe for the taking. He enjoyed the violence that followed well enough, as long as he was on the winning side, and when they found a woman on a ship...

He was distracted by a movement at the tree line. His first impulse was to call for help, but then Ginandjar thought of how the others would make fun of him when it turned out to be a monkey or a little forest deer. Nothing at all, he told himself, but then decided he should check it out. If nothing else, the lonely walk down toward the forest would prove something to himself.

Ginandjar reached the spot where he'd imagined movement, but he saw nothing. He was no woodsman, granted, but he knew enough to recognize footprints in soft, wet earth. There was no sign of— Wait! Was that the imprint of a boot heel, behind the tree?

He stepped in closer to investigate. Ginandjar held his rifle ready.

But it didn't help him as an arm came out of nowhere and the cold steel of a knife blade kissed his throat.

"One word, one move," a voice told him in English. "One twitch, and by the time I kill your playmates, you'll be cold."

Sanctuary

A RUNNER CAME for Nguyen when the seaplane was still five miles out, before its twin engines were audible from the beach. Nguyen went out to wait for it, taking a pair of security men with him down to the sand. A boat was already standing by, so Lee wouldn't have to get his feet wet when he came ashore.

Nguyen had been a bit surprised that Lee planned to visit. Even after learning the enemy had phoned Lee's home, suggesting that he might be next in line for an attack, the move made little sense from Nguyen's point of view. If *he* were running from a foe who'd already attacked one island base and wiped out thirty men, he would've tried to lose himself in some great city for a while. Not Singapore, of course, but possibly Manila, Bangkok or Yangon. If it was serious enough— and this appeared to qualify—he might run as far as Calcutta or Tokyo, kill a few weeks in some place where no one knew his face or name, until the trouble at home had blown over.

Lee had a different idea. Instead of getting out he was on his way to the very island where their hostages were caged. Nguyen hoped it wasn't a fatal error, but he hadn't felt entitled to give Lee advice when none was sought. He had been ordered to prepare his master's quarters and provide extra security. Beyond that, nothing was required of him except to squeeze some useful information from the woman he had bagged in Singapore. He had but one job at the moment—and so far, it had defeated him.

Nguyen admired the woman's spirit, even as he tried to break it. She frustrated and infuriated him, but he controlled his feelings with an effort, knowing that a fatal slip would scuttle any chance of learning what she knew—and, at the same time, would make Nguyen fresh meat for Lee's exterminators. He'd failed once already, and Lee had made it crystal clear that he was living now on borrowed time. One more mistake, one failure to complete a mission of whatever magnitude, and he could be the next one strapped to a table, screaming his life away.

He saw the seaplane now, a speck on the western horizon, growing larger and more distinct by the moment. For a mad instant he wondered what would happen if that speck suddenly vanished or exploded into roiling flames. He would be free of Lee's orders, but was he strong enough to lead the pack himself? Would anyone support his bid for power? How many challengers would he be forced to kill—and would the men obey him willingly, without Lee's threat behind him? Did they blame him for their losses of the past few days?

It would be risky to challenge Lee, all the more so just now, when so many enemies were out for his blood. The wise thing, Nguyen reasoned, might be to hang back and see what became of his master in the next few days. The problem might well take care of itself, and if someone eliminated Lee, Nguyen could always step into his place on a temporary basis. Once the men became accustomed to his leadership—and once he had Lee's elite security team in his pocket—it would be that much harder for a challenger to unseat him.

Something to think about, at least. But it meant nothing if he wound up dead beside Lee, at the hands of their persistent foes. The enemy had seen him now, and nearly killed him on the waterfront in Singapore. They might not know his name, but Nguyen couldn't count on it. He would assume the worst and act accordingly to save himself.

Lee's plane was losing altitude, throttling back as it prepared for touchdown in the sheltered cove. Nguyen signaled the boat crew to push off and meet it. Lee's mood wouldn't improve if lackeys kept him waiting, and since Nguyen was about to greet him with bad news, he needed all the help that he could get.

Surabaya, Indonesia

THE CAPTIVE'S NAME was Abadi Ginandjar. He had required no great persuasion to inform them that Lee had left the estate several hours earlier, around the time of Bolan's phone call. Lee hadn't precisely fled the premises, but there'd been no time wasted packing for his unexpected trip. The pirate chief had taken half a dozen gunmen with him, leaving others at his home to wait for any trouble that might come their way.

Yun had interrogated enough prisoners—watched them sweat under hot lights while their brains churned, fabricating lies—that he could tell their man was holding something back. He couldn't say exactly what it was, or whether it would help them find Lee, but there was something this one didn't want to share.

After discovering that Lee had eluded them, they'd dragged their prisoner back to the car at gunpoint, Yun riding with him in the back seat while the American drove, seeking a place where they could have some time alone, uninterrupted, to extract whatever knowledge Ginandjar possessed. They'd found a rest stop outside Surabaya and marched their prisoner into the lavatory built of breeze blocks, squalid on the inside from a lack of maintenance. It was as good a place as any for the man to talk or die.

Yun watched the door and waited while his partner did the work. Their captive spoke enough English to understand the questions and respond coherently, although he seemed intent on pleading ignorance to everything except his own name and the time of day. He claimed to think Lee was a "famous man" who needed armed guards at his home because of "business competition." On his own behalf, the hostage claimed he'd never been arrested—a transparent lie, exposed by crude tattoos from prison artists on his arms—and then admitted that he'd had "some little problems" in his youth. Predictably, he'd seen no hostages and he knew nothing about murder, kidnapping or piracy.

Yun knew his partner's patience was exhausted when he heard the *click-clack* of a pistol slide. Abadi Ginandjar began to speak more rapidly, but it was still the same evasive patter, offered with a mounting note of desperation. He would gladly help, of course, if he knew anything, but since he was a simple peasant, kept in total ignorance—

The first shot echoed through the lavatory blockhouse like a thunderclap. The hostage yelped and cowered, pleading for his life. When Yun glanced cautiously around the corner, Ginandjar was crouching in a corner of the wall, between a urinal and the partition of a toilet stall. He held both hands in front of him, as if his palms were somehow bulletproof.

"We're out of time," Bolan said. "If you've got nothing useful for me, try a prayer."

The pirate blubbered, pleading for his life. Yun didn't know if they were honest tears, but he'd have bet the fear was real. His partner listened for another moment, shook his head, and aimed his pistol at the Ginandjar's face.

"No! Wait!" the hostage wailed.

"What for?"

"There is a place where hostages were taken in the past. I'm told that some were held for ransom there. Myself, I've never seen—"

The second shot drew blood.

Yun flinched, surprised at the move and the ungodly scream that followed it. Ginandjar clutched his shattered knee and wallowed on the filthy concrete floor. Bolan watched him, resolute, the pistol in his hand unwavering.

"The place," he said, raising his voice above the pirate's moans and curses. "You've got one last chance."

Ginandjar raised his hands again, blood dripping from the palms. "An island! I believe it has no name."

"Give me directions, then," Bolan said.

"South of Lombok, maybe one hundred kilometers. Not sure."

Bolan glanced across the room at Yun, a question in his eyes. "I know Lombok," Yun told him. "It's two islands east of us, beyond Bali. As for the rest, who knows?"

The American turned back to the prisoner and said, "I think you're lying."

"No lie!" Ginandjar said. "You boss!"

Bolan's face was grim when he asked Yun, "What do you think?"

"I think he tells the truth," Yun said. "He's too frightened to lie."

"Too frightened, yes!" the pirate groveled.

"Not quite," Bolan said, and fired another shot that silenced Abadi Ginandjar's fawning voice.

"We've got no coordinates. You know what this means, right?"

Yun wasn't sure. "Tell me."

"We need your flying friend again."

South Java coast

SHAZRIL HADZRAMI TRIED to cop an attitude the second time Yun called him on the cell phone, but he finally agreed to make another run at the same rates as last time, when Yun promised it would clear the slate between them.

"Until next time, anyway," he said, after the link was broken.

Bolan left the choice of meeting points to Yun and the pilot, less concerned about a trap this time, since Hadzrami had proved himself earlier. Bolan would still be on guard, but he let his thoughts ramble, examining hazards that still lay ahead on the last, desperate leg of their quest. Driving south in the sedan, Yun silent and thoughtful in the shotgun seat, Bolan had time to examine the upcoming hurdles.

The first and most obvious problem would be simply finding a nameless, presumably uncharted island for which they possessed no coordinates. It would be easy to miss in the Indian Ocean, searching with a single, small seaplane. They might never find it at all. And if they did, there was no guarantee that Lee or the captives they sought would be there. It might all be for nothing, a huge waste of time and energy, while Lee slipped away to parts unknown and his soldiers got rid of the hostages.

There was no point in dwelling on that bleak scenario, so Bolan moved on. The rest of their potential problems all revolved around scenarios in which they managed to find the island with Lee and/or the hostages in place. It might come down to one or the other, Bolan realized, and if they had a chance to free the prisoners without eliminating Lee, he'd have to settle—for the moment, anyway. Hirawa might be ready for another round of fighting, if the pirates hadn't injured her too badly, but the Ryans were straight-up civilians with no battle skills of any kind. Bolan had been dispatched to bring them home, not drag them from one deadly situation to another while he chased Lee around the Asian continent.

The flip side of that play was if they found Lee on the island, but the hostages were either dead already or imprisoned somewhere else. Bolan was ready—more than ready—to confront the pirate chief, but there was no way to insure that they could capture Lee or any of his men alive for questioning, if Hirawa and the Ryans were missing in action. Revenge might be sweet, but it couldn't compare to the taste of success. And in Bolan's mind, anything short of a live rescue across the board would rank as failure.

If and when they found the island they were seeking, the approach would be a problem. Only gliders and balloons were silent on an aerial approach, and sound would carry farther over open water than on land. If there were sentries posted, it would be a challenge to avoid them, and it might well prove to be impossible. An unarmed seaplane made an easy mark for any shooter worth his salt, or Lee could always let them land and have a firing squad greet them as they came ashore. Toss in the fact that they had no idea how many shooters would be posted on the island, or what kind of hardware they were carrying, and it came down to one hell of a gamble.

Bolan's mind harked back to the question Brognola had asked him at Arlington, the day he laid out the mission: What else is new? And Bolan's answer was the same.

Nothing.

Long odds and shaky futures were his stock-in-trade. He'd stayed alive this long by applying skill and nerve in equal measure to problems that would've sent the average man— hell, the average soldier—running for cover in a heartbeat. Uncertainty didn't frighten Bolan, but it did make him more cautious. Wild-ass warriors who thought nothing of the hazards in their path were normally short-lived and buried with their medals. Bolan, for his part, was in no rush to join them.

They found the spot Shazril Hadzrami had selected for their meeting, waiting in the car and talking through their options one by one, until the sound of airplane engines cut through conversation, drawing Yun and Bolan to the sheltered beach. Hadzrami greeted them with smiles and pocketed the money Bolan handed him without stopping to count it.

"So, where are we going this time?" he asked Yun.

The cop briefed him, Hadzrami frowning at the vague directions. Bolan half expected him to say the search was hopeless, but instead he startled them.

"Pirates, you say?" Hadzrami said. "I think I know this place."

12

The Island

Flying south, their pilot briefly told them how he knew the place. He kept it short on details, but it wasn't hard to fill in the blanks, since Bolan knew Hadzrami was a smuggler. He'd been hired to ferry certain merchandise—most likely arms and ammunition—from a dealer in Malaysia to the island stronghold of a group he first believed were revolutionaries. Politics didn't concern him, if the price was right, but on arrival he'd seen things that made him wonder who the island people really were.

Two things in particular had struck Hadzrami as unusual. First, he'd seen two luxury boats—a yacht and a large cabin cruiser—anchored in the cove where he off-loaded his cargo, both vessels receiving a hasty paint job where they sat. Second, and stranger yet, had been the sight of two men walking on the beach. One led the other on a kind of leash or halter, the bound man blindfolded and naked, except for baggy shorts. Hadzrami couldn't swear to it, but he thought the blindfolded man bore a strong resemblance to the French captain of a hijacked oil tanker who made headlines in Kuala Lumpur some weeks later, after he was ransomed from pirates.

It was good enough for Bolan, as a start. The best part, though, was Hadzrami's assurance that he could set them down on the south shore of the island, three or four miles away from the north-shore pirate camp. Circling wide of the mark, he was confident they could approach the island without being seen. Unless someone happened to be standing watch to the south when they landed. Or hunting in the woods. Or any of a hundred other things that could go wrong and strand them on a beach bristling with guns. They could be dead in an instant—but that was the risk Bolan took every time he went out in the field.

They were eighty minutes outside Java when their pilot found the island. It sat small and dark on the horizon, barely visible with the tropic night coming on. Hadzrami had already killed his running lights, and now he held a course that would take them well west of the island until he circled back for a sea landing in the dark. He gave them a don't-worry smile and flew on, leaving Bolan and Yun to double-check their gear for the assault.

Bolan had used roughly one-third of his ammunition for the AKMS rifle so far, and three of his ten frag grenades. He could've used more ammo, but the good news was that he could likely pick up more from his enemies during the strike. David Yun had already put on his war face, frowning as he cleared the chamber of his AK-47, then reloaded it and worked the bolt. He checked the Daewoo pistol last, topping off its magazine before he slid it back into the pistol grip.

When he met Bolan's eyes, Yun asked, "You think she's dead?"

Bolan didn't have to ask who *she* was. "I don't know," he replied honestly. "There's a chance that we don't even have the right place."

"It feels right. I have faith."

Couldn't hurt, Bolan thought. But it might not help, either. An old aphorism said there were no atheists in foxholes, but he knew from personal experience that praying didn't guarantee a soldier's safety when the feces hit the fan.

Bolan felt the seaplane banking, looping slowly into its long turn back toward the island. Soon they were losing altitude, dropping toward touchdown. It was full dark outside the Grumman's windows, nothing he could do but trust the pilot's skill and knowledge of the sea. Their landing was smoother than he expected, and he took it as a hopeful sign that they hadn't drawn fire coming in.

"Go now!" Hadzrami said. "Not much time."

Their transportation from the seaplane to the beach was an inflatable raft with two small aluminum oars. Unlike most life rafts, colored red or bright orange for high visibility at sea, this one was black, the oars spray-painted to match. They would make less conspicuous targets that way, but it would still only take one bullet to sink them.

They shoved the raft clear, Bolan yanking the rip cord to inflate it as soon as they got it through the Grumman's door. It inflated in seconds, Bolan holding the tether while Yun went aboard. The Executioner followed close behind him, careful not to tip the raft or let his weapons gouge the rubber skin.

Shazril Hadzrami had arranged to wait for them this time, but he wouldn't wait there. He closed the door behind them, watched them paddle clear, then switched the Grumman's engines on and powered off into the dark.

Alone, the warriors paddled silently toward shore.

"YOU WERE CORRECT," Nguyen Tre Minh announced, reentering the hut. "The watchers heard a plane."

"What did they see?" It took an effort for Lee to keep the anger from his voice.

"Nothing," Nguyen replied.

"No lights?"

"No, sir."

"Do you not find that curious?" Lee asked.

"Perhaps it was too far away."

"Or else the pilot wanted to remain invisible."

Nguyen let that sink in before he answered. "Searching will be difficult at night, sir."

"Not along the shore," Lee replied. "We have no airstrip, so a landing must be made at sea. Send out the boats."

"Yes, sir."

Lee heard Nguyen shouting outside, rallying a handful of men to take the speedboats and search in opposite directions, following the island's coastline. It was relatively small, no more than fifteen miles around from start to finish. If they hurried, they might still be able to surprise a seaplane on the deck before the pilot had a chance to flee.

Or maybe they would find nothing at all.

Lee admitted to himself that he was suffering from an attack of nerves. Why not? He had been dogged by unknown, unseen enemies for days on end, his soldiers slaughtered in a series of engagements that should rightfully have ended any threat to his domain. It was enough to trouble any man who still possessed the instinct for self-preservation and the common sense to recognize a threat. Lee was concerned enough to leave his home and travel there, to share primitive quarters with Nguyen while they tried to resolve the issue, and his fear had traveled with him.

There was nothing necessarily mysterious about an airplane passing in the night, and yet...

He heard the speedboats revving at their dock, accelerating into open water, then retreating as they nosed in opposite directions. They'd meet and pass each other on the north side of the island, each team covering the full perimeter before returning to the pier. If they met any strangers on the way, his men knew what to do.

Nguyen returned, a satisfied expression on his face. "We'll soon know whether there is anything to see," he said.

Lee knew his first lieutenant would be pleased to let the subject of their interrupted conversation slide, but he wasn't inclined to let that happen. Straight-faced, he reminded Nguyen, "You were just explaining why you've failed to make the woman talk, so far."

"She is resilient," Nguyen said defensively. "Your observer will tell you—"

"*Has* told me," Lee said, interrupting. "Have you done your best? Are you finished?"

"No, sir. She will talk, I promise you."

"But when?"

The question troubled Nguyen, but he tried to put a brave face on it. "Certainly within the next—"

Lee never heard his estimate. Instead, a burst of automatic rifle fire tore through the camp and several voices started shouting simultaneously, cursing, barking orders, asking questions. Lee felt his stomach twist into a knot, a headache pulsing silently to life behind his eyes.

"Your guards?" he asked Nguyen, his voice tight with apprehension.

"I'll find out, sir!" Nguyen turned to leave, was reaching for the doorknob when the shock wave of a powerful explosion rattled walls and windows in his quarters.

Not the guards, Lee thought. Most definitely not.

"I want a weapon," he commanded. "Now!"

THE TWO-MILE MARCH was rigorous but not prohibitive. Yun held the pace his partner set, and might've tried to pass him, but the tall American clearly had more experience and greater skill at jungle fighting. Yun would be no use to Hirawa if he blundered off a cliff or walked into a trap before he learned if she was even on the island.

Yun wasn't sure exactly when his feelings for Hirawa had begun to change. The American saw it in his eyes but kept the knowledge to himself, not criticizing Yun for his unprofessional emotions. It kept the peace between them, but he felt his partner watching him more closely now, as if expecting him to take some foolish action that would kill them both. Yun understood the big man's attitude, but he had no designs on martyrdom.

He was simply, amazingly, falling in love.

He pushed those feelings from his mind as they approached the pirate camp. They'd heard speedboats behind them, prowling on the south coast of the island, after they were well ashore. Their raft was hidden in the jungle, and he had no fear that searchers on the water would detect it in the dark.

Scanning the compound from the tree line, he was instantly reminded of the camp on Wewak Island, but Yun reckoned there were more men there than in the other settlement. More men would mean more guns, and thus a better chance of getting killed. He searched in vain for any vestige of Hirawa or the other hostages, but knew it was unlikely they'd be let out after nightfall. There were several huts that might serve well as makeshift prison cells—or quarters for Lee Sun and Nguyen Tre Minh.

Bolan nudged him, pointing toward the cove that lay beyond the camp's pale strip of beach. A fair-sized seaplane rode at anchor near the wooden dock that ran some fifty feet from shore into the water.

"Lee's plane?" Yun asked him, whispering.

Bolan shrugged. "Whoever it belongs to," he replied, "we need to take it out before they have a chance to fly."

The plane was close enough to hit with rifle fire from where they were, but Yun couldn't have guaranteed the shots would damage it beyond all capability of taking flight. The American seemed to share his thought, sweeping the camp with narrowed eyes before he said, "I'll take the left and you find a place that suits you on the right. Wait for my signal."

"Okay."

It hadn't taken long for Yun to find his place and settle in to wait. He knew the signal would be something obvious, impossible to miss. Yun spent his time gauging the distance to prospective targets, plotting fields of fire. When it was time to kill, he would be ready and he wouldn't hesitate.

Yun noted pirates moving freely in the camp, most of them armed. Despite the speedboats out on what appeared to be security patrols, there was no visible excitement in the compound. He was unsure whether anyone had heard their plane approaching or, if so, whether they'd paid attention to the sound. From what he saw now, there was no attempt in progress to prepare the camp for an attack.

So much the better. They might still have a chance.

He didn't see his partner moving closer to the camp, but

Yun knew when he got there. Suddenly a muzzle-flash lit up the darkness on the far side of the compound and he saw two pirates fall as if their legs were suddenly yanked out from under them by trip wires. Others poured at once from huts and tents, presenting Yun with several dozen targets on the move. They weren't returning fire so far, but that would change as soon as one of them decided that he'd found a likely target in the shadows ranged about the camp.

Instead of giving them a mark to shoot at, the American lobbed one of his hand grenades. Yun didn't see it coming, but the impact was impossible to miss. One of the larger tents near his position on the west appeared to swell, floating on tongues of yellow flame, until the canvas vanished in a cloud of smoke. The thunderclap of the explosion swallowed screams, as men and parts of men were airborne, fleshy shrapnel hurtling through the night.

Yun sighted down the barrel of his AK-47, picking out a clutch of pirates running toward the scene of the explosion, shouting among themselves. They all had automatic weapons, but there'd be no opportunity to use them if Yun did his work efficiently.

He took a breath and held it, tightening his finger on the rifle's trigger, and began to cut them down.

BOLAN WAS MOVING by the time his first grenade exploded, taking down a tent he guessed was large enough to house three pirates, maybe four. The blast spread chaos, drawing some defenders, even as it frightened others into flight. They recognized a raid in progress, but they couldn't get behind an organized response until they had at least one clear-cut target, and he meant to keep them in the dark as long as possible.

He moved along the tree line, staying under cover while his enemies fired random bursts into the forest. Two or three of them were close enough by accident to make him duck and dodge, but most were firing back along the dark line of trees near the flattened and smoldering tent. Bolan had nearly reached the point where jungle gave way to open beach. He was calculating his next move, when a figure rose in front of him. The stranger held a pistol, uttering some indecipherable question or command. Without a second's hesitation, Bolan slapped the gun aside and drove his rifle butt into the pirate's larynx, feeling the cartilage snap on impact. The dying man slumped backward, trying desperately to breathe, and Bolan followed him. He brought the AKMS down a second time, crushing the pirate's skull, but not before his adversary squeezed off a reflexive pistol shot.

The Executioner stood for a moment and waited, watching to see if any other pirates responded, but the gunshot was lost in the general din from the camp. One shot, more or less, meant no more than a sneeze in the midst of a cyclone.

Bolan moved toward the beach, marking the sound of firing on the far side of the camp, where Yun was keeping more of their enemies busy. Bolan hoped the cop would be all right, but Yun was on his own for now. Before the Executioner could start to think about a hostage search inside the compound, he needed to cripple the seaplane and boats.

The speedboats on patrol hadn't returned, but there were three more tied up to the pier, along with the seaplane he thought might belong to Lee. If there'd been sentries posted on the boats and plane, they'd long since fallen back into the camp and joined the chaos there. Bolan found no one to oppose him, no one watching as he left the trees and ran across the moonlit sand to reach the pier.

He moved quickly, firing two rifle shots into each speedboat's engine, glancing back toward the camp after each report to see if he'd been noticed. So far the pirates were distracted by Yun and their dueling with shadows along the western edge of the camp. Bolan was aiming at the seaplane's engine cowling when a roar behind him announced one patrol boat's return. A spotlight framed him, and an automatic weapon started hammering across the water, throwing slugs his way.

Bolan spun to face the new threat, dropping prone on the

rough planks of the pier. There were two men in the speedboat, and he concentrated on the pilot, squeezing off a short burst through the windshield as the streamlined craft sped toward him, locked on a collision course.

The pilot doubtless meant to turn away before he hit the pier, but Bolan's rifle fire erased that option when it drilled his chest and stopped his heart. The pirate toppled forward, slumped across the open throttle as his sidekick tried to pull him back. Deadweight resisted the intrusion, and the boat held to its course, while Bolan broke and ran back toward the beach. He turned in time to see the speedboat hit, then somersault out of the water, flipping over once before it struck the seaplane and exploded into leaping flames.

HIRAWA SACHIKO KNEW it was a trick when her interrogators released her, but she didn't care. The walk back to the hut she shared with Kim and Jeffrey Ryan had been painful, but the relief of simply standing and moving after hours on the table compensated for the pangs she felt in joints and muscles. Dressed in an old man's shirt and jeans, she made a curious spectacle, wincing when she sat, the Ryans making useless sympathetic noises, but she'd learned a critical lesson. Every second of freedom was precious—and certainly worth fighting for.

She'd made her mind up to resist when they came back for her, as Nguyen and his goons inevitably would. Or so she'd thought, at least, until the storm of gunfire and explosions rocked the compound and her captors suddenly became the hunted.

The Ryans were huddled in a corner, cringing, as gunfire raked the camp. Hirawa stretched out on the floor, making herself the smallest target possible, though part of her felt she should jump and shout for joy. The shooting had to mean that David Yun and Mike Belasko had arrived. No other explanation was conceivable. And yet, while that thought gave her hope, she also knew it didn't guarantee she or the Ryans would survive.

"Get down!" she whispered at them. "Lie on the floor!"

Kim Ryan blinked at her. "What did you—?"

Her question was cut off by bullets punching through the wall above her head. Kim squealed in fright, her husband cursing as he took both of them down, winding up huddled on the bare dirt floor. Hirawa watched them for a moment, knowing she should feel more pity, but there was something about her fellow captives, even in adversity, that set her teeth on edge. Perhaps it was a combination of moneyed arrogance and wide-eyed innocence that made her wonder how they'd managed to survive this long.

They were nothing to her, after all she had suffered—from loss of her parents to torture by Lee's goon squad. The Ryans were her partner's problem, his commitment. Hirawa, for her part, would be satisfied with revenge.

And yet...

"We have to get out of here," she told them, repeating it when they gaped at her, as if she were speaking Japanese instead of English.

"What?" Kim asked, bewildered.

"How?" Ryan demanded.

"I don't know," she replied honestly. "But we can't wait for them to find us."

"Them?" Ryan's confusion had deepened. "Who's them?"

"Never mind. Will you help me or not?"

He shook his head. "Help you do what?"

"We obviously don't have time to dig a tunnel," Hirawa said, as if explaining to a child. "It has to be the door."

"The door's locked," Kim reminded her.

"Which means we'll have to break it down."

"The guards—"

"Are busy now, in case you hadn't noticed. We won't have another chance like this."

Ryan frowned at the idea. "Hey, I don't know."

"Stay here, then," she suggested. "And to hell with both of you!"

Hirawa stood, braced for the impact of a bullet if more wild rounds came her way, and moved to stand before the door. Her first kick sent pain lancing through her body, but she bit her lip and tried again. Around the third or fourth kick, Ryan rose to stand beside her, stopping Hirawa with a hand on her shoulder.

"Let me try it," he said, and dropped into a football crouch before flinging himself headlong at the door. He rebounded with a curse, but tried again before the pain could register. On his third try, the door ripped free and dropped him sprawling in the dust outside.

Hirawa half expected someone to shoot Ryan at once, but the pirates were obviously too distracted to notice the breakout in progress. Seizing the moment, she turned to Kim and said, "Come on! We haven't got much time."

Kim hesitated, trembling where she sat. "I can't," she said.

"They'll kill you if they find the door like this," Hirawa told her, almost certain it was true.

"Oh, God!"

Ryan grabbed his wife and hauled her to her feet. "Come on, for Christ's sake! Let's get out of here!"

He let Hirawa lead, which would've pleased her if there'd been time to consider it. Without a backward glance, she left the hut, the Ryans on her heels. They were in time to watch the generator-powered lights wink out and plunge the compound into darkness streaked with fire.

NGUYEN TRE MINH crouched in the shadow of a hut, some sixty paces from the beach, and watched the seaplane burn. Its detonation had splashed burning fuel across the speedboats tethered to the pier, and they were burning, too. Their fuel tanks blew up, one after another, as if some high-altitude aircraft was dropping bombs around the pier.

Nguyen clutched the Walther MPK machine pistol he'd taken from the camp's communal armory and watched as flames devoured his only means of escape from the island. No, he realized, that wasn't strictly true. One speedboat still remained, from the pair he had sent on patrol, but it hadn't come back yet and might not return if the pirates on board decided to save themselves instead of joining the fight. Nguyen wouldn't blame them if they made that choice, but if they did come back, he'd gladly commandeer the boat, giving them the chance to jump or take him north out of harm's way.

Lee Sun could look out for himself.

Nguyen was finished. He was out. Assuming he could put the camp behind him without getting killed, he didn't care what happened to his leader or the men he'd once commanded. There was obviously nothing left for him—or for Lee—that wouldn't be destroyed before their enemies were done.

All over two Americans, he thought, and shook his head, disgusted. Typically, he didn't blame himself or even stop to think that he might share responsibility for the debacle. Lee ran the show. He made the rules, and anything that followed from his orders was the master's ultimate responsibility.

Thus self-absolved, Nguyen returned his thoughts to getting out alive. He didn't know if it was possible, but one thing struck him as a certainty. He'd have a better chance if he had an insurance policy—and what better protection could he have than the hostages? They could serve as human shields for his getaway or as bargaining chips if he ran out of luck and was halted in flight. If he could slip out undetected, it would be a simple matter to dispose of them at leisure, somewhere in the forest.

Fired up with new determination, Nguyen left his hiding place and worked his way back toward the hut where the three prisoners were kept. He'd meant to fetch the Japanese woman before this, for further interrogation, but the surprise attack had canceled his plans. She should be waiting for him now with the Americans. Show them a gun and they would follow orders quietly—or he could simply kill them where they stood and flee the camp alone. In either case he'd have the satisfaction of destroying those he blamed for his misfortune of the past few days.

It was a perilous advance, strangers firing from the camp's perimeter while his own men sprayed bullets at shadows, but Nguyen reached the hut at last. He came in from behind it, circling cautiously around—and stopped dead as he found the door not only open, but completely off its hinges, lying in the dirt.

The hostages were gone.

Rage seized him as he scanned the darkened camp, searching for someone—anyone—to serve as fitting target for his wrath.

BOLAN PICKED himself up, shook the sand from his rifle, and ran for cover in the shadow of the nearest hut. The camp had gone dark and it wasn't his doing, leaving Bolan to speculate that Yun or one of the trigger-happy pirates had damaged the compound's generator. Bolan would've done it himself, given half a chance, but someone had beat him to the punch and he was thankful for the darkness as he made his next move, easing cautiously around the hut and homing on the heart of the compound.

He still didn't know where the hostages were caged, but it stood to reason they'd be kept in a location that was easy to guard, conveniently located. They wouldn't be kept on the outskirts of camp, where a short run would bring them to cover and stymie pursuit. If they were in the middle of the camp, surrounded by enemies, it made escape doubly difficult, doubly dangerous for hostages and would-be rescuers alike.

The darkness helped him navigate, giving the Executioner at least a fighting chance to pass unnoticed through the milling ranks of his foes. Where one or two of them marked him in transit, passing close enough to see his face or noting the discrepancy in size, he dealt with them individually. Single shots or crushing buttstrokes with the AKMS's stock cleared his path through the compound, leaving crumpled bodies in his wake.

And still he wasn't sure exactly what he was looking for.

A hut, he calculated, rather than a tent. Lee and his aides would want the captives penned by something more secure than canvas. That reduced the structures he would have to search by some two-thirds, since tents were dominant throughout the camp. Most of them served as sleeping quarters for the pirates, with a larger, open tent filling the function of a mess hall on the east side of the camp. The huts, made out of corrugated tin or plywood, occupied the center of the compound, situated in a layout that was roughly square. Somewhere nearby, in one of them, Bolan was hopeful he would find Hirawa and the Ryans still alive.

Bolan was startled when he found the prison hut almost by accident.

It was his second try, the first hut having housed a radio, which he disabled with a burst of AK fire, though none of Lee's pirates had so far tried to use it. By removing the temptation, he insured that there would be no reinforcements riding to the rescue while his back was turned.

His next stop was a six-by-ten-foot structure, windowless, that would have served well as a cage—if it had still possessed a door. At first he thought the fallen door had been jarred loose by gunfire, but a closer look revealed no bullet scars to wood or hinges. Rather, Bolan saw, the door had been knocked down from the inside. Raw wood revealed where a secure hasp had been broken free at the same time. He glanced around for enemies, saw none in striking range, and quickly knelt to check the door itself.

It had been locked from the outside, before brute force defeated hasp and hinges all at once. He ducked inside the hut, found no one there and quickly doubled back. Where had they gone? Were they pursued by pirates as they fled or had they slipped away unseen?

The answers still eluded Bolan when a shout revealed that he'd been spotted and a swarm of bullets sang around him in the dark.

13

David Yun fed his AK-47 a fresh magazine as he moved along the tree line, circling to the east. Behind him three or four pirates leveled a blistering fire into the cover he'd occupied moments earlier, their bullets flaying bark from trees and chopping forest undergrowth to ragged stubble.

When he'd put some space between himself and the shooters, Yun paused for a moment and surveyed the camp. Several huts were in flames now, their flickering light casting surrealistic shadows, concealing as much as it revealed. Along the pier speedboats and Lee's seaplane had burned to the waterline, and the dock itself was on fire. A handful of pirates ran up and down the beach, waving and shouting at the blackened hulks of their getaway vehicles, but they could go no farther, short of swimming out to sea.

Yun turned back to the pirates who believed they'd pinned him down. He checked for other enemies nearby, then stepped from cover, kneeling as he leaned against the nearest tree for balance, sighting on his targets in the firelight. They were easy, clumped together and distracted by the sound of their own weapons, pouring rounds into the forest. It only took one burst, raking the group from left to right, and they went down like bowling pins.

Yun felt nothing for them, and wondered if that should

disturb him. He didn't have time to consider it now, but perhaps at some time in the future, away from this place—if he lived through the night. If he didn't, then none of it mattered, regardless.

But while he lived Yun had a job to do. There were hostages to be found and delivered from bondage, Hirawa and the Ryans waiting for him somewhere in the camp. Or were they? Yun still had no proof that they were there, but he was bound to look. That meant leaving the shadows and scouring the camp, danger be damned.

His first route brought him to a crude brick oven someone had constructed at the south end of the mess tent. He thought it smelled of smoke and charcoal, but that could've been the fires in camp. Yun scanned the mess tent and found no one hiding there, then broke for the next nearest cover, sliding in beside a hut whose plywood walls were pocked with bullet holes. Moving around the hut, he found the door ajar and nudged it open with the muzzle of his weapon, leaning in to check for lurking foes.

A pirate leaped at Yun from the shadows, swinging a machete overhand. Yun raised his AK-47 to deflect the blow and thereby saved himself, but toppled over backward as the charging man slammed into him. They rolled together in the dirt, Yun taking hits along his flank with the flat of the machete blade, feeling a burn across his rib cage as the cutting edge found flesh. He fought with knees and elbows and the rifle in his hands, clubbing his adversary with the butt and barrel, back and forth, until the pirate shuddered and lay still. Yun struck him twice more in the face and throat to keep him down, then rolled away and scrambled to his feet.

The wound beneath his arm bled freely, but it wasn't deep and wouldn't slow him, if he could stand the nagging pain. Yun doubled back to check the hut again, found no one else inside and moved on to the next in line. The door on this one had been battered from its hinges, seemingly from the inside. He ducked into the hut, checking the space where someone had been recently confined, wishing that he had skills to let him read the tracks outside and thus pursue the fleeing hostages.

The hut was scarred with many bullet holes, firelight showing through the walls in abstract patterns. Spent brass crunched beneath Yun's boots, and when he stooped to roll a cartridge case between his fingertips he found it warm. The last shots fired outside the prison hut were recent, but he searched in vain for bodies of the hostages. If they weren't shot while fleeing, Yun decided, maybe they'd been rescued. By Belasko? There was no one else to help them in the compound.

Yun could make nothing of the evidence, such as it was. For all he knew, Hirawa and the Ryans had escaped, but then had been recaptured and removed to some other location. Where? Another hut or someplace well outside the camp?

Another hand grenade exploded in the compound, shaking Yun out of his private thoughts. Without a clue where he should seek the prisoners, Yun knew he had to start somewhere, anywhere that he hadn't already looked until he'd checked them all.

And then?

He didn't know, but he would search the whole damned island if it came to that.

Dogged and relentless, Yun moved on in search of someone he could save.

LEE SUN WASN'T afraid of death. He didn't welcome it, but he had seen enough of life, from slum to palace, that he had no fear of any higher power lurking in the wings to punish those who died. Men made their own heaven or hell on earth, he was convinced, and Lee had seen both in his time. As far as hell on earth was concerned, he thought the camp offered a fair preview.

The trick now would be getting out of hell alive.

One of the bodyguards he'd brought from Surabaya was already dead, dropped by a stray round outside Nguyen's quarters. The other crouched beside Lee now, doing his best to protect his master. Unfortunately, there was only so much he could do, and finding a way off the island didn't seem to be included.

The seaplane was gone, as were most of the speedboats. Lee knew there was one boat remaining, but it hadn't returned from patrol and he feared the men aboard it had turned coward, fleeing for their lives to parts unknown. Without some method of communication, he couldn't appeal for them to come back and retrieve him.

Stranded.

Lee had no fear of being permanently trapped, but neither was the distant future foremost in his mind. He was in danger now, and if the raiders didn't kill him, there was still a possibility that military or police patrols might find him and attempt to prosecute for any one of several hundred felonies he had committed during recent years. Lee needed to get off the island soon, but he was at a loss as to the method of escape.

Logic dictated that the first thing he had to do was to get out of the camp and seek refuge in the forest. Lee hadn't explored the island—this was only his third visit since the compound was established—and he wished that Nguyen hadn't run off and left him on his own. It was the last straw with his *ex*-lieutenant, Lee decided. If he saw Nguyen again, he'd waste no time on conversation with the spineless traitor. And if Nguyen managed to survive the night, he'd be a hunted man until the day Lee's trackers overtook him, wherever he tried to hide.

First, stay alive, Lee thought. He nudged his bodyguard and spoke to him in Cantonese, directing him to follow Lee and watch their backs as they made their way out of the camp. The pirate had a Daewoo K-1 A-1 carbine, while Lee carried the only weapon Nguyen had been able to find on short notice, an SR-88A carbine made in Singapore. The latter weighed nearly ten pounds, with its curved magazine of thirty 5.56 mm in place, and Lee had no extra ammunition for the unfamiliar weapon. Once again he cursed Nguyen, wishing the bastard would appear and make himself a target. It would only take a moment to—

"Come on!" Lee snapped himself out of his morbid reverie and started moving cautiously in the direction of the trees. It meant traversing eighty yards or so of open ground, littered with bodies where his men had been cut down by unseen guns or by their own undisciplined fire. If he could make it that far, Lee believed, he had a fighting chance.

It might've helped to know how many adversaries were involved in the attack but Lee had no way to determine numbers, much less who they were. Gunfire rang out on every side, and while he knew most of the shooters were his own men, firing at shadows, he couldn't be certain which muzzle-flashes belonged to hostile weapons. Neither could he take the risk of calling out to those he passed in the darkness, identifying himself by name, in case one or more of them were enemies.

It was humiliating, slinking out of camp like a deserter, but embarrassment was preferable to sudden death. If Lee lived to see the sun rise, he would find some way to name his enemies and punish them.

Lee and his bodyguard had covered half the distance from their starting point to the tree line without being halted, when they paused beside a tattered, sagging tent. The next bit would mean running flat-out, no cover for the final thirty-five or forty yards. It would be dangerous, but Lee thought they could make it if—

A thud behind him made Lee turn just in time to see his guard bolt from a crouch and take off running, back the way they'd come. Another heartbeat passed before Lee recognized the hand grenade and hurled himself away from it, too late to gain much distance from the lethal egg.

A blast of superheated air caught Lee in midstride and sent him somersaulting through the smoky air.

BOLAN HAD DROPPED below the spray of sniper fire outside the prison hut, spotting a muzzle-flash that seemed to match the rattle of incoming fire. It took two bursts from his Kalashnikov to put the shooter down, then Bolan rushed for new cover before another pirate had the chance to zero in.

He ran without particular direction, seeking only to avoid incoming fire. A bullet tugged his sleeve, another burning past his face so close that Bolan felt its hot breath on his cheek. He dropped and rolled against the north wall of a Quonset hut that could've been the compound's recreation hall or arsenal. The metal walls offered better protection than plywood, but only by a matter of degree. Full-metal jacket rounds from any modern military weapon would cut through the corrugated metal without losing their lethal velocity, and Bolan stayed close to the ground, worming his way along while the firefight blazed around him. He reached the northwest corner of the hut and risked a glance around it, scanning the camp for enemies or friends.

There was no sign of Yun or Hirawa, no trace of the Ryans from his present vantage point. Bolan was starting to believe the search might be a waste of time, but if he couldn't find the prisoners, at least he had a change to thin the ranks of his opponents. Only when the field was clear and he had time to search in peace would Bolan write off the others.

Movement across the compound drew the Executioner's eye. He watched two men running in fits and starts, ducking from one hut to the next. He couldn't be certain by firelight, but one of the runners bore a passing resemblance to Lee Sun, from the photos he'd seen in Kuala Lumpur.

Mirage or hard target?

Bolan didn't know, but the runners were definitely flesh and blood foes. It was enough for the moment. He reached down to his belt and freed one of the NR-330 frag grenades, slipping an index finger through the ring to draw its pin. Pushing up on his free hand, Bolan gauged the distance, cocked his arm and let fly, watching the deadly canister arc high across the intervening ground to drop between his targets.

One of them bolted instantly, running for all he was worth

to the north, flinging himself out of shrapnel range. His companion, the Lee look-alike, was slower to identify the danger, recoiling from the grenade when his brain recognized it. He was tossed like a rag doll when the blast caught him in a storm of smoke and shrapnel. Bolan couldn't see where he touched down at first. The soldier still waiting for a clear view of the fallen pirate when a bullet struck the metal wall above his head.

It was immediately followed by another and another, echoing on impact as they drilled the metal, making it vibrate with concussive force. Bolan turned to seek the source of danger, swinging his AKMS around to meet two gunners rushing toward him from his flank.

The closer of the two was twenty yards away when Bolan hit him with a rising burst that knocked the pirate tumbling through a wobbly back flip, landing crumpled on his side. The second pirate saw his comrade fall and veered off course, still firing as he ran but losing focus on his target, more concerned now with self-preservation than an easy kill.

Bolan tracked him, sighting down the length of his own prostrate body to lead the runner by a foot or so, stroking the Kalashnikov's trigger to release a short burst. At least a couple of the bullets found their mark, jolting the pirate off stride and spinning him around, his legs tangled up with one another as he fell. The shooter kept firing, but his rounds were wasted as he sprayed the camp behind him, burning up the last rounds in his magazine on empty air.

Bolan turned back to seek the man he thought might be Lee, but there was no trace of the fallen runner now. A shallow crater marked the point where Bolan's frag grenade had detonated, but the pirate it had downed was nowhere to be seen.

The Executioner rose and went to find him, searching for his quarry on the killing ground.

HIRAWA WAS AMAZED by the change in herself, her attitude and demeanor. She had always considered herself indepen-

dent, but that assessment had been made in the context of tra-
ditional Japanese family values and gender roles. A month
ago, if anyone had suggested that she would be fighting for
her life against pirates and drawing confidence from the experience, she'd have laughed in their faces and said they were
insane. Hirawa now wondered if perhaps she was the crazy
one, shrugging off her recent pain and throwing herself head-
on into the grim tasks of survival and revenge.

For even with the Ryans trailing her, trusting her to help
them escape, she knew that one achievement would be mean-
ingless without the other. If her family went unavenged, her
journey would've been for nothing—a colossal, agonizing
waste of time and energy.

She felt as much as heard the pirate rushing toward them
from the darkness on her left. He didn't seem to know or care
that they were prisoners, en route to freedom of a sort. She
only saw his features for an instant, as she launched a stunning kick into his face and took him down.

The impact didn't finish him, but he was groggy, stretched
out on his back, as Hirawa stood over him. He blinked at her,
confused, blood welling from his flattened nostrils, one hand
groping blindly for the weapon he had dropped. She hesitated
for a beat, then slammed a heel into his throat and finished
it. He shivered out the final seconds of his life before her,
while Hirawa claimed his fallen rifle for herself.

She recognized it as the same kind David Yun carried, or
possibly a knock-off. Yun had let her practice briefly with his
AK-47 on their boat ride, in what now felt like another century, another life. Hirawa was turning away from the body,
weapon in hand, when she remembered to check for extra ammunition magazines. The pirate wore a bandolier, which she
removed with only modest difficulty, somewhat startled to
discover that she didn't flinch from contact with the dead
man's still-warm flesh.

Hirawa found the Ryans watching her after she donned the
bandolier and checked the AK-47 to make sure it had a live
round in the chamber. Both of them were staring at her, but

with different expressions on their faces. Kim looked dazed, while Ryan couldn't conceal a hint of admiration. "You've got moves," he said, half whispering.

"I do what must be done," Hirawa replied. "Come on."

She still had no coherent plan. Belasko would've counseled her to lead the Ryans out of camp and hide them in the forest, find a safe place and wait for daylight to reveal the victors in the battle for the compound. That idea made sense, in terms of seeking safety first, and while Hirawa knew she shouldn't jeopardize the hostages, she likewise didn't want to leave the compound without punishing the men who had destroyed her family and made her past two months a living hell. She had responsibilities in both directions, but her blood cried out for vengeance, claiming priority over any obligation to strangers she barely knew.

All this she considered while they were in motion, moving in fits and starts toward the northern perimeter of the compound. Even with her mind racing, she was aware of movement all around them, dangers in the dark. She saw the pirate stepping out in front of them before Kim gasped aloud and Ryan pulled his wife back from the young man with the submachine gun in his hands.

Hirawa shot him without thinking, a short burst that almost got away from her before she fought down the AK's muzzle, but it did the job well enough. Her adversary dropped as if his legs had been yanked out from under him without firing a shot. She stooped to seize his weapon and was handing it to Ryan when a cold, familiar voice called out to her.

"There's more to you than I imagined, Sachiko."

She dropped the SMG and turned to face Nguyen Tre Minh. He stood no more than twenty feet away, holding an automatic rifle leveled from the waist.

"I hoped we'd meet again," Hirawa said.

"Did you?"

"Our business isn't finished yet."

"You're right," Nguyen replied. "I need your help to get away from here."

"We won't be traveling together," she informed him.

"No?" He twitched a smile at her. "Why not?"

"I'm not a pallbearer," Hirawa said.

"Your confidence is admirable, but misplaced. It's time to drop the gun and—"

"No!" Jeff Ryan blurted out. Hirawa heard a scuffling sound behind her, but she couldn't see what Ryan was doing. Whatever it was, Nguyen gave the two hostages his full attention for an instant, pivoting to aim his piece their way. She saw orange flame spring from Nguyen's muzzle toward the Ryans. Hirawa took the opportunity and dropped to her knees and found the AK-47's pistol grip with her right hand, squeezing the trigger to unload approximately half a magazine.

Nguyen took it all, twitching and dancing as he skittered backward, bits and pieces of him outward bound from impact, tumbling in grotesque slow-motion through the smoky air until he hit the turf facedown. Hirawa grudgingly released the trigger, covering his corpse until she satisfied herself he wouldn't rise again.

"Are you all right?" she asked the Ryans.

"Fine," Kim said.

"He grazed me," Ryan replied, pain in his voice. "It's nothing, really."

Hirawa saw blood on his arm and knew she couldn't help him in the middle of a combat zone. "Right, then," she said. "Both of you follow me. And don't forget the gun."

THE SHOT THAT nearly killed him flew past David Yun's face with an inch or less to spare. Recoiling from the noise and sudden heat, he tripped over a corpse and thereby saved himself, as more rounds sliced the air where he'd been standing. Yun used the momentum of his fall to roll for cover, fetching up beside a tent whose occupants had long since fled.

He hadn't seen the shooter who had come so close to dropping him, but he had a fair fix on the origin of those near-miss rounds. Another burst cut through the tent above his head, confirming it, and Yun began to worm his way backward, circling around to get a better angle on the shot. It cost him precious moments, and he cleared the northwest corner of the tent in time to find two pirates moving forward, separating as they tried to flank him.

He took the closer, firing from a prone position and cutting the man's legs from under him, finishing it with a second short burst as he fell across Yun's line of fire. The dying pirate triggered one more burst before he lost his weapon, the bullets coming close enough to blind Yun with a spray of sand.

Yun cursed, squirming away while he swiped at his eyes with one hand, suddenly aware of how vulnerable he'd become. He couldn't see the second shooter, couldn't even hear him with the racket all around. Blinking, he had a blurry vision of a figure moving toward him, looming overhead, the dark shape of an automatic weapon raised to take him out from point-blank range. Yun fumbled with his AK, knowing in advance that he wouldn't be quick enough to save himself this time.

He flinched at the clatter of gunfire, awaiting the impact of slugs tearing flesh—but it never came. Instead, Yun opened his burning eyes in time to see the second pirate fall, collapsing like a scarecrow whose supporting rod has snapped. Behind the dead man there were three more figures, with the foremost leveling an automatic rifle.

Yun swiped at his eyes again, reluctant to believe them now. Hirawa stepped forward, lowering her weapon, while her fellow prisoners stayed close behind her, glancing nervously about.

"If you can stand," Hirawa said, "we should be going now. It isn't time to rest just yet."

A rush of sweet relief brought Yun immediately to his feet. It took another beat for him to realize that she was wearing different clothing from the last time he'd seen her. There were also bruises, like a smudge of charcoal, on the left side of her face.

"Are you all right?" he asked.

"Better than you, apparently," she answered, smiling. "Who'd have thought I'd ever save your life?"

Yun matched her smile and answered her impulsively. "Tradition says it now belongs to you."

"Later, perhaps," she said. "It won't be worth much if we linger here."

"Agreed."

"Where's Belasko?" Hirawa asked.

The echo of a hand grenade's explosion answered her. Yun tracked it, pointing. "Over there," he said.

BOLAN REACHED the spot where he'd seen Lee Sun or his twin hit the ground moments earlier. He scanned the nearby huts and tents, seeking a runner, and he was rewarded with a glimpse of movement to the south. He caught a flash of dirty white, arms pumping as the runner covered ground, charting a course that bore him toward the tree line.

Was it Lee? Bolan couldn't be sure, but the clothing looked right, from his earlier sighting. The choice was to follow or let this one go. His instinct took over, propelling him after the runner. Another pirate loomed out of the shadows, snarling incoherently. Bolan shot him in the face and swept past before the body hit the ground.

His quarry didn't seem to know that anyone was in pursuit. The man was running like his life depended on it. Bolan kept pace with him at first, then pushed a little harder, catching up. He meant to overtake Lee—or whoever it was—before his adversary reached the forest and it turned into a creeping hunt by sound and smell.

Closer.

Bolan was never sure what made the runner glance back at him, but he recognized the face, even in shadow, from the mug shots David Yun had shown him. Lee seemed to recognize him, too, although they'd never met. Perhaps it was more accurate to say he recognized Death's shadow on his heels and knew that he was running out of time.

The pirate had a choice to make: pour on the speed and hope the trees would cover his retreat, or stand and fight. Bolan thought Lee would run for it, so he was taken by surprise when the pirate stopped dead in his tracks, spun and cut loose with an automatic rifle from a range of thirty yards.

Lee was too shaky for precision fire, but it was close enough to send Bolan leaping aside from his path, tumbling head over heels in the dirt while bullets swarmed past in the night.

The Executioner came up firing, tracking with the Kalashnikov as his target did a rapid fade to Bolan's left. He gave Lee points for thinking on his feet, correcting his aim as the pirate returned fire. The hit came as Lee reached his cover, vanishing around the southwest corner of a Quonset hut. One round or two, it was impossible to say, but impact staggered him and squeezed a cry of pain from him before he disappeared.

Bolan closed in, circling the hut, unsure of anything except that a wounded enemy was often the most dangerous. He didn't know how badly Lee was hit or whether it would even slow him. He approached the hut cautiously, stalking his prey, concerned that Lee may have kept running despite the hit, slipping away into the dark woods unseen while Bolan played tag with a phantom.

Gunfire from the remainder of the camp had begun to sputter out, dying as the last of the pirates died or fled into the jungle for safety. Bolan heard a scuffling of feet as he approached the southeast corner of the Quonset hut, still uncertain if the sounds issued from his target or some other hidden gunman.

The approach was critical at this stage. He could blow it, literally, with another frag grenade—but if he scored a hit, he might never be able to identify his adversary. By the same token, if he went rushing blindly in to the attack Lee might kill him before he could get off a shot.

What to do? Compromise.

Bolan took a grenade from his belt, leaving the pin in

place, and tossed it around the corner, shouting to the darkness as he made the pitch, "Grenade!"

It wasn't much, as tricks went, but it did the job. Lee, already stunned by one grenade, burst from cover with a cry of panic, running hard to Bolan's left. The Executioner tracked him with his AKMS, leading, and fired a burst that caught Lee's ankles like a trip wire, jerked them out from under him and dropped him on his face.

To his credit, the pirate leader recovered swiftly. Clenching his teeth around the pain, Lee found his weapon and pushed himself into a seated position, looking around for the enemy. By the time he found Bolan, Lee was covered, his own rifle pointed harmlessly off toward the cove.

"It's finished," Bolan told him.

"When *I* say so," Lee replied.

"You need to look around and check the score."

"You feel like winner now?" Some of the polished English from their prior phone conversation had to have vanished when the bullets hit him.

"You want to call this winning, be my guest," Bolan replied. "The only thing I need from you is three live hostages."

Lee sneered, then flicked a glance away to the soldier's left. A subtle change in his expression raised Bolan's hackles. "You want your friends?" Lee asked him. "Look behind you, white man."

Bolan heard a scuffling footstep at his back, saw Lee start to shift the rifle in his lap. It was the kind of cross fire that was hard—if not impossible—to beat.

The shot rang out behind him, Bolan pivoting, his finger on the trigger of his weapon. By the time he realized he wasn't hit, he'd recognized the four figures standing behind him, Hirawa with an AK-47 at her shoulder. Glancing back toward Lee, he found the pirate stretched out on his back, a fresh wound leaking where his nose had been a moment earlier.

"My parents are avenged," Hirawa said.

"Suits me," the Executioner replied. The others stared at him expectantly. "If no one wants to hang around," he told them all, "we've got a plane to catch."

Epilogue

Arlington National Cemetery

They were back where they'd started, communing with heroes. Brognola wore an overcoat that matched the slate-gray sky, snap-brim fedora firmly planted on his head in defiance of the latest fashion trends. For once, it pleased Bolan to know that some things never changed.

"How was your flight?" the big Fed asked him, starting off with small talk.

"Long," Bolan replied. "Routine." In fact, he'd slept most of the way, catching up for the days when he'd gone without sleep altogether, or made do with less than his body required.

"I heard that," Brognola said. "You're all right, otherwise?"

"Five by five," Bolan told him. "What's doing out east?"

"Everyone's sifting through the fallout right now. I've been calling around, touching base, but it's early to tell."

"You've got something, though," Bolan suggested.

Brognola shrugged. "Odds and ends." He took a small spiral notebook from the right-hand pocket of his overcoat, holding it loosely in his hand without referring to it, as if simple contact with the paper helped him to recall its contents.

"Off the top," he said, "the Indonesian cops are claiming Lee Sun had some kind of falling out with various unknown associates—maybe a mutiny, the way they make it sound. No details, since they can't back any of it up, but it keeps us out of the picture any way they sell it."

"Fair enough."

"I didn't think you'd mind. There'll be some stories in the press out there, about the pirates, but the lid's on anything official that would make it seem like Lee was operating with a license or the boys in charge are just too dumb to know what's going on. They'll say he had his HQ in Malaysia or the Philippines, and that'll start a whole new round of arguments."

In short, the usual, Bolan thought. Denial and evasion, shifting of responsibility until it came to rest somewhere at sea. In a world of see-no-evil, Bolan understood, the buck stopped nowhere.

"What about survivors?" Bolan asked.

"They've got a couple dozen on the line," Brognola said. "Nothing to prove involvement with ongoing piracy, the way it looks right now. They'll probably go down for being part of Lee's swan song. If they get tagged for murder, it's the firing squad. They're done."

Bolan would shed no tears for Lee's men. They'd picked the bloody road they traveled and could ride it to the bitter end. If any of them were released, he knew, the odds were strong that they'd return to lives of predatory crime before the ink dried on their walking papers.

"That's it, then," Bolan said. "Until the next batch comes along."

"Smart money says they're already at work. I wouldn't bet on any great reduction in the local crime statistics."

Bolan knew that dismal tune by heart. He met the predators, dealt with them one by one, and there were always more waiting in line to take the place of those who fell. It was a grim commentary on the human condition, unchanged for all he knew since primitive man climbed down from the trees and lit his first fire at the mouth of a cave.

"The rest?" he prodded Brognola.

"The brass in Kuala Lumpur is impressed with your buddy, David Yun," the big Fed replied. "He's in line for some kind of promotion or medal, I think it was, as soon as he comes back from his leave of absence."

"Where's he going?" The soldier had a fair idea before he asked the question.

"That's a funny thing," Brognola said. "Word is, he's taking time off to help the Hirawa woman with her kid brother, something like that. Does that make any sense to you?"

So, Hirawa was out of the hospital. Bolan kept his face blank, responding with a casual shrug. "Hard to say," he replied. "They were friendly, I guess."

"Friendly, right. Nothing like a little gun smoke to get the hormones cooking." Brognola shook his head. "Thank God I'm too old for all that."

"You're as young as you feel," Bolan said.

"That's my point." Brognola raised the notebook, tapping it against his temple like a psychic, reading by osmosis. "The newlyweds are stopping over in Tahiti, if you can believe it. Daddy Ryan is sending out another yacht to pick them up. I guess he has a few spares standing by, in case one of them hits a squall or something."

"Are they holding up all right?" Bolan asked.

"That's one thing about the filthy rich," Brognola said. "You hear they can't buy happiness, but I suppose resilience is the next best thing."

"It couldn't hurt," the Executioner agreed.

"The rumble out of Hollywood is that their story's earmarked for a feature film, production starting in the spring. Brad Pitt and his wife—what's her name?"

"Jennifer Aniston."

"That's her. They're 'passionately interested' in bringing this 'great romantic drama' to the screen, supposedly."

"How are they handling the rescue?" Bolan asked.

"The usual bullshit. Jeff Ryan is telling anyone who'll listen that they fought their way out of captivity with minimal assistance from your buddy Yun and Hirawa."

That was fine with Bolan. He'd impressed the Ryans with the need to keep their lips buttoned concerning his involvement in the getaway. A movie struck him as the perfect vehicle to cover any latent tracks and thoroughly confuse the issue. Nothing short of a congressional investigation could've done a better job of burying the truth.

"That leaves the families," Bolan said.

"It's a touchy subject, that one. From what I hear, the Ryans and the Strouds won't be spending any great quality time together for a while—if ever. Old man Stroud's thumping his chest and making noise about his stance on terrorism being vindicated, but he can't go into much detail about how he supposedly came through to save the kids. His friend on Pennsylvania Avenue has one hand on the leash, and Stroud's not getting too much slack."

"Sounds like a wrap," Bolan said.

"Cut and print," Brognola replied. "You want to have the cast party at Spago's?"

"I'd settle for a cold one and a few days of uninterrupted sleep."

"You're tired?" Brognola asked.

"I'm getting there."

"Okay. I've got this other thing working, but it can wait a few more days."

"I'm glad to hear it."

"Hey, who ever said I was a slave driver?"

"I'm sure I heard it somewhere," Bolan answered, smiling. "Let me check my notes."

"I've got your notes right here," Brognola quipped. He sobered then, adding, "The Bureau wants to take a look at piracy, if you can picture that. Same thing as their arrangement with Moscow to keep tabs on the Russian Mafia, if they can get Jakarta or Manila to play ball."

"And then what?" Bolan asked.

"More paperwork," the head Fed answered. "Reports up the wazoo. Don't hold your breath waiting for any great accomplishments. They've got no jurisdiction, anyway."

Another make-work program, Bolan thought. Cosmetic patch-ups that accomplished little or nothing. The FBI could no more wage effective war against foreign pirates than it could stamp out terrorism in the Middle East. Some folks would still take comfort from the knowledge they were trying, though—and others might increase their annual appropriations if they climbed aboard the band wagon.

"I'd just as soon stay out of that," Bolan said.

"That makes two of us." Brognola slipped the spiral notebook, still unopened, back into his pocket. "So, what were you thinking of for R and R?"

"I hadn't thought beyond the sleep we talked about," Bolan replied.

"If you were in the mood for salsa—"

"We can talk about it next week," Bolan interrupted him.

"Spoilsport."

"You got that right."

"Okay. I'm nothing if not generous," the big Fed replied. "But if you're hanging out and start to get a little bored—"

"I've got your number."

"Hey, that's all I'm saying."

They walked on in silence for a while, the markers all around them, row on row. It seemed to Bolan that the valiant dead were just a bit more peaceful now than they had been the last time he and Brognola had passed among them. Less watchful, perhaps, if only for a moment.

Bolan wondered sometimes if they ever really rested. Were they constantly on watch or was it simply his imagination when he walked in such a place?

No matter. If he felt the dead, believed in them, then they were real. And so, then, was his debt to their enduring memory.

The Executioner passed on and felt the silent shadows around him, keeping pace.

God keep, he thought. I'll see you soon.

But not today.

James Axler
Outlanders

SUN LORD

In a fabled city of the ancient world, the neo-gods of Mexico are locked in a battle for domination. Harnessing the immutable power of alien technology and Earth's pre-Dark secrets, the high priests and whitecoats have hijacked Kane into the resurrected world of the Aztecs. Invested with the power of the great sun god, Kane is a pawn in the brutal struggle and must restore the legendary Quetzalcoatl to his rightful place—or become a human sacrifice....

Available May 2004 at your favorite retail outlet.

Or order your copy now by sending your name, address, zip or postal code, along with a check or money order (please do not send cash) for $6.50 for each book ordered ($7.99 in Canada), plus 75¢ postage and handling ($1.00 in Canada), payable to Gold Eagle Books, to:

In the U.S.	In Canada
Gold Eagle Books	Gold Eagle Books
3010 Walden Avenue	P.O. Box 636
P.O. Box 9077	Fort Erie, Ontario
Buffalo, NY 14269-9077	L2A 5X3

Please specify book title with your order.
Canadian residents add applicable federal and provincial taxes.

GOUT29

TAKE 'EM FREE

2 action-packed novels plus a mystery bonus

NO RISK

NO OBLIGATION TO BUY